TWO MUSICIANS And THE WIFE WHO ISN'T

Syd Goldsmith

Two Musicians and the Wife Who Isn't is a work of fiction set in the late 1970s and early 1980s. While historical figures who enter the story, including John Updike and the former President of Suriname, are portrayed as accurately as memory permits, any resemblance of the imaginary persons in this novel to particular individuals living or dead is unintended, as is the use of names which might belong to real people.

ISBN-13: 978-0-9854446-2-4

Two Musicians Publishing
Dallas Taipei
www.sydgoldsmith.com
syd.goldsmith@gmail.com

1

Sally Pendergast

No Man Carries My Baggage

I really should have left the lace panties hanging on the front doorknob for Michel to stick his nose into when he gets home, but I need them more than him.

I'm a classical guitarist, and my Juan Carlos Marin goes everywhere. It's his best instrument. He made it for my hands when I was studying with Segovia in Spain, and I am never without it. Juan Carlos loved me too. He said Sally Pendergast is the best guitar talent of this generation – that's me.

My soon to be ex-husband Michel Sevigny was the first American violinist to win a medal in the Tchaikovsky competition. He used to carry the guitar for me sometimes, but ever since he changed his name from Michael Schwartz he's bitched just getting it from the house to the car. I still can't figure out why it took more than a year before I told him to fuck off and stop telling me it isn't a legitimate instrument.

I save my right hand for that guitar. The left hand hauls everything else I own as I walk out on Michel. It's all stuffed into the duffel bag; purple concert dress and heels, a pair of jeans and a sweatshirt, a decent skirt and blouse. And don't forget the lingerie. The bra size I need for my petite frame is impossible to find. Whenever I lean forward or take a deep breath, men drool.

There's also the pair of sneakers I grabbed from the closet on the way out because the heels are coming off my boots. Had to take the makeup kit I hate, but I'll need it if I ever get a TV gig. The framed picture of me and Segovia playing duos in Seville goes everywhere too.

Michel did his best to drown me out. He insisted I use an amplifier whenever we performed together. That's the next closest thing to forcible rape. Outside of domestic labor, all he ever wanted off of me was to get inside those panties. I was always generous about that, but can't afford a new pair now. I pulled them off the doorknob and jammed them into a side pocket. Michel will have to make do without.

No man will carry my baggage, so I travel real light.

2

Lex Kennan

Accelerando

Sally Pendergast's head was in my lap, bringing waves of disbelief. We met only two weeks before, at Katya Tenbroek's. Neither of us planned to go to that party, and my stomach was roiling at the prospect of being unwelcome in the coterie of Washington's best musicians. Like half the Class of 1969 that graduated from Juilliard ten years ago, I gave up on making a life in music, even though people who didn't know any better said I was the best flutist around.

Lost in the crowd at Katya's Capitol Hill townhouse, my fingers ran over the wallpaper in the hallway, yearning to enter its scene and come upon the Greek garden with grape leaves dangling from trellises and goddesses cavorting nude by a marble fountain. A nymph beckoned. I could not go there. I should not be here.

It isn't that my wife would block my way. Vera is as supportive of my musical urges as any non-musician wife could be, but I screwed her out of her high school class reunion in Connecticut. When I told her I must go to this party, she did no more than ask, "How can you do this when you committed the weekend to me months ago?" Then she went quiet. Her anger rumbles through me like a thunderstorm brewing from eerie calm.

Vera's so damn good at that. Never raises her voice. I'd dare anybody to find a visible sign that she was royally pissed. But she knows exactly how to turn my intestines inside out with guilt. She comes into my room when I'm wrapped up in a solo flute partita and says, "Why don't you spend a little time with the kids?" I considered trying to explain how important it was for me to practice before going to Katya's, but the tired attempt died in my throat. Then when I suggested a babysitter just this once so she could go to her reunion, she seared my skull with her stare. "You saw that headline. 'Au Pair Strangles Toddler in Bathtub.' I'll stay home, thank you."

With Vera you never know whether it's a whisper or a hiss. She must have swallowed bile to wave me out the door to go to Katya's. Perhaps she had finally come to understand how desperate I was to play flute with the pros again.

Most every musician in Washington has heard about Katya. She is a young widow from Amsterdam who opens her elegant townhouse to the best musicians. She serves brie, grapes, Gewurztraminer and sometimes, it was said, special favors to hungry stars of the music world.

My own flute playing, though good enough to play second chair in the Meadowdale Symphony when I was still a Juilliard student, had never merited an invitation to Katya's. That didn't deter Ralph Greenberg from dragging me there. He claimed to be Katya's bosom buddy and insisted I should just come. Ralph is the self-appointed greatest amateur cellist in the world, and surely deserving of the title. His uncle is the cellist of Ars Nova Trio fame.

When I first learned of this, I asked Ralph why he didn't make a career out of music. "You kidding?" he said. "Ars Nova rehearses every day and the players won't even speak to each other. They detest as passionately as they make music." Ralph snorted, "Far better to be the best amateur than some professional orchestra slave. I get to play the great quartets with the pros all the time."

Ralph had chosen not to make it big in music. I'm way too cowardly to risk a career of it. His pride and my fear led us to share an office and responsibility in the Department of the Interior for staffing studies for the National Park Service. Stultified fellow travelers in the bureaucracy, we are stiffs at work on mounds of paper that never get smaller. We curse our inboxes and seek escape to the wordless poetry of music.

Ralph told me that many of the party guests are from the National Symphony. "This place is respite from the tyrants on the podium. Make it into an orchestra and you have no say about what you perform and how you have to play it."

"I know that conductors are feudal lords, but chamber music is intoxicating."

"That's why I brought you here," said Ralph. Come on. Go in."

I couldn't move. Too busy tucking my nerves under a blanket of envy, peering out at nude nymphs prancing on wallpaper and paragons of music strutting into the salon. Ralph clutched my hand in his and pulled me forward, the peacock shepherding a cornered rabbit.

I hadn't planned to bring my flute this first time, but Ralph called me chicken until I was pissed enough to show him I'm not. It's a Powell, and the case trembles in my unsteady hand. I had practiced ten years on a student flute and waited five more on a long list of buyers to get that instrument from the most revered of all flute makers, and now I was afraid to play it.

If you opened the case you would be struck by the black on silver. That heavy tarnish is evidence of years of sweat from fingers and my failure to wipe it off with a sliced rectangle of undershirt too frayed to wear any longer. I might explain that some people tarnish even gold flutes, though I hide my embarrassment that I would be one of them if given the opportunity.

I gave up dreaming of a life in music after learning that it takes longer and is harder to make it as a musician than to become a doctor or lawyer or just about anything else. The only flutists I ever heard of who made it as soloists were my own teacher and Jean-Pierre Rampal. How many musical hopefuls count the measures of their lives passing by in streams of failed auditions and talentless students?

There was no room for another star soloist, and I had neither the chutzpah nor the talent to try. Vera made sure of that. She was the sensible one, but she never knew anything like Red Fox Music Camp. There, music had been unadulterated adolescent passion that promised to smolder for a lifetime, even though those embers would not burst aflame in the real world of hundreds of flutists vying for one job. It wasn't her fault that I settled for government work.

When Ralph took off to find his friends, I squeezed into a group of string players quaffing Gewurztraminer and asked if any of them would be willing to play Mozart's D Major Quartet with me. "Yeah. Maybe later. You got anything more interesting than that?" The two guys closest to me turned away and joked that the only sound worse than a flute is two flutes. That's what Mozart told his sister Nanerl, and his voice was ringing in my ears more than two centuries later.

I retreated to the hallway and was about to leave when the front door swung open and a rather petite woman with shoulder-length black hair came in carrying an instrument case that wasn't big enough for a cello. Her lips puckered in animated conversation as she turned to face her friend. She couldn't have noticed me staring at her outsized breasts.

But she caught me before I could look away. "I'm Sally," she said. "What do you play?" Tiny dimples accented her open smile.

In the hallway by the Greek garden, Sally became the nymph at the fountain. I could see her as a Renoir nude, succulent, inviting. "Flute," I said, glancing away, "but I haven't practiced seriously in years."

I couldn't tell her that giving up the music had muted my zeal. Two mortgages on the house and a job classification that promises chafing at the bills aren't the only dampers. Conscientious Vera demands more for the little ones than I know how to give. Nobody taught me to read fairy tales to toddlers with the same fervor that once marked my flute-playing. "I was one of those great talents that didn't quite make it," I added. "What about you?"

Sally seemed to grow taller as she looked up at me, richly proportioned in a tight-fitting purple top. Her eyes were so alive yet so near tears. I had seen those eyes before, in people who believed music would give them everything.

"I'm going to make it," said Sally. "By the way, I brought the 'Entr'Acte' for flute and guitar. Ibert. Want to play it with me?"

I wondered if I could still sight-read, scared silly that the professionals would look away and cough – I felt their thumbs squashing my testicles. But I came to this party determined to overcome fear and meet musicians, hoping that snooty string players would give another instrument a chance to play with them. "Sure," I said, not sure at all.

Katya summoned us into the kitchen to eat and drink our fill. In the center of the crowd, she paid no mind to some guy's stray hand lingering on her shapely, silk covered rump.

We loaded up on wine and cheese and sliced sausage on crackers, juggling plates and our instruments as we made our way back into the parlor. Ralph Greenberg assembled two violinists and a violist to form his exclusive club. "There is no higher art than the string quartet," he announced, echoing minions of strings who wouldn't play with anybody else, except maybe a pianist.

That rattled my resentment. I couldn't help but think of the time he rounded up some string players so I could play those Mozart flute quartets. At the end of it he said, "I guess that's it for decent stuff with flute. And the cello part is boring as hell." Once, and we never played together again.

Ralph's quartet played Brahms, filling the void with sounds that bring musicians together and tear them apart, though they may hardly know each other. But this was a party, so they didn't stop to argue who should play louder, who softer, or how much space there should be between the notes.

Sally turned on her tiptoes as they started the Andante and whispered in my ear, "I ran away from home at fifteen to study with Segovia. Who was your teacher?" She was hugging her guitar case like she would never let go.

A coterie of aficionados clapped in unison with the quartet's last chord, like the chorus in an ancient Greek ritual. They must have been friends of Katya's who do not play music but are essential to the tender egos of those who do.

Katya did a slow dance around the salon, casually elegant and almost beautiful in blue silk. She greeted people she didn't know as warmly as those she did. "And who did you come with?" she asked, flowing toward the center of the parlor. "What will we hear next?" A violinist took out his instrument and tightened his bow. His face twisted into a frown as he looked around in vain for his partners and lost the chance to play before an adoring audience.

Sally moved quickly to the center of the room, tugging me behind her through the devotees. A portly woman of about fifty who looked like she could afford the arts pushed the extra chairs aside as Sally opened her bag and handed me the music to the "Entr'Acte." The tempo marking was 176.

"This is going to be hard," I said.

"You can play it." Sally looked straight at me. Eyes alight, she conveyed everything and nothing between joy and tears.

Yes, I could play it, I think. Sally pushed me through the piece with fierce rhythmic drive. Even the symphony players applauded. Later, we told each other that there weren't any musicians who would play with a flutist or a classical guitarist – not even a Segovia protégé – just for fun.

"I'll play," I said, and she liked that.

Vera played along too, though she was no musician and couldn't really fathom why I would want to be one. "Of course," she said, when I told her there's a classical guitarist I would like to invite over for chamber music. "It will be good for the children to be exposed to it."

Sally Pendergast came by the Metro on a chilly Saturday afternoon. We played up a storm, going through all the music she had for flute and guitar. She was ready to go home the way she came despite the freezing late autumn drizzle, but it was after dark and Vera was adamant. "It is only proper that you see her home. You know as well as I do that women do not travel alone at night."

Neither Sally nor I said much as we drove around the beltway. I thought about Vera, watching us from the living room sofa with six year-old Aaron leaning on her shoulder and Jennifer, a year younger, on her lap. She had no idea of the depths from which the music sprang, but she was always so damn good about what's good for the kids, so sure about what's good for us. So good about everything until she said, "You can't run from reality to chase after some crazy passion. I never would have married you if I thought you would give up everything for music."

Had Sally not told me, I would never have guessed that she left her husband the very day of Katya Tenbroek's party. I was cruising at about sixty-five when she whispered, "The principal second violinist – she's my best friend – dragged me there to banish the pain of one musician with the promise of others." Then Sally said she was tired and sprawled across the front seat of the car.

My foot went down on the accelerator. It must have been the weight of Sally's head on my thigh, my leg, my foot on the pedal. Or was it her outstretched hand and the movement of her fingers?

No doubt I am distracted by what had never happened to me before. All that feeling, through groin, belly, nipples, lips, escaping to heaven around the Milky Way. I did not know whether it was a bridge or a tunnel just ahead. The structure loomed ever larger in mind as I was blinded by the high beams of an oncoming car. Frozen in grim fascination by all that I felt but could not see, I swerved to avoid the abutment.

3

Vera Prudhomme Kennan

In Vera's Kitchen

My husband Lex wouldn't realize that my kitchen is my refuge. To tell the truth, there's nothing special about it except that it doesn't even fit me. The counters and cabinets are much too high, but Lex said our 1939 cottage was the only thing in the area we could afford. He squelched thoughts about the quirkiness of this house, even though he usually questions anything and everything.

My neck and shoulders ached every time I did the dishes in that elevated sink, but it was six months before Lex got around to getting the step-up built. He was always too busy with work or unsuccessful investments. If not that, he was practicing his flute and grumbling that he had nobody to play with. Whenever I mention the kitchen, Lex tells me to be patient until we have the money to redecorate.

I don't know if we'll ever have enough money. First we gave up the accoutrements of middle class life to make the down payment. There's no replacement in sight for our old clunker and we don't even think about nice clothes or entertainment. We hardly ever go out since the children came along. I can't figure out why we don't save a penny. It's been more years than I care to count and I still have to step up and down and move things around every single day.

No doubt you must be wondering why I call such a dysfunctional kitchen my refuge. It's very simple. Lex never comes in.

There is always some good reason. It was another numbing day in piles of paperwork in the Department of the Interior and he has a splitting headache. Bills must be paid tonight or we'll get stuck with late fees. More often than not he's off somewhere in dreamland, reading a book on how millionaires make their money.

When I asked for a blender to make fresh fruit juice, he told me our stock took a dive. "Wait until it recovers, dear, and I can get you whatever you want." It goes without saying that his stocks never recover. I feed him Tang and Maxwell House instant in the morning and he tries not to complain too much. He knows what I will tell him.

What a change it has been since he started making music with Sally Pendergast. He smiles. He's half out of his seat when he's playing. I can feel the excitement flowing from his instrument. He even wraps his arm around me again. For far too long Lex had been facing the wall instead of me at night.

Now, when he plays that flute of his, it's almost like when we first met during his days at Juilliard. I had stopped taking violin lessons years earlier, but I loved to go to the free student concerts. Lex had just performed a Beethoven Serenade and the sound of him just flew out to me. It actually sent chills up my spine.

I went backstage afterwards. There were a lot of people in line, and they all seemed to be his friends. I was really nervous and almost left. By the time I told him he played beautifully we were pretty much alone except for the violist packing up his instrument.

"I could play for you sometime if you let me know who you are and how to find you," he said. It was almost a whisper, halting and tentative, as if he was afraid I would reject him. Of course I didn't. He borrowed a pen and had me write my name and telephone number right on the back of his flute part.

He was very much alive back then. His slim build made him look taller than he really is, and what struck me was that he always seemed to be in motion, gesticulating like Italians in the movies. I wondered if his arms were long because he played the flute.

He had season tickets for a series at the New York Philharmonic. They were half-price for students, and there we were every couple of weeks in the first row balcony, dead center. He swayed with the music and conducted with his index fingers. When he was really into a Schubert or Dvorak symphony he leaned way over the railing, arms extended, still conducting. I was afraid he would end up crashing into the audience in the orchestra section below.

After the concerts he would sing the main themes of the symphonies to me and explain how the composers developed them as he walked me home. One December night we were out by Columbus Circle and he started singing Beethoven's "Ode to Joy." He belted the solo out right in the middle of a crowd and drew quite an audience.

And what did he do? He waved his arms and summoned everybody to sing with him. Quite a few people joined in, right there on the street corner. He conducted and sang as if he were the whole orchestra.

After the last crescendo the others started singing Christmas carols, but Lex lost interest and we moved on. That's what happens when I mention the kitchen.

4

Lex

Bit Parts

I asked Sally, "Are you sure you want me to play a couple of pieces with you at the University of Maryland in March? I haven't played a real concert in living memory."

She laughed. "Of course. It's time I had someone carry my guitar for me."

"How can you be so certain I won't make a mess of it?"

"You were great at Katya's party, so stop worrying."

When we rehearse, Vera sits the kids down on the sofa, Aaron on one side of her and Jennifer on the other. Aaron is already beginning to look like me. He's long and lanky, with unruly light brown hair and eyes that tend to fix on whatever he's looking at – until he's distracted elsewhere. Jennifer is rather short and compact. Her neatly brushed hair curls at the chin, making her face seem heart-shaped. Vera is a grown-up version of Jennifer, but she cuts her hair shorter.

The three of them are an attentive audience. If anything is on Vera's mind besides educating Aaron and Jennifer to appreciate classical music she doesn't reveal it. Dutiful and proper as always, she puts her index finger over tight lips and admonishes the children, "You have to be perfectly quiet and listen to the music." Then she goes into the kitchen and leaves Sally and me alone to meld passion without words.

Sally took charge of tempos and interpretation. I learned early on that she would keep smiling only as long as I didn't give any advice. My suggestion that she try playing an accompanying passage differently was met with a scowl. "You can carry my guitar, but don't muck around with my musicality. Tell me how to play my instrument and you can get your ass out of my life."

The bit part Sally promised was anything but. Sandwiched between her solos, we would play Giuliani's "Gran Duetto Concertante." Flute and guitar was a very popular combination around the time that Beethoven was losing his ability to hear them. He composed nothing for us, but this piece is our equivalent of the "Archduke Trio." I think it could be passed off as Beethoven with some audiences.

The opportunity to perform in public motivated me to practice like mad. Driving Sally home after our last rehearsal, I confessed that I hadn't realized how much I missed making music. I thanked her profusely for getting me going on the flute again. She brushed off my gratitude. "Thank yourself for not equating music with getting paid. This is good for me too. You'll add variety to the program."

When I pulled up in front of Sally's place she opened the door to get out of the car, hesitated, then turned to me. "Do you have any regrets about that first night you drove me home…about that blow job I gave you?"

I shuddered involuntarily at the intoxicating memory of Sally's erotic lips and fingers turning into sheer terror as I came within a split second of pulverizing us on that bridge abutment. Amazing that she didn't dismember me when I finally saw the danger and swerved.

I didn't know what to say. Sally looked at me expectantly. Finally I asked, "Why did you do it?"

"Needed to be close to somebody," she mumbled.

I put my arm around her and said something about not having any regrets, "I don't think."

She lifted my arm off her shoulder. "Don't get any ideas, buster. You're a married man, and that was a one shot affair."The drive back home set me to wondering. Just who is this Sally Pendergast?

Glistening eyes were the first thing I noticed at Katya Tenbroek's party. I still can't tell whether they express come-hither hope or tears about to flow. She is busty, short, always looking up, with sexuality written all over her face. Maybe I should say she only invites friendship, but there was that incident in the car and the putdown just now. All I can see are contradictions from this shy but brassy guitarist who said she was feeling old at thirty-one.

Sally told me about fleeing, and not just from her husband. She couldn't stand her mother and three sisters all trying to outdo each other. Two of the sisters look to her like they couldn't possibly have the same father. Sally is the only one who was musical. She had to get out of that house, so she took off to study with Segovia in Spain.

Sally is usually unemployed, but somehow she gets along. I envy her that. Better a slave to her music than to an office in the Department of the Interior.

"No doubt about that, but sometimes I wonder," she said. "You're a slave to one master. When I need money, I'm a slave to any master"

5

Sally

Make a Living – Make Music

When I came back from Spain I got a job in Lord & Taylor to support my guitar habit. Better pay than the cash register slaves in Wal-Mart. Nice ambiance, with plenty of expensive things I'd never be able to afford and don't even want.

Rich bitches would come in with their noses somewhere on high, feigning interest in the Parisian designer du jour. They paw through the whole collection of ten thousand dollar labels perfectly stitched on ten bucks worth of cloth. I would smile sweetly at whomever I was waiting on, all the while wondering how she could stand the smell cloaked by her perfume.

It was hard to tell which were worse, the snobs who came in the store wearing that stuff or all the trash trying to steal it. Both would try on the entire collection of designer dresses and toss them at me one at a time when they finished prancing around in front of the mirrors. "Nice but not quite right," they said. I cursed under my breath and cleaned up after them.

There was a nice little bonus if I ever sold one of those outfits, but if you believe that happened often, you're dumber than I think. I started offering to tell these hotshit ladies where they could get a perfect knock-off for a tenth of the price if they gave me a piddling $50 dollar fee.

One of them must have told my supervisor because Mrs. Penny told me to gather my things and get out. I was supposed to get paid for the hours I worked, but it took two months to get my check. I was about to become a beggar. Would have too, if a violinist I met at a party I crashed didn't put me up for a while until I found a job in the Georgetown Mall selling yoghurt.

I get a new student every so often and a couple of gigs for peanuts. My life is one bit part after another. But…At a time when employment is uncertain and I have no idea whether I can pay the rent, there is one certainty. Lex worships my playing.

He stops right in the middle of a passage to watch my hands. Then he tells me how amazing it is that I can roam the fret board so freely. He asks, "How is it you don't make scratching sounds like other guitarists? None at all, even when you slide from neck to throat." He can't believe that my little fingernails produce such an incredible range of tone colors when I pluck the strings. I tell him, "They're my fingernails, you know. None of this glue on stuff. Real classical guitarists never use those plastic picks. Segovia would have a fit."

Lex looks at me as if I brought all this technique from another planet. Actually, all it took was practicing all day for the better part of my life. "Incredible," he says.

My ex-husband never said anything like that about my playing, not once the whole nine years we were married. Certainly not when we concertized together. What idiocy led me to idolize him in the beginning?

Lex never made it in music like my ex, but he plays with guts and passion. You would never believe it if you saw the way he acts around Vera. Half the time he isn't there when she talks to him, and the other half he looks sort of numb. "Can you do the dishes for a change tonight?" She drones.

"Yes dear."

"Would you mind helping with the kids, just a little? They want their daddy." She stares him down until he asks, "Do you want me to read them a story?"

I don't think she's nagging so much as hoping for him to volunteer. If I had kids I'd want some help too, but I don't want to struggle to get it. Least of all do I need a husband who snarls under his breath, "See Dick. See Jane. See them run. Why don't they just run off into the woods and…?"

Lex isn't really like that, but I bet that's what runs through his head when he asks, "Don't we have anything else I can read to them?" He doesn't show much annoyance, he just lives it.

He's somebody else entirely when he takes up the flute. He's animated, he's vibrant, and sometimes he plays out of tune, so I tell him.

"Give me another chance," he says. "I promise to get it right next time."

Vera tells me about his passion for music. "When Lex gets back from taking you home he wakes me up humming what you practiced in my ear."

6

Lex

Another Place to Rehearse

Vera took the kids to visit her parents in Pennsylvania because she knew I would be stuck in the office all weekend on a crash report about the future of the C and O canal. We want to refurbish the original tow path for biking, all the way up to Cumberland.

By mid-morning Sunday I'd had it with the freaking project. I called Sally. "Why don't we just rehearse at your place? It would save a lot of time running around the beltway."

"Sure, but don't expect much. I'm a guitarist, not a housekeeper."

I couldn't keep my jaw from dropping when Sally opened the door. She turned and led me into the small living room with its scatter rug, desk, sofa and a couple of folding chairs for musicians while I wondered what I was supposed to do about a woman who welcomed me in nothing more than a bra (could it have been a halter?) and hot pants.

She offered a tour of the place. I gaped helplessly at her hips in perfect rhythm as she led me through the kitchen and opened the door to a bedroom that featured a pile of dirty laundry. Other than that, her apartment was as tidy as anyone could expect.

I was still intent on her gorgeously exposed body as Sally led me back into the living room. Before I realized it she turned around and caught me undressing her with my eyes. She smiled, or frowned, I'm not sure.

"I was giving you a tour of my apartment, not my ass," she said. "This is the way I dress. Nobody has a right to tell me how to live in my own home, so if you have any ideas, forget it. Go grab your flute and put your urges into the music."

She handed me an eighteenth century Serenade by Fernando Sor. The notes and the tempo were easy, but I had to play it several times to learn its lilting beauty. Sally's part was also easy enough technically, but the sound she brought to the strings was soul music for any century, and that's not a simple matter at all.

We made beautiful sounds that day, and I learned something about Sally too. The way the guitar covered her, she might as well have been playing in the nude. I'm sure she knew that, but she was all business, and I didn't dare challenge her insistence that her head in my lap was once and only once.

That night I dreamed about her every move as she made love to music and I soared with the flute. After we worked on the Serenade until it sounded the way we wanted it, she smiled and lifted her guitar, exposing a large tuft of pubic hair. "Did you mean what you played?"

"Every note, but I could put even more into it. Any suggestions?"

"I'll show you." She stood up and unlatched her halter, revealing a body made to model for Renoir's bathing nudes, like the ones that led me to buy print reproductions of the masters to decorate my living room wall.

I started to get up. She put her arms around my neck and kissed me quickly. "You played it beautifully. More music later."

I put my hand around her waist and motioned to her bedroom. No," she said, pulling me down. "Right here."

So vivid, that dream talk. I woke up. There was a good sized stain on the sheet.

7

Vera

Back Home from Parents

The trip back home was awful, as usual. My father ranted, "How can that man you call a husband be so irresponsible that he doesn't accompany his wife on a trip back to her parents?"

"How do you put up with him?" Mother asked.

"Would you mind watching the children while I go out for a little walk? Please."

I don't expect Lex to clean house, but it would have been nice to see the bed made when I got back. Instead the covers were all over the place, like he twisted and turned all night and left everything the way it was when he crawled out of bed.

I wasn't used to measuring such things, but the stain looked huge and it certainly wasn't me. I had changed the sheets just before I left. I mentioned it to Lex. "Tell me about your midnight affair."

He blushed and stammered, "No. No. I was dreaming about you. Honest."

"Oh Lex, really now. Don't worry. I'm joking."

It isn't that Lex doesn't love me. He just doesn't know how to show it and he doesn't know how to do it very well either. He needs his sex with such urgency that I can't help but think that it matters little to him whether I'm there or not when we have it. Rather than real electricity between us, I feel a riptide of disappointment along with the shudder I offer when Lex explodes inside me.

I don't know whether he thinks he makes me happy or doesn't understand that he should. Brenda Scotton, my maid of honor, told me I really ought to do some reading, "And Lex isn't going to learn anything without a book."

"How do I get him to read without making him feel like he's been castrated by his aggressive wife?"

Brenda shook her head. "That's the hard part. He'll hate you if you shatter his macho ego."

The clerk at Kramer Books was much more open than my parents ever were. He recommended "The Joy of Sex" when I blushed and asked for some good reference books on, well, you know, sex.

Lex would wonder what I was doing with a book like that, so I hid it and read while he was at work. After I went through it twice I started experimenting with my body. When I finally came to the joy that the book talked about so much, the guilt that almost stopped me from trying began to fade, as if the stranglehold of ghosts was finally overcome by pleasure.

I had trouble understanding why Lex didn't think to satisfy me. I could do it myself but when images of Lex popped up feelings turned hollow. He would be so deeply hurt by any hint that he isn't the perfect lover. I couldn't bring myself to give him the book.

I almost did one night when he was drying the dishes and putting them away one by one so I didn't have to climb up our little stepladder and stretch to get them in those ridiculous cabinets. "Someday when we can afford it, I'll get you new cabinets placed right," he said.

"That would be so lovely. Maybe a dishwasher too?"

He dropped the dinner plate that he was wiping, but after a muttered curse he picked up the pieces, got behind me while I soaped a plate, and kissed me on the back of the neck.

I sighed as a shudder tingled down my spine. "That feels good." I proposed wine and cheese.

We sipped and gazed at each other through flickering candles and glanced away when the silences got too long. I love him and I'm sure he loves me, though he never actually said so.

Back when he was courting me it wasn't even necessary. I could see it in his effervescent smile as he sang to me after the concerts we attended. His brown hair was longer then, swaying in the wind as he turned to look into my eyes. His gait was always in time with mine when we walked together. But now we often seemed trapped in clear glass bubbles staring at each other, unable to get out and touch.

I had wanted to ask him for a long time. "Do you like having sex with me?"

"What do you mean by that?"

I could not tell whether he was bewildered or insulted.

"Just curious. Maybe I wanted to hear that you're satisfied."

"Of course." He went silent.

"They say that men think about sex all the time. Do you?"

He blushed. "Not all the time. But yeah, more often than I get it."

It was as if the words slipped out from some place deep in his unconscious.

"I didn't mean it that way. It's just that…I do think about it pretty often."

"With other women too?"

Lex didn't answer my question.

"I don't suppose it's so terrible as long as you don't do anything about it. Do you ever fantasize about me?"

He was silent just a little too long. A frown crossed his face before he gave me an artificial smile. "Of course, but you're for real."

"Does that make it any different?"

"I don't know. Why are we talking about this anyway?"

Because I didn't want to grunt to please him, and I didn't want to be frigid, and I didn't want to have to take care of myself. That's part of what a husband is for. Isn't that the way it should be?

I called my gynecologist's office to make an appointment for my annual pap smear. The nurse told me she could schedule Dr. Cooper in three weeks. That was a long time to ponder what to say and bite my nails. I wasn't afraid of cancer or embarrassed about the exam, but the shame of talking about our sex life was almost more than I could bear. I had real trouble facing the fact that this was the reason for my visit to the doctor.

I wondered how Dr. Cooper could be so totally unfazed peering at women's most private parts. He was calm and gentle, a master of small talk to divert attention from the task at hand. After the examination, he brought me into his office to go over my chart and recommend a mammogram. "You're fine, but you seem to be anxious about something. Is everything all right?"

He was looking straight into my eyes, but gently, concern in his voice and wrinkles in his forehead. It was as if he had taken my hand in his. Tears rolled down my cheek.

"How can I teach my husband the basics of lovemaking without crushing him? He's so sensitive that when I asked if he ever fantasized about women he looked at me as if I had accused him of having an affair. He couldn't even talk about it. All I want is more intimacy from my husband, and I don't know how to go about getting it."

Dr. Cooper took the time to hear me out, even though his waiting room was full when the nurse called me in. He offered tissues to dry the tears and rubbed his nose with his index finger as he mulled over my problem. "Making this a joint research project might be less threatening. He could read Kinsey's 'Sexual Behavior in the Human Male' and tell you all about it. You could read the companion book, 'Sexual Behavior in the Human Female.' Promise to share what you learn with each other. Remove the problem from yourselves and get at it by studying what other people do."

"How can that help? I am not one to probe into other people's sex lives."

Dr. Cooper seemed surprised by my question. "You'll see. Then you can get serious about studying what it takes to make you happy. Give it a try."

I had heard of the Kinsey books. And I heard my mother's insistent refrain that I should not be curious about such things. She shut me up every time I had an adolescent question.

"Come to think of it," mused Dr. Cooper, "you could even offer him a choice. He might be more intrigued at the thought of reading about female behavior. Ask him."

It didn't take a great effort to convince Lex. Dr. Kinsey's book gave him permission to peer at naked females openly. Since this was supposed to be a joint research project, I gave myself permission to read about men. Lex read avidly in bed at night.

I couldn't get him to talk to me when he had that book in his hands. We promised to share what we learned every day, but that did not happen.

8

Sally

Vera and Lex

In the beginning I thought Vera would squash me. When I made music with Lex the first time, she watched us like a hawk to make sure there's nothing between us. Whatever her reasons, Vera trusts us now. She listens for a few minutes and then leaves the kids on the sofa, engrossed in the music. She counts it a big success when her darlings tug her back to the living room at bedtime, begging to hear more.

After rehearsal Vera took me aside in the kitchen and whispered, "Thanks for making music with Lex. I see the spark in him again, like before we were married and he was free-lancing around New York in opera orchestras."

Vera laughed. It sounded dry and harsh, but I don't think she resented me giving him what he wanted – in music. If she ever suspected that I gave him head she probably would have killed me.

It's not just that Vera tolerates us. She wants us to play together because she can't make Lex happy by herself. She isn't a musician and I bet she doesn't know any other way to please him. Far too practical. Not at all like Constanze Weber getting up at four in the morning to keep Mozart company after he composed all night, singing his songs and playing his instrument whenever he had the urge.

I don't know whether Vera is frigid or just rigid. She directs all her energy toward the kids. Lex is just a regular paycheck and a dick whose satisfaction is her obligation. Vera never said straight out that he was a burdensome duty, but she talked about how Lex wants music more than her and the kids.

"Even if he has no idea that's his message, it's clear to me," Vera said. "He picks up the flute when I need help around the house. When he hands over his paycheck for me to take to the bank, he says he would rather be a musician and starve."

I shared my feelings about this burdensome duty stuff. "My ex never thought of anything but himself. He cut me off whenever I mentioned anything else. Once he won that Tchaikovsky medal he ticked off everybody who helped him and treated me like I would ruin his run to stardom."

"Men don't understand that the weight of keeping things together is on our shoulders," said Vera. "They're too busy struggling to get to the top of the anthill to notice. They don't know how to satisfy us women and won't make the effort to learn."

Vera doesn't satisfy Lex either. They never do anything spontaneous, though I've offered to baby-sit so they could go to a nightclub or a show. He says, "I'd rather stay home and make music." She mumbles, "That would be nice." They try so hard not to argue in front of anybody, but they can't always hide it.

Vera finally took me up on my babysitting offer. Lex wanted to hear Stern, Istomin and Rose do the Beethoven Triple Concerto with the National Symphony. She wanted to see Twelfth Night at the theater where Lincoln was assassinated. They went to see the play and Lex came back scowling.

9

Vera

Invitation to Dinner

Aaron and Jennifer sit quietly on the sofa, surrounded by cushions and holding hands. They weave along with their daddy as he sways back and forth playing Giuliani. Sally plucks the strings with a passion that makes her guitar sound seem bigger than it really is.

Aaron follows every move Lex's fingers make on the flute. Jennifer is transfixed by the dance of Sally's hand on the fret board. My babies are enthralled by the music, but sometimes I wonder if they are so quiet only because they know that I'll shush them if they make any noise.

Sally has been coming over every week for more than two months now, and I decided that I really ought to invite her for dinner since she probably doesn't get anything to eat before rehearsals. She came a little early and you might say that the two of them played for their dinner. I got the kids to bed and we sat down to steak tartare by candlelight, a hurriedly tossed salad, and a bottle of cabernet that Lex brought home from Eagle Wine and Liquor.

Sally dominates the discussion whenever we talk, but I like it that way. Although the incessant stream of babble that colored my college years at Sarah Lawrence gave me a strong preference for letting talk go in one ear and out the other, Sally is an exception.

She's like Scheherazade, with stories about her escapades with Segovia in Spain and her performances all over Africa sponsored by the International Communications Agency. She tells us how so many people mixed up our government's ICA propaganda machine with the CIA that they changed the name back to the U.S. Information Agency.

The three of us were sitting around the table, finishing up the last of the steak, when Sally asked, "Why don't men ask me out for a second date?"

That's something I used to ask, but I couldn't imagine it coming from Sally.

Lex said, "You must be kidding. Of course they would come back."

"I wish it were so, but it isn't," said Sally. "I must have dated a dozen men since my ex and I broke up, and not a one of them asked me out again."

"That many?" I asked.

"Maybe more, maybe less. So many came and went that I lost count. I never hear from them again, even when I run into someone and invite him to give me a call."

"That's hard to believe," said Lex. "You're really quite attractive. And you tell terrific stories."

I glanced over at Lex. He was looking hungrily at Sally's breasts. Personally, I think they are too big, but when he finally saw me watching, color came to his face and he turned away. "Did these men have a good time?" I asked.

"They said they had a wonderful time. It sounded like they were interested in a serious relationship. No way could all of them lose my phone number."

Sally's eyes glisten when she gets animated telling stories. I had always taken that as a spark that makes a person really alive, but now the gleam seemed like a shroud covering deep sadness inside. I asked, "What did you do with all these men?"

"Most anything," answered Sally. "Concerts, movies, museums, even picnics in Rock Creek Park when the weather was nice. I was happy to do whatever they suggested."

"But what did you do afterward?" I asked, surprised at my temerity. I wanted to know what turned Sally's men off, because I had a really hard time keeping men interested when I used to date. My sorority sisters said it was because I was a cold fish.

"Everything. They all wanted me. So I gave them what they wanted. And they said it was the best time they ever had. Then they never called back. Not a one of them."

Lex looked like he was struggling with a sudden bout of diarrhea. He squirmed in his seat and wouldn't look directly at either of us. I was about to ask him if he had any ideas about this, but decided against it. Sally shrugged her shoulders, as if to suggest that these jerks are incomprehensible.

Lex finally broke the silence. "You made it with them on the first date?"

I really wish Lex had been more discreet than that. It's none of his business and I certainly wouldn't answer a question like that.

"They were so hungry for affection – so sincere about it. So I felt sorry and gave it to them."

Lex looked like he was going to choke. Maybe I did too. I had trouble imagining that Sally was a nymphomaniac or so anxious to please that she acted like one. I couldn't ask her if she enjoyed it.

"Maybe that's why they didn't call back," said Lex. "It's not my place to say it, but I would bet they thought that going to bed on the first date means you're doing it for everybody. That's not good because most guys like to think they're the one that got through and stole the chick's virginity."

"You men are so full of crap. These guys knew I'm no virgin. They said I sent them straight to heaven. They came down from the clouds and asked for more."

I'm surprised that Sally has no interest in Lex, nor he in her. I guess music is their sex, and that's acceptable as long as it stays that way. I went over to Sally and put my hands on her shoulders. "Maybe those lechers only wanted to use you once they sensed you were willing. Since they got what they wanted there was no reason for them to come back. Best be careful about the men you keep company with."

I went back to my chair, not bothering to look over to see Lex's reaction. Instead I studied the defiance and then the little girl devastation on Sally's face as she must have come to realize that to most men she is an over-endowed plaything to be toyed with by any man crass enough to ask.

10

Lex

After That Dinner

Vera and I were in bed trying to go to sleep, and she was staring at the ceiling. I reached for her hand and asked, "Is something the matter, dear?"

"I wish you would have thanked me for the dinner. Tell me, why would a talented woman let any man who comes along have sex with her? Is that what musicians like you and Sally are about?" Vera turned on her side and dug in to me with her eyes. "Do you take any opportunity you can get?"

I started to sweat, though it wasn't very warm under the covers. Vera wasn't going to let me get away without answering. "I probably would have before I knew you, but I never met girls like that. If I had… anyone who wasn't a marriage possibility was fair game."

"So you were an animal too."

"But I wasn't an animal to you. You were marriage material from the start."

"I confess you were the first guy I had met in a long time who didn't make a pass before telling me who he is. The others thought that accepting a date meant sex, and it was up to me to wiggle out of it. Some of the sweetest sounding boys were really crude when it came to saying goodnight. That Joe Clifton friend of yours wasn't the only one ending the evening with 'Wanna F…?' You know what the word is."

"That's not such a bad idea. Wanna make love?"

Vera laughed and draped an arm over my shoulder. "Sure. Take what you want."

She had to be the giver, never the taker, the always good wife. That Vera would never want or need from me ran down through my constricted throat, twitched as it crossed my gut, and lodged below my belly button.

"You can have me now," she said.

Some weeks later, Vera's mother fell and broke her hip. I pleaded too much work and told her she should just take the car and go on up with the kids. For once she did not argue that I should at least visit her parents for the weekend, no matter how much they dislike me.

I called Sally from the office and asked her to come over Saturday afternoon. She had given me a lot of new music and I was anxious to know what it sounded like with the guitar.

We get right down to business when we rehearse. I sorted out the parts while Sally turned the tuning pegs on the six strings of her instrument to bring them up to pitch. The G string slipped and she had to start over. I asked her to play each note with me for two octaves so I could tune to it.

"You're the first person I know who does that," said Sally.

"How else am I going to be 100% in tune with your instrument?"

"Nobody else ever bothered. They didn't give a damn whether they were in tune with me or not." Sally looked up at me and our eyes locked. "Put your flute down. Over there on the coffee table."

She got up and kissed me with such force that I almost lost my balance. I hugged her tight while her tongue articulated all the mood changes in the Prokofieff Sonata. Dancing staccatos, soaring arpeggios, fortissimo attacks, and when she finished there was a moment of tranquility like in the third movement.

She started unbuttoning her blouse and led my hand there to continue. My fingers trembled with anticipation. I took her blouse off slowly, not quite sure of myself. Vera wasn't the kind to let me undress her.

Sally turned her back to me, a silent invitation to unhook her bra. I fumbled with the clasp and moved closer, wrapping one arm around her waist while sliding the bra straps off her shoulders. I cupped her breasts in my hands.

"They're too big, aren't they?" Sally asked. "Someday they'll hang down to my waist."

I finished removing her bra and turned her to face me. "Luscious." She took my hand as I bent down to kiss a nipple and led it to her underpants.

I led her to the guest bedroom. There, tangled memories of my mother's fury when she arrived home early from a trip to find me playing house with a co-ed invaded my intoxication with Sally topless. I looked down at the bed, hungry for it, half-paralyzed by the thought of evidence that could be found there. "Are you sure?" I whispered.

Sally did not answer. She went to the bathroom and brought back a towel. "A couple of minutes in the washer and this will be like new." She wrapped the towel around my shoulders and slipped off her underpants. "You really shouldn't be doing this," she whispered. "Can you face your wife?" Sally smiled, wicked.

"In my own house? I'm not so sure."

"Guess you'll have to deal with that when it comes. When did you say she'll be back?"

"Another week or so."

"You still have plenty of time to put on that serious face of yours."

"Vera used to say that faces don't lie."

"Let it go and you'll be all right."

Afterwards she said it felt so natural, "Must have been the music. Needed that."

"Me too." It came from deep inside, that part of me that's still free. "But please don't misunderstand me. I have a good marriage and can't give it up."

Sally flashed anger faster than I could swallow the words. "Sure, because marriage means servants for you men. Women get married and their lovers become slave drivers. You know what husbands say? 'Where's breakfast?' Or, 'Why isn't dinner ready? You know when I get home every day.'"

"I guess I shouldn't have said that."

"Damn right you shouldn't. Why should I have to stay home preparing for a man?"

Sally's tirade drowned the honeysuckle of love-making in a sea of venom. I gasped for air and choked on her rage. She wasn't finished.

"My ex-husband – the bastard – said all I do is play guitar all day. When I told him I'm a musician too, he retorted, 'Why don't you get a real job and help out?' The jerk had all the connections and he wouldn't lift a finger for me. He let me play with him at minor gigs in Michigan and resented it all the way."

Her words dug in like a pick-axe. I tried to hold on to her. She shoved me away.

"He did his best to drown me out when we played together. Get amplification, he told me. Sure, so the audience hears all the squeaks and fingerboard scratches. All he wanted was somebody to cook and clean and fuck for him."

Sally pulled my head to her and snarled in my ear. "Do you understand what I'm saying? You men get to work with people. Try going it alone all day with squalling babies crying, 'Mommy. Mommy. Mommy! Waaaaah.' You think that's lonely. Husband gets home and demands service. That's when the real loneliness begins."

"I didn't know you had children."

"Are you out of your mind? Who needs children? My ex had a solo career handed to him on a silver platter. That Tchaikovsky medal got him the best management in the business and more than a year of bookings with major orchestras for starters. He thought that meant he should be treated like visiting royalty. The jerk demanded to be waited on hand and foot wherever he performed – to say nothing of what he demanded of me."

Sally cursed him with an impressive repertoire of gutter talk. "His reward for offending everybody from Boston to San Francisco was that no conductor would have anything to do with him again, no matter how well he performed. Word spread like wildfire that they would rather shove their batons up his ass than conduct for him. It wasn't two years before he was back playing local gigs for peanuts like before he won that medal. That killed my hopes for making it too."

Sally heaved with anger. If we had just made tender love, I couldn't remember it.

I tried to hug her and offer some comfort. She pushed me away. "You get to make the bed. I'll get this towel washed. If Vera ever asks if you did anything with me, look her straight in the eye and ask if she's crazy."

11

Vera

I Don't Like Stan Goldman

Lex's closest friend is much taller than he deserves to be. I don't doubt Stan Goldman would love my ultra-high kitchen cabinets, but only if he were a woman. His nose is a little bit too big for his face, but otherwise he is strikingly handsome. He boasts a smirk that says he knows it.

I met Mr. Goldman not long after Lex started thinking he wanted to marry me. That came about because my parents didn't like Lex at all. Mother harassed me constantly about finding somebody better, but I couldn't.

I had to get out from under her thumb, so I moved to Washington to be with Lex and three other men in a house on Van Ness Street that belonged to some Foreign Service people assigned overseas. Mr. Goldman was one of the roommates, a new diplomat in Washington to train for an overseas assignment. He behaved like he already was a big shot in the Foreign Service. That is why I call him Mister.

This was not your typical group house. Along with a living-room full of Chinese rosewood furniture, there was a complete set of Wedgwood china, real silverware, and an antique grandfather clock that stood taller than me. How I wish our shabby home had just a few beautiful things like those we enjoyed when we lived there.

Elaborate ivory carvings of a Buddha and an old fisherman graced the mantelpiece over the fireplace. They had a much simpler carving of a stiff naked woman for company. Mr. Goldman explained, "Chinese doctors used these for diagnosis. Women pointed out the location of their problem on the ivory figure rather than remove their clothes for examination. Not my kind of women." He guffawed whenever he thought he was funny, though he was not.

Lex's housemates switched around and gave us the master bedroom. I offered to make dinner for them but they rarely came home to eat. Except for Mr. Goldman, I was barely aware of their presence. When we did have a meal together, his smirk punctuated every conversation.

Mr. Goldman and Lex became good friends, but he is not the kind of person I would have in my home voluntarily. Ten years after we left the group house Lex still insists on bringing him around from time to time despite my distaste for him. I just have to bear it.

This time was better than usual, thank goodness, because Sally was here to share the burden of Mr. Goldman's incessant chatter and bad jokes. It pains me that Lex hangs on his every word while he looks right over my head and acts as if I'm not there at all. I'm sick and tired of hearing him brag about how Donovan Q. Zook and Outerbridge Horsey were the names to watch in the Foreign Service until Goldman and Abramowitz came along.

Afterwards I gently suggested to Lex that it would be nice if Mr. Goldman came over to our house as little as possible.

Not for the first time, he answered, "But this is how I learn what's going on in the world. Let other people go numb watching TV that doesn't tell you anything worth listening to."

I wondered if that's me he was referring to.

When we got into bed Lex hugged me and apologized for Goldman's behavior. "It's OK," I said.

"Let's make it even better," he whispered.

I usually try to oblige him, whenever and wherever, but this time I pleaded exhaustion.

He smiled. "I hope I'm not wasting my time reading 'The Joy of Sex.'"

"Tomorrow, can we please?"

I'm not sure I heard it right, because Lex had already turned facing the other way, across our bedroom and out the window – but it sounded like he whispered tomorrow, and tomorrow, and tomorrow. It's a good thing I was still focused on detesting Stan Goldman. That allowed me to believe he only said it once.

12

Sally

Invitation

Bernice Berberger from USIA called, gruff as ever. "Come in at 9:15 next Wednesday. We need to talk." She hung up before I could ask what the meeting is about, but that ranking muckety-muck in our make friends for America agency holds my life in her hands.

There's only two reasons she would see me. Either I'm off their recommended musicians list because I don't perform any more with my ex-husband, or she's desperate for someone to go to Africa again. I come cheap and the Africans love flamenco.

I trembled all week waiting for the axe to fall. When Wednesday finally came I got there at 8:30. First I circled the dirty gray building housing the agency. Then the labyrinth these people go through every day led me everywhere but the office of the program director. It was getting much too close to nine by the time I found it and was ushered past a phalanx of desks to a chair jammed between a file cabinet and a paper shredder. Nobody was at the desks except the lone secretary, who took to polishing her nails as she guarded the entrance.

Nine-fifteen and nine-thirty came and went, with barely a rustle of papers from some desk in the distance. Another ten minutes and I was fighting to save my fingernails for guitar playing instead of chewing them off.

It was almost ten before Miss Berberger ambled over, took my hand, and directed me into the office. She didn't even offer me a seat.

"I will get right to the point. We still have funds to commit and I intend to get the money allocated this week. I can give you three to four weeks of concerts for our programs in Europe."

My heart went through the roof.

"The pay is modest, but don't you ever forget that I'm doing you a favor by putting you on at all. Yes, we will cover the plane fare."

My heart skipped about six beats. There's nothing I ever wanted more than a European tour. In Schubert's day it was my instrument that was all the rage. I'll show everybody why.

My daydream was interrupted by Miss Berberger's impatience. "I need to know right now whether you can take this on, before my next meeting in exactly two minutes." She looked at her watch with the intensity I associate with learning a new piece of music. "If you won't do it there are plenty of people who will."

I had to ask. "Would it be possible to take on another performer, maybe a flutist? The combination would make a really great program."

"Understand this. We don't support unrated artists and we already broke the rules to rate you because your husband won a medal in the Tchaikovsky competition and insisted on it. This is what we offer."

She didn't repeat what it was, but I could care less. All I want to do is perform in European concert halls.

13

Vera

In the Living Room

My neck takes its ire out on me in the living room. The sofa we bought at a garage sale sags and the frayed piping shows white. Tension creeps up to the base of my skull when I turn my head and am reminded that everything here is second-hand; the end tables, the lamps, the rocking chair that nobody sits in, even the drapes. Standing there in the middle of our very own flea market makes each fiber of muscle scream. I retreat into the kitchen and massage my neck until it calms down.

I had wanted to wallpaper the living room with an elegant floral pattern, but Lex insisted on grass cloth and was adamant about doing it himself. Mr. Troon at House Beautiful explained everything. "Don't try standing on a ladder and eyeballing the alignment. You have to use a plumb line to get it right."

I was Lex's girl Friday, handing him the brush and paste and bracing him on the ladder. We forgot the plumb line. Worse yet, I looked all over the house and couldn't find any string to improvise one. I wanted to go and buy some. Lex insisted he could hang it in perfect alignment.

When I told him the living room is just a little bit off the perpendicular, he was adamant. "Nothing's wrong. In a day or two and you'll get used to it."

It has been years, and I still get dizzy. When Mr. Goldman comes to dinner he thinks it's very funny to greet me with, "Your wallpaper's out of alignment," before he even says hello. Lex says, "It really doesn't matter, does it?" I'll bet that when Sally Pendergast tells Lex he's playing out of tune he wouldn't dream of suggesting that it doesn't matter.

I have some hand woven wall hangings that I bought when my parents took me to Guatemala during a high school vacation. They're real folk art created by the Indians in the mountain villages, and the vivid colors brought life to my college dorm room. I hoped to see them on my walls again.

Lex had different ideas. "I want some real art. That's why we picked grass cloth, so our collection wouldn't be cluttered up by some flowery pattern. I learned about all the great works in a fabulous course with the grandson of the designer of the Brooklyn Bridge."

Lex's idea of real art was reproductions printed on thin cardboard in chintzy frames. He hung several of them with great care, proving that there is nothing quite like wavy grass cloth out of alignment to draw your attention to Renoir, Goya, and Modigliani. I had to line the pictures up with the wallpaper, crooked for all to see.

From time to time, Lex stares at Renoir's bathers on the side wall, totally oblivious that I'm standing right behind him. His head bobs up and down, probably hoping they will come alive and flock to him. When he's had his fill of these nudes he turns around and, startled by my presence, asks if we can make love now. I should tell him we don't make love until he gets me a new sofa, but he wouldn't hear it. When he gets engrossed in his cardboard art, I'm invisible.

With Aaron and Jennifer now in school I was going nuts cooped up in this house with "La Maja Desnuda" and all the other nudes hanging crooked on our walls. I couldn't help but wonder if Lex's sex urges hung with them.

I suppose I could have spent my days reading books, but try reading for a couple of days straight with nothing else going on and you will see why I cannot do it. In desperation I decided to get a grip on the kids' education and make a social life for myself by joining the Woodbridge Elementary School Parent Teachers' Association. The first thing they asked me to do was be the President. I was fool enough to be flattered. The outgoing officers realized they had a sucker.

I would like to say I enjoy being in a respected position of authority, but authority over nothing is much closer to the truth. At PTA meetings a handful of parents argue endlessly over how their children should be educated. Even when there was consensus nobody volunteered to do anything. The principal listens to my reports with the vacuous look of a mind far away. If the school ever implemented a PTA suggestion, nobody bothered to make me aware of it.

Outside of the meetings, there is no social interaction whatever. You would think we parents have something in common, but the only reward for all this effort is an overwhelming veneer of distant politeness. Varnish smells better.

None of these people will allow me to resign as PTA president. Some of them are parents of children the same age as mine, and they are neighbors, but nobody knocks on my door except a motley collection of obnoxious missionaries. I tried drawing and knitting and fancy cooking, but nothing fills the void that settles in the minute I get home from walking the children to school, not even working in my garden.

Maybe shopping for antiques would help. How nice it would be to have some real ones to complement the cheap second-hand furniture we bought at garage sales. There is no reason we should be broke now that Lex has been promoted, yet he still moans when I suggest we do something to make the house more livable. The irony of his poor boy talk is that I've been writing the checks and paying the bills ever since he got so busy playing the flute, but I never have any money I can call my own.-

On one of those rare nights Lex helps with the dishes I told him, "I feel like I'm chained to this house. I desperately need to get out and get a job."

"So go ahead and see what you can find out there. Just make sure you can take the kids to school and be with them when they get out."

"I doubt there will be any decent possibilities if I have to quit in the middle of the afternoon. I'll need a baby-sitter"

"That's a new twist. You're the one who always refuses to have baby-sitters."

"The situation is different now. This is daytime and the children are bigger. Maybe one of the PTA mothers in the neighborhood would take Aaron and Jennifer for a couple of hours. I could arrange to take in her children when they want to go out so there wouldn't be any money involved."

"Don't you think it would be better if the children are with their mother?"

Lex is a specialist with that line, and he knows just where to find support for it. My mother's voice still yells at me from inside, "A woman's place is in the home."

I want to shout, but I mumble, "I'm with them all the time. You wouldn't notice, would you? I'll ask Sally if she wouldn't mind doing it."

"She's a musician," pouted Lex.

"The children really love her, and she seems to love them too. She certainly could use the money."

"I can't imagine you making her into a baby-sitter."

Wrong again, dear husband.

14

Lex

The Offer

Could I be a friend of Ludwig's in 1815, playing Giuliani with the best guitarist in Vienna for intoxicated royals celebrating Napoleon's downfall at Waterloo?

In reality, Beethoven was a little jealous in my dreams between twice a week rehearsals for the concert Sally arranged at the University of Maryland.

I'll perform almost half the program, with our duos sandwiched between her solos both before and after intermission. Besides the "Gran Duetto" there's the "Entr'Acte" and memories of those nights we met and almost ended up splattered on the bridge abutment. We'll also perform Dowland's sublime "Lachrimae Pavane." It's the oldest piece in our repertoire, but it demands more practice than any of the others.

This was to be my first public performance in close to ten years, and I hadn't been a soloist since college days. I should have been a bundle of nerves, but Sally told me to cool it and my only choice was to listen to her. Don't ask me how I did it, but I forgot the jitters once I got on stage and the concert was a success.

The next time we got together to rehearse Sally whispered in my ear, "Come with me. I'm scared to do this all alone."

"What are you talking about?"

She told me about the European tour. Just like her to spring this when Vera is upstairs putting the kids to bed and could be back any minute.

"You've got to be kidding. I'm not good enough for that." I really wish I didn't mean it, but that's what came out before I could give it any thought.

"Yes you are."

Vera came down the steps and the conversation ended as suddenly as it began. She sat on the sofa just a few feet away while I struggled mightily to keep my mind on the music. The rest of the rehearsal our talk was limited to the minutiae that must be mastered to make it worth listening to.

I drove Sally home and saw her to the door. She fished for her keys, and then we just stared at each other. She pleaded, "You'll do it, won't you?"

Without a word I tried to pick her up and carry her across the threshold. Sally wouldn't let me. "Not that. I mean you'll do the European tour with me."

"Can we go inside and talk? Taking off like this is pretty complicated. Besides, it's been too long since…"

"Cut the pillow talk. You really think you can do me quick, take a shower, and go home and fool your wife? Come on." Sally looked at me like I had lost my mind. "You've been lucky you didn't arouse suspicion before, but you'll never get away with it when she's home in bed waiting for you."

Sally went on before I could answer. "I'm serious about taking you on my European tour. I've got concerts all over, and we'll even get to play in the Salzburg Mozarteum. Doesn't that send shivers up your spine? To play where Mozart himself played."

"To tell the truth, I gave up that fantasy a long time ago."

"So what do you spend all your free time practicing for?"

"To make music… but there are all kinds of flutists around Washington who have more performance experience in a week than I've had in ten years. I bet they would die to take a European tour with you."

Why am I doing this to myself? If I must choose I would rather perform in Salzburg than make love to Sally.

"Why not stop the false modesty crap and start planning our music for the heavens."

"Play for the heavens? Maybe play while looking for my soul."

"Make love with your flute in Europe."

I drew back a step from Sally, not knowing what to say about the most important thing that was happening to me in memory. I couldn't even tell her that I loved her for the invitation and was terrified of Vera's reaction.

"Stop looking at me like I'm going to let you in and go take care of your wife – all the time, because I have to convince her that we'll be going to Europe on a concert tour, not a fuckfest."

15

Vera

Vera Gets a Job

Lex might not have taken my quest for employment seriously, but I certainly did. You cannot believe how many ads I answered. Washington Post ads, Washington Times, even the Northern Virginia Daily. No, I cannot take dictation. Yes, I can type, but you can't expect me to type well enough to be a secretary. To tell the truth, secretarial work is so pre-liberation. I consider myself at least a little bit liberated.

I'm not a nurse or a teacher, but I should be qualified to be a store clerk. I called about a few of those ads and it turned out that the wages are hardly enough to pay a baby-sitter. The receptionist listings seemed to be the most promising, but as soon as I revealed my interest in working from nine to three, their interest dried up. I was about to give up the search and accept my role in life when I came across an ad in the Washington Post: Receptionist for doctor's office. Must be mature and outgoing. Full or part time. Tel: 879-2345. Certainly I'm mature, but I wonder if my outgoing hasn't been superseded by being homebodying.

The phone number was familiar. As I suspected, it was for Dr. Cooper, the OBGYN who delivered my babies and advised me to read Kinsey. When the pain got really excruciating, he gave me drugs that made my long labor manageable. Am I thinking Demerol – or those books?

The doctor's office is on 17th and I Streets, in an old building whose drab cement façade is badly in need of a sandblasting. When I got there for the appointment I learned that the same could be said of the receptionist. She looked older than the building and her eyes were as opaque as the frosted glass door.

Her sharp angular face did not suggest a welcome. Nor did her gravelly, "There will be a short wait." This must be somebody Dr. Cooper hopes to replace, because he certainly is not a grouch. When he summoned me into his examining room his lips opened into a broad smile. "How are those beautiful babies of yours?"

I felt strange that Dr. Cooper remembered the birth of my babies five and six years ago but asked what I'm here for today. "Are you pregnant again?"

"Heavens no. Two little rascals are enough for me, thank you."

"I also have you down for the mammogram I recommended last time."

"Oh, my, there must be a mix up. I'm actually here to inquire about your ad for a receptionist."

Dr. Cooper looked at me with a spark in his eyes that sent a shiver down my spine.

"We missed a trick here. The nurse handed me your file and we assumed you were in for an examination."

"I guess I'm due for one, but could you tell me about your job opening."

"There are several applications, but I haven't selected anybody yet. Are you asking for yourself or for somebody else?"

"I could do a very good job for you. I like to work with people, and I majored in psychology in college."

"With those credentials you should be able to earn more money elsewhere."

"Perhaps, but everybody wants a full-time employee. I need to be able to pick up Aaron and Jennifer from school."

He chuckled. "You know what's really important. That's what I need in my office, so consider this your job interview and tell me when you can start."

"Yesterday. I'm so happy about this." I surprised myself gushing like that, since I hardly knew him. "I hope next Monday will be OK. I want to give my husband a few days to learn to do the dishes more often."

"Don't worry about that," said Dr. Cooper. "In a couple of weeks you'll have a paycheck big enough to buy a dishwasher."

"That's great news, but I will have to teach him how to load it."

16

Lex

Why Not Tell Me These Things?

It was the anniversary of our first date, and I was washing the dishes while Vera toweled them dry. That's a propitious time to get through to her, so I asked, "Why is it that I first learned about this new job of yours from Sally Pendergast?"

Vera looked out the window into our back yard. "If you would really like to know, I was worried that you wouldn't approve. We're a pretty old fashioned family, one breadwinner and one dutiful housewife doing everything at home and raising children."

"But that's great news." I took Vera in my arms and gave her a big hug. "You'll earn enough money that we can do all kinds of things we couldn't afford before."

She put her arms around me and I was about to carry her up to the bedroom when she recoiled. "Ugh. Your hands are all wet. I feel it right through my blouse."

I released her quickly. "Sorry. I didn't think of that. I just wanted to celebrate with you."

Vera rubbed her back. "I didn't mean to jump like that. I guess I'm just super-sensitive to soapy dishwater, but it's good to have you in the kitchen helping out."

She slipped a plate into the rinse water and turned to give me a light kiss on the cheek. "I'm so glad you approve. Now it's your turn to tell me why you haven't said anything yet about *your* upcoming job."

"What do you mean?" I looked straight at her. She didn't turn away from my gaze.

"You know, that concert tour Sally asked you to take with her. She's terrified that European reviewers will crucify her if she goes it alone, and tells me it is almost impossible for a mere mortal to pull off a solo guitar recital. What do you think of that?"

I shuddered.

Vera rattled on, "Sally said she looked all over Washington for a flutist, or even a violinist who would take the tour with her. She thought about Naomi Goldman, but said her sound is so mousy it wouldn't add much color to the guitar. Two string instruments just cannot offer the variety of sound that a flute can."

Vera dried her hands, but wasn't about to let me say anything just yet. "Everybody Sally asked wanted far more than she can afford to pay, and the decent musicians told her they would only be able to rehearse once or twice before the tour. Sally was almost in tears when she told me there is no way she can perform that way. She asked whether you might be able to go and pay your own expenses. She said she wouldn't dream of proposing this without my permission."

I could already feel dinner juices in my throat. Is Vera babbling on just to taunt me, or is all this talk her way of giving permission?

She stared at me the way she stares at the kids when they misbehave. "It was pretty awkward hearing it first from Sally. Don't you think this is something you should have told me about?"

I stammered. "Maybe for the same reason you didn't tell me about the job in the doctor's office. I was worried you would think we're plotting some kind of affair."

"Are you?"

That's not a question I'm going to hesitate to answer. "I just want to make music, that's all. It's what I always hoped to do before the reality of supporting a family set in."

"Very well." Vera looked me straight in the eye. "You're already having a passionate affair with the music. I see that every time you bounce off the chair when you're playing. Just don't get any ideas about having sex with Sally. She told me she'll lop your whatsis off if you try."

"I'm sure she would. But I won't give her that opportunity."

My wife is a boa constrictor slowly twisting around my torso, tighter and tighter, before swallowing me whole. She won't take her eyes off me, or that tone of voice. "I still don't know why you don't talk about these things with me."

"I don't know either." I stared out the window at Vera's crocuses, in full bloom in an otherwise scroungy garden. I couldn't face her when I said, "I told Sally to wait until I asked you about it first."

I am not a very good liar. Sally had insisted that she be first to ask Vera about the concert tour. She was certain I would mess it up, and she wasn't about to let me give Vera any excuse to squelch the idea.

17

Vera

Accepting Dirt

I find gardening to be hard, dirty work, but I want to do it, for reasons I don't fully understand. Mrs. Reiner next door tells me that the topsoil here is just wonderful. Anything will grow in it. The weeds agree with her but my cantaloupes are not quite like those pictured on the seed packet. They're no larger than tennis balls, and the birds have taken their share.

Thank goodness I don't calculate the number of hours it takes me to produce lettuce that the insects transform into Venetian lace and tomatoes that Lex and the children leave uneaten in my salad bowl because they're all spotty. For me, gardening is more about getting my hands dirty than cultivating anything edible.

Dr. Eisenberg, the psychiatrist we met at Stan Goldman's party, explained that caressing dirt is compensation for hands being slapped by mothers when little girls are naughty.

"It's surprising how mature women compensate for childhood trauma this way when they should want nothing more than to demonstrate that they are not peasants who must till the earth. You don't find many liberated women gardening unless they're repressing some pretty serious trauma."

When I asked him where that theory came from, he pontificated. "Sexuality starts in infancy. For reasons that can only be called Victorian or Holy Roller, a lot of mothers do everything they can to prevent their babies from discovering their bodies."

I wondered whether this could somehow explain why Stan Goldman is so obnoxious. More than that, I was tempted to ask Dr. Eisenberg whether my timidity might be traced all the way back to being swatted by mama when masturbating before the age of conscious memory. That's when Stan sauntered over, dragging Lex with him. "You two analyzing your sexual prowess?" Stan asked.

"Of course," I said, surprising myself. "Would you care to join the discussion?"

"That's a bold invitation for somebody as repressed as you are," said Stan. Has the good doctor told you how to overcome all your hang-ups?"

I started to raise my hand to slap him, but stopped. He probably didn't notice.

"Now you can understand why we psychiatrists focus on repressed desires and trauma," said Dr. Eisenberg. "That's what underlies these presentations."

"What am I presenting, dear Doctor?" Stan asked.

"Yourself. Since we're in polite company, I'd best limit myself to that for now. We can take up the details in your regular session next Tuesday."

I have no doubt that Mr. Goldman needs a psychiatrist, and maybe I need one too, because I'm convinced that relating to seeds and soil is so much simpler and more rewarding than most other relationships. When I get my hands dirty I can wash them whenever I please, or not. Sometimes I sit with my hands covered in dirt for who knows how long, just gazing at soil until I can visualize the shoots growing, like my Aaron and Jennifer. With adults, I'm more likely to look right past them. You have to wash your hands of so much dirt just to accept people with all their warts, and that's before a friendship can even begin.

Make no mistake. I can wash away all the mistrust and resentment to do just that. Take Sally, for example. She comes into my house and takes over. She's the performer. I'm the audience whether I want to be or not. She plays so beautifully that I can't help but listen even when I'm not in the mood for intrusions, or should I call it company?

She entrances Lex with her music. Watching him respond with such energy and drive in his flute playing depresses me with the certain knowledge that I can't give him that. I might try, but after all these years I wonder if Lex would recognize joy from me if it stared him in the face.

Don't ask me how I have come to feel close to Sally, because I cannot find a reason for it. We couldn't be more disparate personalities. She sparkles everywhere she goes. I might as well be invisible. Her radiant glow snares people because she shows interest in everybody. I confess to finding most people rather boring and it probably shows, although I do not want it to.

It's a bit strange that I can still feel this way about Sally when she proposes to take my husband off to Europe. The idea was bothersome at first, but not so much now. Am I grateful for the vacation from marriage? I'll admit that. Worried about an affair in front of my nose? I don't think Lex would dare. He's straight-laced and pretty repressed himself. What will it look like to the neighbors? None of them looks at us. We might just as well be living in a Manhattan skyscraper.

Sally enters our life and gives Lex the music he has always craved. That leads me to understand how the two of us became so close. She keeps both me and Lex happy. With Lex it is the music, pure and simple. That has taken the pressure off me to give him contentment that he doesn't seem able to create on his own.

For me, it's a complex mix. Besides being relieved of the burden of responsibility for Lex's happiness, Sally is a voice – in the cacophony that swirls around in my head – which I find fascinating to listen to. She tells incredible stories about running away from home, the excitement of being Segovia's kitten and protégé, of seducing the stars of the guitar world and becoming an emerging star herself. She also listens, even when all I have to offer is complaint. She helps in the kitchen and takes care of the children whenever I need her to. You can't ask any more from a friend.

This European tour seems innocent even as it appears to be not so innocent at the same time. She needs a melody instrument to make her tour a success. Lex comes free and has been playing with her regularly. Paying another musician to accompany is beyond her means. I believe her when she says USIA won't do anything to help. That is so typical of government.

Lex doesn't care if he pays to play. You have to see them rehearse to know how much heart he puts into the music. Sally too, even though she is a professional and says that playing guitar is pretty much all she does. The two of them ponder every note and play everything a dozen different ways, just to see which sounds the best.

Sally plays her solos for us too. She has such an extraordinary range of expression that it is difficult to believe she cannot pull off wonderful concerts all by herself. Sometimes I think it would be better that way, but I know how badly Lex wants to do this, and it would ease Sally's anxiety too. Evidently she is not ready to pretend she is Segovia and she really does need my flutist husband to make this concert tour with her.

You might think it is beyond belief that nothing is going on between Lex and Sally, but she shows no interest in him at all. Maybe her saturation with other men explains why the disinterest is mutual. Lex seems to prefer being the counselor who gives her advice on how to keep a man coming back. He must believe he's sharing wisdom, but it seems to me that for Lex, authority trumps wisdom.

I wonder if he is able to pursue a truly intimate relationship. No doubt he tries, but the more I see him engrossed in his music, the keener I feel that is the only place he dares put all his passion. Sometimes I wonder if Lex has gotten over the trauma of being told what he needs to do during our bedroom lessons.

Lex trumpets his love for music. He is matter of fact about me. He did not beg to go off on a concert tour of Europe with my best friend, but I do not doubt he would have gotten down on his knees and done so if I wanted that.

Sally and Lex have become best friends too, rehearsing like they do for hours on end. Lex tells me, "Making chamber music is another kind of orgasm." Am I crazy to think that one orgasm won't lead to another in Europe? Maybe, but I must think this way. If I say no to this tour, my husband and my best friend will detest me for the rest of their lives.

18

Lex

Indispensable Employee

Why must I always hang on doggedly to subway straps, swaying and bumping into strangers at random intervals? Mornings the Washington Metro is crammed to the gills with sleep-deprived commuters, their eyes glazed over with the remnants of restlessness in the wee hours. They push each other to get out before the doors close and the train lurches forward again. Like most of them, I'm headed for lifeless buildings of depression-era architecture, the bony structures of the nerve center of world power.

Everything in this city is defined by rank in the government. I'm in the middle of that rank race, rather young for my station in bureaucratic life, supposedly someone with bright prospects. In the Interior Department, I'm drowning in the mid-levels of a huge morass.

My reward for excellence in a government slush factory is to be put in charge of planning and development for restoring the Chesapeake and Ohio Canal towpath. I learned soon enough that this is another one of those projects where the work of weeks and months drags on for years. I'm not really in charge of anything at all. The title is just a sham to justify laying on more drudge work.

Every couple of years they delay my promotion for another year or two and blame it on budget constraints, pay freezes and all that shit. When it finally comes, the pay raise barely keeps up with inflation. Some time shortly before brain death I might dream of making it to the top of the civil service so I can report directly to a political hack who knows nothing about what we do. Rather than learn, these people usually bring real work to a halt.

Some consider the drudgery a fair exchange for a regular paycheck and a secure job. My jaundiced view is colored by the fact that I have not been able to take leave in almost two years because my work is so absolutely essential. For many reasons, I have swallowed that line since my all too ambitious beginning.

Now it's different. All I want is the leave I'm entitled to so I can take this European concert tour with Sally Pendergast. You know what the boss said? "We've got to finish the budget first." He wants me to hang around and create a budget for an idiotic project of his that is certain to be killed by Congress, if not by my own department. My assistant can do that. No, he wants me here to supervise it.

B. George Rollins, the Deputy Assistant Secretary for National Park Development, didn't bother to look up from his desk when I got up the guts to take my leave request up with the next bigger boss in line. "This is very important to me, and I stand to lose the leave if I don't take it now."

"So. What else is new?" Rollins smiled. He looked at me as if he was going to laugh in my face. "You know very well that I don't set the deadlines around here."

I pleaded, "This concert tour is a once in a lifetime opportunity."

"Concert tour? You must be pulling my leg."

"No sir." I handed him my formal written request for leave. He stared at it as if he had never seen a leave request before. A frown colored his jowls as gray as the dingy walls. "Nobody has the right to force you to lose leave, but this is a most inconvenient time. Maybe we could compensate in other ways."

He said it in that saccharine voice of deliberate civility that slicked-down senior officials display when they are certain their genteel request will be understood as a command to be slavishly obeyed.

I couldn't strangle him as I wanted, but there was nothing to stop me from imitating his voice, unmistakably sarcastic in its obsequiousness. "Yes sir. Of course I understand that it has been a most inconvenient time to take leave for more than two years now. I've already arranged for Sam Ziegler to cover for me while I'm gone. He knows the details of our budget at least as well as I do."

"You put us all in an awkward position." Rollins's voice was so flat it was hard to tell whether he meant it, but he went on about the seriousness of my absence, much like a devout mother lecturing a preteen son who balks at going to church on Sunday. "I'm not going to deny this leave request, but you should know that insisting on it at this critical juncture lets your colleagues down. In truth, it is not very healthy for your budding career."

I had nothing to say to Rollins, but I sang the opening of Beethoven's fifth all the way out of the building, not giving a damn if colleagues in the corridors thought I was nuts.

19

Sally

Dreams of Europe

I'm having dreams of playing in palaces. We start with Hapsburg heaven in Vienna, and then calm mad Ludwig under that huge crystal chandelier in *Schloss Neuschwanstein.* I see John Dowland coming to hear us perform his Lachrimae Pavane in the Uffizi Palace salon that the Medici grand duke built for us. Lorenzo the Great applauds wildly and his whole entourage demands encores until we can't play any more. And there's the Mozarteum in Salzburg, where I let Mozart know he should have composed for guitar.

I'm adored as a musician, but feel sorry for Lex having to put up with his government job. That's when I'm jolted out of sleep wondering if I wouldn't be better off going to work and getting paid whether I actually accomplished anything or not.

Is it never-ending frustration with work that translates into passion when Lex makes music? None of the professionals I know play with his fervor. Maybe it's because we have to struggle so hard to make a living out of it. I play for the passion of it too, but I'm starving. I know he cares about music more than anything, but I wonder if he really cares about me – or is it the animal hiding in him on those rare occasions we make love.

I still can't fathom why Vera isn't suspicious – is she playing a game too? Cross your fingers that Lex can face Vera without guilt showing in his face. So far it's OK as far as I can tell, but who knows what she'll think after we go off touring Europe together for a month?

Vera already told me while we were waiting for Lex to get back from the office for rehearsal. We were sitting at the dining room table chatting about nothing in particular when she blurted, "Musicians have a reputation for having affairs with just about anybody they ever perform with." I was about to duck then and there. All I could think of to say was, "Not always." I couldn't even look at her.

Vera just laughed while I squirmed. The front door opened and Lex walked in as she continued, "I imagine you wouldn't want to break up the duo that way, would you?"

"What are you two talking about? Lex asked. "Sorry I'm late."

"Just sharing a few thoughts about Europe," I said.

"Let me get something in the oven," said Vera. "I'll be right back."

We've got a lot of work to do this evening," said Lex.

"Right." I felt the tremor in my voice.

Vera came over as Lex and I were setting up our music stands and arranging the parts in the order we would be performing them in Europe. She waited until we sat down and started to tune up before putting a hand on each of our shoulders. "Now you two make sure to behave yourselves during this trip."

I'm sure I saw Lex's heart drop into his stomach. How could Vera miss it? He stiffened up like he was having an attack of acute heartburn and mumbled, "Of course we will."

"Yes, I know," Vera said it so softly it was barely a whisper.

It took everything I had not to look away. "Don't worry. I won't let him get near me. He's not my type."

Vera gave us a wan smile. "Make music," she said, on her way out to the kitchen.

I could hear her thinking…and not love.

20

Lex

Final Rehearsal

After that performance of Vera's – was it make music not love she said? – our playing was shakier than it had ever been. Dowland's wildly intricate "Lachrimae Pavane" turned my fingers to butter. Worse, I played out of tune and didn't realize it until Sally dug into me with a snide remark about tin ears. "And why are you playing with so much vibrato?"

I couldn't help it, and I couldn't say anything either. I was scared out of my wits that Vera might overhear the cause of my tremulous tone. To say nothing about my wrong notes.

"Let's play some of the easier stuff until we get warmed up," said Sally.

"Good idea."

"Sounds super." Vera's voice floated in from the kitchen. She is not in the habit of tossing praise from the kitchen. I wondered whether she was trying to rub the guilt in our noses.

I used to think I could figure out what was on her mind, but she has proved me wrong time and again. Sometimes she tells me what she's thinking after making me feel like an idiot. More often silence is her way of letting me know I don't understand her as the storm brews.

Vera cooked spaghetti and meatballs while we were rehearsing. She didn't say a word as she filled our plates, but once she sat down at the dinner table with us she was ebullient. "You two will be famous. I was looking at that copy of Musical America you gave me and there's only one flute and guitar duo listed there. You need to get listed."

Vera turned towards Sally. "Lex still cannot believe that he will get on a plane next week and perform in Europe."

"He better play well for me. If he plays like he did today, his dream will turn into a nightmare."

If Sally thinks I'll blow it, she ought to look in the mirror. I'm not going to take all the blame for today's disastrous rehearsal. I looked at her and at Vera in turn. "Look who's talking. If you're going to be unsteady, how can I follow you without sounding like a beginner?"

Vera shushed Sally before she could retort. "I don't know what's with you two today. Why are you skewering each other?"

"It's not that. If I perform like I played today I'd be hissed off the stage."

"Stop being such a worry wart," said Sally. "I'm steady as a rock."

"That's right," said Vera. "Every other time you've played together it's been beautiful."

"Don't you know that a disastrous dress rehearsal means a great concert?" Sally asked. "That was our mantra at Juilliard," I said.

An image flashed across my mind and I broke out laughing. "Remember that mad Russian refugee and his wife who worked seven days a week to rent Town Hall so he could conduct his so-called world famous balalaika orchestra? When I was free-lancing in New York he hired me and a batch of other ringers to cover the string and wind parts. Instead of sticking to Russian folk music, he brought in a friend to open with the Schumann piano concerto. Imagine performing Schumann with balalaikas and laughing ringers.

"It should have been a hoot like P.D.Q. Bach, but the poor woman at the piano was so pathetic during that long opening solo that half the hall emptied out before she was through butchering it. So much for great concerts after dress rehearsal disasters, but we ringers weren't asked to do the rehearsal and had absolutely no idea what was in store for us until the conductor took up his baton. He flailed until none of us could keep a straight face."

We all laughed at that, but Vera knew my mind better than I did. "That's a great story, but you should forget about how you played today and enjoy the evening. You're going to be gone for the better part of a month."

"Right on," said Sally. "You'll play just great if you stop wallowing in doubt."

"Time to stop ganging up on Lex, even if he is male and we outnumber him. It would be much better to smile through this," said Vera.

"Agreed. Just give me a second. I'll be right back." Time to get away from these women and get my little present for Sally.

21

Sally

Electrified

Lex left Vera and me at the table and went upstairs. He came back down with a cardboard box about a foot or so in each dimension and put it in my lap with a big smile. "I have a little present for you."

"Help me with it."

Lex opened the box and I jumped out of my seat. "How can you do this to me?"

I must have been screaming bloody murder because little Aaron tiptoed down the stairs with a very upset look on his face. "Mommy. Mommy, what's the matter?"

Vera rushed over and wrapped her arms around him. "Everything is just fine." She took his hand and led him upstairs.

Everything is not all right. I was about to spit in Lex's face when the kid interrupted. That didn't stop me from yelling like he should never forget it. "No classical guitarist worth a damn uses an amplifier. What do you think I am?"

Lex put on a voice like that psychiatrist at Stan Goldman's. "Just a minute, Sally. You are the one who said guitar is such a soft instrument that it's extremely difficult to carry the hall. Who said it's a crime to use amplification if the hall is dead?"

"Turd. Segovia didn't use amp and neither does Bream or Williams or anybody else who counts. You won't catch me dead with that thing."

Lex begged me to listen. "You don't have to use it if you don't want to, but some halls are so dead I wish I had an amplifier. They had to spend millions to get Avery Fisher so the New York Philharmonic doesn't sound like some high school orchestra from Kansas. If the hall is good, don't use it. I only got it for insurance."

"Some insurance. Maybe I should get another flute player for insurance."

Vera ran down the stairs and entered the fray. "Stop it, you two." She put her arms out between us, like a referee at a boxing match. "What are you doing, screaming at each other like banshees?"

"Damn if I know," said Lex. "I got Sally this tiny Pignose amplifier in case we have to play in a lousy hall, and she blows up to high heaven."

"Don't you know when to shut up?" I drowned them out.

Vera turned to Lex. "For goodness sake, keep quiet."

"I…You don't have to use it Sally, but nobody in the audience would ever know. I wouldn't have to play so softly that people wonder if I'm running out of breath."

I wanted to drown Lex in the bathtub. "If I knew you were going to pull this shit on me I never would have invited you to play. We've been balancing perfectly all along so take your Pignose and chuck it into the nearest dumpster."

"Stop it, please. Both of you." Vera looked at me, all sympathy. "I don't think he meant any harm…"

"How can you possibly know that?"

"…he just doesn't know any better."

"Oh yes he does. He knows guitarists who use amps are worse than whores. I'm not taking that thing to Europe. Throw it out."

"Don't worry." Lex choked on his own voice. "I'll carry it and you don't have to use it."

"Did you have to say that now?" Vera asked.

"Chauvinist pig. Get me a cab."

"Please don't misunderstand. I was just trying to help."

"Get me a cab. Jackass."

"No." Vera insisted, "It will cost you a fortune and you don't want to waste the money. Lex will drive. We'll sit in the back and our chauffeur shall keep his mouth shut. Hold on and I'll get a scarf so I can gag him if I have to."

22

Lex

No Joyride

I was too upset to catch Vera and Sally's conversation as I drove her home. Can't she get it into her head that I'm just trying to save her from musical suicide?

Heavenly sound doesn't help if only the front rows of the audience can hear it. It's one thing to play in our living room, but something else entirely to fill a hall that holds hundreds of people. They dampen sound and the guitar just dies. Try to balance with it and the flute sounds like a mouse squeaking in a trap.

I'm desperate to explain all this, but Vera was serious about gagging me if I opened my mouth. The last thing I needed going around the beltway was getting choked and crashing into an abutment without Sally's tongue inside my pants. The thought sealed my lips tight.

"Slow up," said Vera.

Maybe she needs more time to get Sally to calm down. The two of them talked constantly, but it was all in whispers, and I couldn't catch it. True to Vera's promise, I didn't say a word, not even goodbye when we got to Sally's apartment.

"Don't even think about getting out of the car," said Vera. She took Sally's guitar and saw her to the door. They hugged. I felt a surge of jealous longing.

On the way home I wanted to make Vera understand that I did this so we wouldn't get panned by reviewers in Europe. She waved the scarf in front of my face. "The gag rule still applies. You really upset Sally, but I don't want to talk about it now. Later you can call her up and apologize."

"Can you do that for me? She'll bite my head off if I call her."

"Shush."

Vera did all the negotiating with Sally to get us to the airport in the same car. She told me Sally wanted to go by herself and she wasn't going to sit anywhere near me on the plane. Vera gave explicit instructions. "If that happens, accept it. If she talks to you, apologize before you say anything else."

Vera drove us to Baltimore Washington International to catch Icelandic Air's cheap charter to Europe. The two women chattered away as if I didn't exist and the air wasn't taut with tension. Aaron and Jennifer sat on either side of me in the back seat. "Where are you going daddy? Why aren't we going with you?" I was distracted. They soon fell silent. The Pignose amplifier, my flute, and the music sat on my lap in a backpack. The cause of all my troubles was heavier than I ever imagined. I couldn't help but wonder if Sally might use the amp to smash my skull in the middle of the night.

At the airport, I undid myself from Aaron and Jennifer and squeezed Vera so tight that she gasped. I planted my open mouth on hers and gave her a passionate kiss of the kind that I associated with Sally. Vera took the kiss and gave me one back, sort of. "Thanks for letting the music happen," I whispered.

"You're welcome," she said. "Play well. Apologize first."

As I waved goodbye, Vera was smiling. I couldn't help thinking she might be happy to see me go.

23

Vera

Relief

Exhilaration surges as I floor the accelerator. It took a moment to fathom an expanding sense of freedom emerging from the fog of hidden feelings. Driving back home on the George Washington Parkway and up through the woods of Spout Run I might as well have been on the Blue Ridge Parkway, heading out on a cross-country adventure. By myself, on my own. This is the first time I'm really unburdened since Lex and I were married. Aaron and Jennifer are still in the back seat, but I never saw them as a burden. They're my babies.

Sailing down a highway with pedal to metal and no dependent adult to care for is independence. Certainly I've been away from Lex before, but it was only for a week or two at most, and then I was always in the clutches of my mother. She still claws at me with the talons of a hawk. Mother would devour me with her intrusive questions and incessant advice.

I help her in the kitchen and she says, "Put your foot down and make Lex behave like a man." When I tried to relax on the sofa or in the rocker on the front porch, she yelled at me, "Make a mensch out of him."

She likes to think she knows all kinds of foreign expressions that other people don't, so I played dumb and asked her what she means. She told me, "There were all kinds of words like that on 'Upstairs, Downstairs.' What? You've never heard of a Jewish butler. Are you telling me I'm getting mixed up?" On and on she ranted. "OK, so it was Sid Caesar. He was Jewish and he was the funniest mensch alive. You don't know he was the Gryphon in 'Alice in Wonderland?' Why do you keep asking me stupid questions about what to do? Just make a mensch out of your husband."

But Lex is a child fearing forty, with all the frustrations and passions that I see in my children. The only difference is that his are buried deep in his music, while Aaron and Jennifer express theirs in every little thing. I wonder how deeply mine are buried, though they seem to be welling to the surface as the speedometer tops eighty.

It's pretty hard to imagine a mensch telling his mother-in-law over the phone how he is going to perform all over Europe with a female guitarist. Lex couldn't believe it when her response was dead silence. Finally she asked him, "Do you really think you're going to do that? Let me speak to Vera."

I don't even want to think about the explosion when I got on the phone. Mother was apoplectic. "If he won't stay home and take care of his family, you should divorce him." I don't wish to remember the barrage of insults that followed. Then she asked why we don't visit on weekends. "You live so close but stay so far away." Her plaintive voice burned in my ear.

Mother understands nothing. She calls her own husband a child, but will never understand that my husband is a still a boy too. She says he's crazy when I tell her that the flute is his favorite toy and he can't put it away. Mother doesn't understand children no matter what their age. She has no idea why Aaron and Jennifer make musical instruments out of tinker toy.

Imagine what would happen if I tried to take Lex's toy away from him. The tantrum would blow the house down. I don't want to be like mother and live with a sulking husband for the rest of my life.

Lex is just a bigger child with an obsession that dominates him day and night. He takes on some responsibility, but like most growing boys, he would really like to get away from it. The flute is his Wednesday softball league, his Friday bowling team getting sloshed on beer, and his weekends playing poker.

He doesn't do any of that. He plays his flute toy at home. Once or twice he played at Sally's place. The music turns him on, because after rehearsals he carries the same faint odor of musk that I associate with our bedroom.

I mother him there too. He's the rooster I take care of along with my two little chicks. His flute saves me the burden of sitting on a rotten egg that might never hatch.

When Sally first asked me if she might take Lex along on the European tour, I was not quite aghast, but then I shouldn't have been, since the two of them had performed together several times. Besides their first concert at the University of Maryland, I went to hear them at the National Air and Space Museum, though what turned out to be memorable that evening was not their performance.

They were background music for a cocktail reception to mark the opening of a major exhibition of art devoted to the military aircraft of World War II. I was strangely attracted to the portrayals of Mustangs blasting Messerschmitts and Zeros being blown up by machine guns just before those kamikazes could get to their targets. There was a picture of torpedo bombers sinking the Yamato, that huge Japanese battleship that was Japan's last naval gasp.

I found it difficult to imagine carpet bombings as art, but there was plenty of that hanging on the walls too. What I didn't get much of was their performance. Flute and guitar was hardly the perfect match for these battles, but the choice of instruments that offered no competition to cocktail chatter seemed deliberate. The guests were much more interested in the canapés, and musicians are supposed to understand that.

I was not expecting to talk to anybody at this reception, and avoided that lonely feeling you get at this kind of event by perusing the artworks. I was intent on the smile on the face of the pilot getting aboard the Enola Gay when there was a voice behind me. "How is my favorite office manager tonight?"

I turned around to face Dr. Cooper, his rather lean, jut-jawed face broadened by a smile not very different from the one I just saw on the face of the A-bomb pilot in the painting. "And what brings you here tonight?" We said it at the same time and both of us waited an awkward moment for the other to answer. Dr. Cooper said, "Ladies first."

"My husband brought me along. He's the flutist of the duo providing the music."

"It's lovely. Quite a few people are standing around listening."

"And you?"

"I started my medical career as a flight surgeon in the Air Force and still head up a reserve unit. Maybe I got invited because they wanted a few more Colonels, but I also support the museum. I'm addicted to aviation history."

"I don't know a soul here." And I can't remember the last time I got a chance to chat with another man.

"Let's wander around. If I run into somebody I know I'll introduce you."

We took cocktail shrimp and champagne from servers and went up front to listen to Sally and Lex playing their hearts out, oblivious to the noise all around them. Dr. Cooper whispered, "It's sad that people who devote their lives to perfecting their art have to perform as background music."

Sally told me afterwards she would never have accepted an engagement like that except the money was much better than she gets for playing in churches and schools. Lex called it a good exercise in concentration. "Think how safe it is. Nobody hears the mistakes, and we get a chance to see what it's like to play under concert pressure."

The trees are flying by on Spout Run. I sing the theme from "The Carnival of Venice." Lex will perform it all over Europe. His flute, my freedom. I wonder what I would do if I ever get to that Grand Masked Ball at Carnival time. I ran a red light and barreled up route 66 for a ride in the country.

24

Sally

Joys of Flight

The S.O.B. at the airline check-in counter said I can't take a guitar on the plane because it won't fit in the overhead. "Yes it will," I insisted.

"We don't allow guitars in the cabin. You will have to check it in baggage." This clerk had a long skinny neck that I wanted to choke with my bare hands.

I refrained from calling him the dirtiest name you can think of and put on sweetness. "Do you know that minus forty in the baggage compartment at 30,000 feet guarantees that the instrument will crack beyond repair? Would you mind insuring it for ten thousand dollars?"

"I'm very sorry. We do not sell supplemental insurance, but we do compensate for lost or damaged baggage in accordance with the Warsaw Convention. Ordinarily I could sell you a seat for your instrument in the passenger compartment, but the plane is full today."

"Which is more worthless, compensation that won't even pay for my guitar case, or your non-existent ticket?"

"I'm afraid that's for you to determine, madam, but you will have to check the guitar as baggage if you wish to board this plane."

I told the jerk I would like to see the rule book. He bailed out and got a supervisor. Someone behind me cursed about the delay. Several people headed for another line.

The supervisor started out on the same tack about guitars having to be checked in.

"But this is no $100 guitar made for pimply high school kids."

"Oh. Concert guitar? I wanted to be a concert violinist, but it was a hopeless struggle. You are lucky this isn't a cello, because I would have no choice but to make you buy a ticket."

I could have screamed, and he must have known it.

"In this special case I can make an exception and check with the captain of the aircraft."

A loud-mouth behind me said, "You're holding up everybody."

"This concert guitar boards with me."

Everybody else got checked in at the adjoining counters. No way this instrument is going in with checked baggage. It's scaled perfectly to my small hands. Nothing can ever replace it.

An eternity passed before the supervisor returned. "You're lucky today. The captain said your guitar is OK if you find space for it in an overhead bin. Board early. Passengers on this flight bring everything they own as carry-on. Once the overheads fill, we take anything that doesn't fit under the seat and check it."

"Looks like the captain knows the rule, even if nobody else does."

The supervisor frowned. "I did you a favor. If you want to get on the plane today you would be wise to put your mouth in the off position and keep it closed."

Lex didn't say a word all this time. I could feel him trembling as we left the check-in counter. We finally boarded the vintage DC-10 charter flight more than an hour later.

All those epithets I muttered under my breath weren't meant just for the airline clerk. They were for Lex too, because he brought the amplifier.

Everybody knows that the best way to put a classical guitarist down is say you need that piece of crap. I haven't said a word to him since he trotted it out thinking he was giving me a diamond brooch.

We're squeezed together on this endless flight, me by the window and he stuck in the middle of our row with a blubbery woman in the aisle seat. She looks as if she wants to start a conversation but is afraid to because of the ice between us. The two of them seem to be settling in to a quiet battle over who gets to put their elbow on the armrest that barely separates him from her corpulent body.

Lex's playing was worse than terrible our last rehearsal. He's sitting there catatonic and I wonder when he'll start crying. I should have chucked him, but too late for that. Nothing like being ready for the unexpected, but I don't have a Plan B. If Lex falls apart on stage I get panned by the reviewers. It takes two to make this tour work, but only one to ruin it.

I really don't want to talk to him now. There's no lousier place to have a serious conversation than cattle class on a plane. I stuffed cotton in my ears but the jet roar is as deafening as ever. Have to get Lex out of his funk, but all I want is sleep.

I was dreaming about performing Tarrega's "Recuerdos de la Alhambra." The chair gave out from under me and I'm falling off a cliff. I tumble weightless in empty space. The audience gasps. Somebody screams. A flash of lightning blinds me. An unsteady voice came from somewhere behind. "Help me. I'm hurt."

My tail plummeted into bedrock. Lightning set the whole sky ablaze as my spine crumpled into itself. I grabbed Lex. "We're not going to die, are we?" He's like the statue at the Lincoln Memorial, except that his arms are twisted around the armrests lifted all the way up to his chest.

"Maybe not." He turned toward me with a Marcel Marceau smile on his face. We took another huge bump. "There isn't much we can do about it."

I'm too frightened to be sick to my stomach. There's more screaming in back. I held on to Lex. He let go of an armrest and put his arm on my shoulder.

And pushed me away. You shit, I started to say…as his head jerked forward and he puked between his legs. He heaved a couple of times and turned toward me, with an apologetic smile and a trickle of vomit on his chin.

"It just came up all of a sudden." He took his blanket, wiped his mouth, and covered up the mess on the floor as if nothing happened.

Good thing he missed me. The stink is bad enough.

"Do you mind if I share your blanket?" Lex shivered.

I wrapped us up in scratchy airplane wool and put my head on his chest. We bounced around for who knows how long. Maybe I didn't puke because I can't stomach airline food, so I hadn't eaten anything.

I can't quite remember when we came out of the turbulence or when I fell asleep again, but I was pretty much face down in his lap when I woke up. Lex was awake, but he didn't respond anything like he did that very first time he drove me around the beltway.

25

Lex

Joys of Flight, II

How can Sally think her career will go anywhere if she can't be heard? I gave her a painless way to face reality and she gave back a screaming fit. She has to get over that ampophobia or we're done for. Ever since I gave her the Pignose the duo sounds like we should forget about making music.

What a god awful trip. Sally has been turning away to stare at the sky whenever I look at her. It makes me feel like she's waiting for me to fall asleep so she can take a knife to my penis like that woman in Virginia did to her husband.

She grabbed me just now, but only because the turbulence must have scared her out of her wits. It didn't bother me much, even though I vomited. My dinner just came up with no warning at all, before I was aware that it wasn't the normal thing to do after an airplane meal.

Sally wrapped me up in a blanket and put her head in my lap like there was nothing but affection between us. How I wish that were so. I had no idea whether this meant she wanted to put us back together again. She's dead to the world.

It isn't just Sally who I can't figure out. I've messed up with every girl who ever was important to me. Worst of all was the girl everybody was sure I was going to marry. Peg O' My Heart adored me since she was thirteen. She was a perky redhead with freckles, porcelain skin, and a seductive smile. Someone to hug and protect.

Peg played Bach and Scarlatti with crisp articulation that dazzled, but her hands were so small she could only stretch an octave. That left her trapped in the eighteenth century. Composer-pianists like Rachmaninoff could reach an octave and a fifth, and it was impossible for her to play music created for big hands like that.

Her piano teacher said that if she really wanted to be a musician she should take up the flute. Her small hands wouldn't matter. Since I was the best flutist at Red Fox, I became her first mentor.

Between lessons she used to slide her bottom up on my belly when I was loafing in the hammock hung between two oak trees near the main house. She'd straddle me and smile while I struggled to control myself. I used to think of it as innocent admiration because Peggy was a child. It took me three years to realize I was wrong.

Peggy was supremely clever at plotting a future inside that head of flaming red hair. She befriended my younger sister and arranged to visit her so she could sit on the edge of my bed while I read the Sunday funnies out loud…and became keenly aware of the power of statutory rape laws to influence my behavior.

When she was sixteen I figured she was finally old enough to date. I was almost twenty and it took only minutes to love her with a passion that sets me aflame even now on this shuddering airplane. All that lightning scares the bejesus out of everybody else, but it's Peggy that makes me shiver.

Back then, Friday afternoons meant finding a park bench and necking until I felt all I could ever dream of feeling, even though we were wrapped in overcoats. She said she felt like making love too. We were building a year-long climax during my junior year at Juilliard.

Opportunity struck when my parents went off for a weekend to visit cousins. They wanted to take me, but I begged off. Palpable disappointment marked another setback in my parents' struggle to draw me closer during my college years.

I phoned to make sure they had already left before I took Peggy home. We couldn't wait to crawl in bed. Strands of rust red pubic hair came out of her underpants, not quite as fiery as the hair on her head, but the sight of them was more than enough to stoke my desire to make her part of me.

I touched those strands, gently, slowly working my hand down from her firm breasts, smelling the seat of love, excitement rising with the tingle on my fingertips stroking her body.

We turned to each other, and those breasts on my chest imprinted themselves forever. Long tender touch of lips on lips, hands not knowing where to explore next. Murmurs, but we did not talk. Hope against hope that she would remove her underpants.

How I wanted to feel her warmth against mine. How we dared not reach for Eden despite our bodies fitting closer together than the pieces of a jigsaw puzzle.

Our souls didn't know where to go from there. Underpants were an iron curtain blocking our flight to freedom – walls of morality thrown up by superior forces.

Was it parents? Church? Self? shouting that you must protect the girl you would marry.

Panties pointing an accusing finger at hands that would breach them. Allow her to give you her virginity with the blessing of holy matrimony, not before. Torsos entwined in flames, but the invisible wall between us unmoving.

Take it, steal virginity, partner willing or not, from any girl, any girl but the one you would marry. Knight on a shining white charger, protect her.

Peggy must have thought differently, that the man she would marry should not leave her hanging in mid-air at sixteen. She must have wondered what's wrong with me, why I didn't or couldn't make love.

But she would not touch me there or lead me to venture inside her. Neither of us said a word. No way to say what we wanted to, no daring to overcome the taboo I forced upon us. No talk of what we could should could not should not do.

The last barriers never came down. I did not even shoot at the border, as I had so many times in the park when we were fully clothed.

Sweat drenched, Peggy got up and took a shower. I took her home. She went on her high school graduation trip. I had finals coming up. More than two weeks passed before we talked.

"It's time I saw some other people," she said. "I'm not even seventeen."

I gasped.

"No, I don't really have anything else to say." She never answered the phone again. Her parents asked me to be so kind as to stop calling. They did not need to threaten to call the police.

Now Sally has her head in my lap, but I think it is only because she's terrified that the plane will get hit by lightning and break up. She won't even speak to me.

It isn't that this kind of thing has never happened to me before. I have a long history of blowing it fatally with every female I really loved. None of them ever told me why. How can giving Sally an amplifier – which she really needs – muck things up so?

Sally has a nerve hating me as she does and then putting her head in my lap to rub it in. Turbulence is no excuse for cruelty.

26

Sally

We Can't Go On Like This

For no particular reason I started moving my head around in Lex's lap. Call it stretching a bit to get the stiffness out of my neck, but if you want the truth, I was getting curious. The naughty part of me wanted to see if he would respond.

There's nothing like sneaky thrills on a plane ride. I once did it in the toilet of a 747 on the way to the Casals Festival with a cellist. Maybe it's not the most comfortable place in the world, but excitement is in ideas, isn't it? A twist on the door latch spurred us on back then, but I was scared out of my wits that we would break the toilet seat cover and the crack of shattering plastic would be heard all over the plane.

Not as frightened then as I am now. Lex is stiffer than a mummy. Our concert tour will be a disaster if we don't make up fast. Uptight musicians don't make good music.

Landing in Reykjavik was uneventful enough. It was a lot easier getting into Iceland than boarding in Baltimore. The customs officer had me open my guitar case for inspection, and asked if I would be giving a concert here. "No? If your playing is as beautiful as your instrument, you should be."

I gave him the biggest smile I could muster. "You make the arrangements and I'll come."

"That's a deal. Give me your card."

I did. Lex looked at me like I did something wrong. I frowned.

We were already on the way to the hotel for our free one-day layover, and there hadn't been a word between us besides Lex's "I'll get it" when he saw my bag coming off the carousel. I whispered into his ear, "You can talk to me now. I won't bite your head off."

"I'm so blotto from that plane ride I wouldn't know what to say."

I wanted to respond that the puking took everything out of him, but he probably wouldn't think it funny.

At the hotel, he waited while I checked us in and followed me as I led him to the room. "Do you have a key for me?" He asked.

"Are you joking? This is it."

"You just got one room? Are you sure you want to sleep in the same room with me?"

This is the first time a guy hesitated when I offered my bedroom. I was about to say I don't have any choice turkey, but I blurted out, "Of course dummy. You can sleep with me as long as you make beautiful music."

Lex tried to say something, choked up, and could hardly get the words out. "I'm truly grateful for that." He whispered so softly I could barely hear it.

If he hadn't come up with that asinine amplifier idea we would be making up for abstinence back home. I haven't had another man since we started making music together. Should have kept my options open, but I was loyal.

I opened the door to one of those tiny rooms where you would have to crawl over one another to get to the bathroom. "Bunk beds," said Lex. "I've never heard of that in a hotel before. Do you want the top or the bottom?"

"Let me try the top."

Lex plopped on the bottom bunk. I peeled off my coat and sweater. On impulse, I yanked off everything but my underpants and slid in the lower bunk on top of him.

"Uh... knocked the wind out of me." Lex didn't make a move.

"Shush." I put my index finger to his lips. "Don't talk." I tugged at his belt buckle, unzipped his pants. He started to push them down. I stopped him. "You don't have to do anything." My breasts nuzzled his face. His cheeks were cold on my skin.

Lex gave me a puzzled look. "What are you doing to me?"

"Don't ask."

His tongue was warm and coarse on my breast. He lifted his hips high enough that I could get his trousers off. I kept my panties on until I had him naked and helpless on the bed, legs spread-eagle. You might imagine that I'm a man and he's the willing but passive woman. "I'm on top. Be my slave."

I was succeeding at what I set out to do. His whole body was trembling.

"Yes master." Lex started to laugh, but it was tentative. "Nothing new about that."

"Learn to like it."

"I hope so."

"Shut up." Good thing he knew enough to let me have the last word.

Reykjavik bunk beds are a good place to kiss and make up. I had been really uptight ever since I asked Vera to let Lex perform with me in Europe. I wouldn't let him get near me, even when Vera took Aaron and Jennifer up to see her mother. We had to be innocent. I wasn't going to take a chance that Lex's guilty conscience would betray us.

An ocean washes inhibition away as surely as it cleans itself. Distance gives permission and Vera gave us permission too. You can't tell me she has no sense of the inevitable.

Music together is intimacy and mutual dependence that bonds far stronger than words. If you heard us playing the "Entr'acte," you would know exactly what I mean. That piece is tumescence, then dreamland, then passion again. It even excited Vera. She let our music happen.

It would be stupid to wallow in guilt, and worse not to make pillow music when the score calls for it…vivace, andante, presto. There is nothing like a terrifying plane ride to make me play life while it lasts.

"You devour me." Lex's hot breath fell heavily on my waist.

"As intended. Tell me you don't like it."

"I can't."

"You don't need to say anything."

For all the insult with that Pignose amplifier, it was still the wildest love-making we ever made. I bumped my head against the top bunk. Lex took my head in his hands and it felt like he kissed every strand of hair on my head. "Don't stop."

I have no idea how he held out so long.

"Encore."

"Bravo."

The best cure for a humongous argument is making love. When we finally lay side by side hand in hand, I told him, "If you perform like that it will be bravo and encore everywhere."

"In bed too?"

"Shut up."

27

Lex

Concert Hall

Was building a cathedral the glue that held medieval societies like *Freiburg im Breisgau* together? Was it that colossal effort that inspired Bach? I studied the spire of this awesome structure and gasped at the enormity of such immortal work as Hans Schering explained, "Our Münster was started in 1200, and it took more than three hundred years to finish it."

Our host, the *Direktor, Kunst und Musik* for the city government, introduced us to the German Renaissance city. "Right here opposite is the 16th century Kaufhaus, built in just ten years. The arches were inspired by Rome, but it is an early baroque style you still see all over Germany. This is where you will perform, in the hall where the dukes were crowned."

There was no reason for this to be happening. I had never even heard of music for flute and guitar. Had I walked out of Katya Tenbroek's party when I wanted to, I would not have met Sally Pendergast. Was I dreaming that I would be making music in the free market town founded in the 12th century by Duke Konrad of Zahringen, and the elves from the Black Forest would show up for the concert?

"The hall will be full," said Hans. "Once people get a subscription to this series they never give it up."

We took out our instruments and began to rehearse. The flute sound reverberating off the wood was glorious, but from the stage it did not feel like the hall was doing much for the guitar. Hans walked between the rows of pews, around the hall, front and back. "Could we have a little more guitar," he said, "for better balance?"

"You mean less flute," said Sally, frowning at me.

"Less flute. OK," I said, keenly aware that the last thing we need is a blowup now. I had been tempted to bring the amplifier along for this, but Sally would have killed me. I cut my sound from the level I would have chosen to a pianissimo to mezzo forte range.

"There's no need to overpower anybody here," said Hans. "Even your softest sound fills the hall."

Sally gave me a look that said a lot more than I told you so. It was the kind of triumphant smile that said what kind of a jackass are you to think about amplification.

We went over the Dowland "Lachrimae Pavane" again. Our playing resounded through the hall even though I was playing as softly as I could while still hoping to produce some dynamic contrast. Sally was making more sound than ever, but I worried about overpowering her and prayed she could keep up the volume at concert time.

"It's going to be beautiful," said Hans.

"Are you sure? It sounds like I'm over-balancing."

"Ah, but with 400 people in the hall the balance will be purrr..fect. The guitar will be resonating like now, and the crowd will dampen the flute echo. You will see. The natural sound of this hall is purrr...fect."

Sally won the amplification war. I swallowed the flute to make it so.

28

Sally

Nerves

Lex knows I'm a bundle of nerves before every recital. I wish I could teach him to calm me down, but I don't know how. In the dressing room he zipped up the back of my gown and put a hot hand on my bare shoulder. "There's no need to be nervous," he said. "You've been wowing people with your guitar all your life."

"Sure. Long enough to know this is my life. Isn't that something to get nervous about?"

"Not really. Maybe we should make love right here and now. That would calm your jitters."

"Fuck you."

"Please do. The concert doesn't start for a couple minutes. If the audience knew what was going on they would wait."

I turned my back to him. "Go ahead. Unzip me if you dare."

Lex put his flute down on the dressing room table and tugged at my zipper. I could feel the tickle down my spine. "Hey! Cut it out." I wasn't at all sure he would stop, and Hans was knocking on the dressing room door.

"Three minutes to concert time."

"We'll be right out." If we can get my zipper up again. This dress is too tight.

"Time to get serious," said Lex.

"Get your parts in order or you'll be playing one piece while I'm off on another."

"Let's tune up here so we don't have to do it in front of the audience."

"That's pretty professional for somebody who all he thinks about before the big concert is getting laid."

"I need a goal in life. Getting laid sure beats getting a case of the shakes."

"How did you get to be such a wise guy? Give me an E. Did you forget how guitarists tune too?"

"Don't worry about it. I have to tune to everything you do."

"Let's get going. They're waiting for us out there."

I walked out on stage in this turquoise taffeta concert dress that Vera said was absolutely stunning. The full house gave us a nice round of applause. We bowed. Then Lex waved and raised his flute in the air like some kind of politician at an election rally. What does he think this is, a rock concert? The audience clapped some more. I was too nervous to do anything but give them a tight-lipped smile.

We sat down and checked our tuning one last time. "Ready to go?" I whispered.

"Just a second."

Out of a clear blue sky Lex got up and faced the audience. "*Guten abend, Herren und Damen.*" That much German even I could understand, but I wanted to grab his butt and tell him that these people didn't come to hear him babble guttural garbage.

Thank goodness Lex continued in English. "The first piece we will play for you is the "Entr'Acte" by Jacques Ibert. Fate brought us together at a chamber music party that neither of us even knew about before friends brought us along. Sally had this one piece for flute and guitar. It led us here tonight, and we will share it with you now."

I sighed with relief that Lex had kept it reasonably short – for him. I should have known better than to expect he would just walk out and perform without thinking of a way to make a spectacle of himself. Then I forgave him, for here it was that we hadn't yet played a note and our audience was clapping like it was encore time.

Lex came back from his one man show and smiled. "Now they're on our side. Play like we're making mad passionate love."

I was going red in the face. Hasn't he ever heard about proper stage manners?

Lex took the Entr'Acte at lightning speed, much faster than we had ever played it. Guess it goes to show that if you really know a piece, you can play it as fast as your fingers can move. The effect was electric, and not just on the audience. As we acknowledged the applause, I whispered to him, "If we were in bed that would have been wham bam thank you ma'am."

"C'mon, let's get out there and do it again while the audience is still hot. You introduce the Dowland."

"Damn you Lex." But I have to give him credit for keeping my mind off my nerves. I have no idea what I said about the piece, except that it sounds as new as it is old, and gives us a claim to be performing music from five centuries, starting with the sixteenth.

Amazing what you can do when you know the audience is on your side. We ripped right through John D's ancient but contemporary-sounding masterpiece, reveling in our combined virtuosity. The whole concert went this way. Afterwards, Hans rushed backstage gushing, "*Wunderbar.* I can't remember the last time this audience demanded three encores." He gave me a hug so strong it squeezed the breath out of me.

There was no such thing as privacy in the dressing room after the concert. Hans brought some of his friends back and introduced them. More names than I could possibly remember in all the excitement. Parents guided their young kids forward to get our autographs on their programs. Lex whispered, "Kids at a chamber music concert. Is this for real?" I shushed him.

At the Mozart café just around the corner from the Marktplatz Hans' patrons and friends went on non-stop about how this was their first ever classical guitar and flute concert, "So much beautiful music we had never heard of before," they said. I love adulation as much as anybody, but all I wanted was to unwind and consummate the performance.

Lex might fall apart when I'm pissed off at him or he's guilty about his wife, but tonight was something else. He was electric with energy and it sent shivers up my thighs. I played with that kind of excitement too. When we sailed through the Carnival of Venice at the end of the program, it felt like… I have to ask.

No doubt Hans thought he was doing the right thing when he got separate rooms for us at the Am Rathaus Hotel. Lex opened the door to his room and asked, "Your place or mine?"

So much for the high cost of being proper. I grabbed him by the lapels of his tux and tugged toward my room.

"Are you sure it's proper to visit an unmarried lady in her boudoir?" He took my hand and kissed it gallantly, European style.

I pulled harder and got him through the door.

He staggered a little and laughed, "Demanding wench, aren't you?"

"Demanding?" I retorted. "I'll show you demanding!" I hooked my ankle behind his and pushed him onto the bed.

"Oh, so feminine, but you were stupendous. Is this an invitation?"

"No. It's an order. Take off your clothes."

Lex started to do a strip tease. I untied his shoelaces and tugged at his trousers.

"Help." Lex was laughing so hard I knew he wanted to be raped. "Where are my pajamas?"

"Don't bother." I couldn't get undressed fast enough. Then I jumped him.

"Oof. Hey. Who's in charge here?"

"What are you, some male chauvinist pig?"

"I give up. You're the boss."

"Now you've got it right. Under the covers." Once we were safely snuggled together I asked him, "Tell me the truth. Did you come when we were playing the Carnival?" I reached below his belly to touch him. "You're higher than the Empire State Building."

"Waiting for the deluge."

"Hush."

Lex clamped his lips shut between his index finger and his thumb. Then he set off fireworks that blew July 4th on the Mall right out of the sky. Never had I seen such color or felt such intensity, not even on the concert stage. Was it the love-making or the music that brought more hues than the rainbow?

29

Lex

What Makes Sally Tick?

How is it that my mind wanders so far as Sally's fingernails rouse the soles of my feet to previously unknown heights?

Office nightmares intrude. The boss and sycophant Szymanski who wants my job must be plotting to get rid of me because I'm taking the leave I earned to go on this concert tour. If they knew what Sally was doing to me now they would hack off my limbs in a jealous rage.

"Not yet," she says. "Don't move. You don't need to do anything."

A Bach organ fugue takes over my body, leading to the frenetic gyrations of the Entr'Acte. Sally's hair flies back and forth, a whirling dervish. I can't move as she works me over like a black widow spider, bringing agony of expectation as I witness her arousal.

I watch in awe as she fulfills herself. She makes exotic love all over me, yet I can't help feeling that I am no more than a dildo to measure the success of her music by, another instrument to be played and mastered.

Is conquering me the key that unlocks her climb to the heights? That's not the kind of thing I can ask. What I really want is to think nothing in the midst of sex, to savor only the pure feeling, one nerve ending at a time.

There was no telling whether it came from me or from her, but I was coming, coming for an eternity. Long enough to hear a groan from a well so deep that it could not have been anything other than our souls speaking.

"Now," Sally whispered, the magic wand of her fingertips barely brushing deep between my legs. "Handel. Royal Fireworks in brilliant blue and orange, all across the heavens. Did you see the colors?"

"Mmm…"

"You don't have to say anything."

We lay under a waterfall of bliss.

"How is it that you weren't even nervous for the concert?" Sally asked. "I get so uptight I can hardly make it out on stage. Answer me."

"Mmm…what was the question?

Sally repeated it.

"How should I know? I was and I wasn't. Somehow the nerves got translated into a public orgasm performing for all those people."

"You're so full of it. Maybe you don't know any better, so you don't get nervous."

"Please don't ask me to understand why I wasn't scared out of my wits. Make me think about it and I might never be able to get out there and perform again."

"Can't you come up with anything better than that? I really have to figure out why I'm so terrified that I'm about to pee every time I walk out on stage."

"I wish I knew what to tell you. I never dreamed of soloing in public before you came along and…"

Sally cut me off. "We're a duo, remember?"

The last thing I wanted to do was piss her off. "Sorry. I must have been thinking we're two soloists coming together."

"Don't let it go to your head."

"Yes ma'am. I was wondering if I don't get real nervous because I'm a government hack with nothing to lose and you're the musician. Maybe you get big-time nerves because you feel you have everything to lose if the concert doesn't go well."

"That's true, but I don't know anybody who doesn't get nervous. How do you do it?"

"Beats me. This is so far beyond my wildest dreams. I felt like we were making love on stage. The music just happened as part of it."

"Me too," said Sally. "But I was scared silly like a proper virgin."

"Virgin? You can't fool me."

"Bastard. I'm very proper."

We laughed together. I gave Sally a hug and she squeezed me harder. Then I told her, "I can't believe how lucky I was that Hans didn't say anything before the concert about Freiburg being the flute center of Europe. If I knew that our Eden is a conservatory town full of famous flutists I would have shat in my pants."

30

Sally

Mozart's Bones

Lex and I had just performed in the Salzburg Mozarteum, an awesome hall which I thought existed in Mozart's time.

I should have known better but I didn't ask whether he actually performed there. By the time Herr Stiftling, the Director, told us that the Mozarteum wasn't even built until a couple of years before the First World War, I could have cared less. We were well received, and glad that our sponsors did nothing beforehand to shatter our fantasies about sharing the stage with Wolfgang Amadeus.

Neither of us could unwind, so we took a midnight stroll out by the Salzach River. I asked Lex, "How in the world could Mozart's home town let more than a hundred years go by after his death before they built anything to honor him?"

"You've got me," said Lex. "I think I read somewhere that in 1781 he was kicked out of the prince's palace by Salzburg's head chamberlain. Maybe that made him *persona non grata* until somebody in power decided it was time to capitalize on his fame."

"That's sick. Poor Mozart never got the big break while he lived. I hear he owed people a bundle even at the height of his fame. I know what that's like. My credit card is maxed out.

"After Salzburg, Wolfie never got any court employment. I still can't believe the royals left him hanging like they did."

"He worked himself to death and not even a dozen people missed breakfast when he died," said Lex. The sadness in his face was clearly visible under the full moon. "I guess nobody will miss breakfast when my turn comes. Maybe you and Vera, if I'm lucky."

"You won't feel a thing, so don't think that way."

Moonlight shimmered on the river, but it didn't calm me. "Lex, they tossed him in a common grave, but Mozart is immortal and I think he knew it. I wonder if I would pay the price he paid for his fame. That would give me three years to live, and maybe I would leave some records and a few pieces for guitar and MasterCard could claim the body."

"Can we change the subject?" Lex interrupted.

"Not yet. If you're not ready to live poor and die young, make sure you keep that good government job of yours with its pension. Then you can have a fancy tombstone and enough left over to pick up my funeral expenses."

"Thanks a lot, but you know what I'd like to do with that good government job of mine. Better to be a starving musician than dying inside."

"The starving part is easy," said Sally. "Being a musician is not."

"All I can think about now is that the music keeps coming and the surge overwhelms anything else. Tell me where it's all coming from."

"Maybe it comes from God."

31

Lex

Flying Fingers

Would I have played as well if I knew that our stage was where the skeletons lay for hundreds of years? I doubt it, but at the time my thoughts were on a very attractive woman in the second row. I picked her out as the person to play for, lifted my arms up to shoulder level, and balanced the flute just under my lower lip. My instrument and my art rested on top of my left index finger near the palm knuckle, steadied by my slightly curled right thumb with the pinkie on the Eb key. It would have taken almost nothing to knock the instrument out of my hands and send it crashing onto the stage. Gripping the instrument tightly is for beginners.

My fingers have to fly with unerring accuracy on that precariously balanced tube of silver. No machine can be expected to match the rubatos, accelerandos, and rallentandos, all those tiny variations that reveal the soul of music. Miraculously, those digits of mine have been hitting all the right notes. It's as if some inner spirit, guided only by the music itself, takes over and does what I must do when I play before an audience.

My playing isn't automatic. I interpret the music differently every time. Don't ask me why. I know this music to the depth of my being. I've gone over every phrase hundreds of times, and every time is new. No matter how easy the piece at hand, I go over it until it's part of me. Yet I'm still afraid to play from memory, though I rarely look at the parts when we perform.

I can't tell you where the difference between knowing a piece by heart and playing it from memory lies. What I do know is that the urge to music is as primal as the drive to survive. It's more compelling even than the drive for sex. Probably for Sally too, though I can't be sure. She says, "Music is sex, and the act is sharing the music by other means. Too bad I've always had more good music than good sex. Most men are lousy at that kind of music."

But after our last concert she told me, "If I can't have Paganini to swoon over, you're the next best thing. There's the devil in your music too."

The concert stage and bed with Sally feel like one and the same place, though our music and our instruments are so different. We were drinking up each other's eyes, neck, and shoulders, and I shared a thought. "Isn't this just like we look at each other when we're in concert? But it takes years and years of practice to even think of making it in music and what we do in bed is just normal human instinct doing its work."

Sally nuzzled up and down my belly. Then she bit, not hard, but enough to know that I have plenty to lose. "Really? A certain friend of mine told me it took you years to begin to understand what satisfies a woman. Should I tell her that you're getting better but still have a lot to learn?"

"You sure know how to kick a man where it hurts." Tell that to Vera and it's the end of our duo."

"Speaking of Vera, don't you think it's time you called to tell her you're being a good boy?"

"Why did you have to mention that?"

32

Vera

Telephone Calls

By the time Lex finally got around to calling I didn't want to answer the phone. I gave him my blessing to go on the concert tour, but I didn't tell him to forget that his family exists. It is just like him to do that, but he can't be making music twenty-four hours a day, so why doesn't he find five minutes to call me. Just five minutes in ten days, mind you. Is that too big an interruption in his ego trip to ask?

My first thought was to hang up on him, but I asked if he really cares at all about us. He mumbled, and I said, "Of course we miss you terribly."

"I miss you too, but phoning from Europe costs an hour's pay per minute. I told you that before I left, didn't I?"

"But we want to know about your success on the concert stage. Couldn't you have taken just a few minutes to tell us about it? I show Aaron and Jennifer a map every day and pretend to know where the famous concert artist is playing, but they just keep asking if daddy got hurt."

I could tell Lex was somewhere else and there was no certainty that he even remembered the children's names. "Why don't you ask how they are? Here's Jennifer."

"Daddy! When are you coming home?"

"Soon, Princess. Are you having a good time?"

"Not good. Bye, daddy."

I should have told Jennifer to hang up, but she handed me the phone.

"All this talk is getting expensive," said Lex. "Is there anything I need to know?"

"No. Of course not. But you haven't said a word about how the concerts are going."

It amazes me how quickly Lex's voice can change from dreary impatience to hot fervor. Is that the difference between family and flute?

He went on and on. Nothing more was said about how much the call would cost, not when he could wax eloquent about his performance.

"I'm so glad that everybody loves your playing." That was the only way I could think of to stop him from talking all night. "And I'm sorry I wasn't in the audience to hear it, but you don't want to waste any more money on overseas phone calls to tell us about your concerts. So I love you and you can get off the line now."

"Me too," said Lex.

Whatever that meant.

I almost forgot about getting the kids to bed, sitting by the phone wondering if he has any idea what he's doing.

"Daddy away for too long. I wanna play catch," said Aaron. "Will you play catch with me, Mommy?"

"See how dark it is outside. Come to bed like a good boy and I'll play with you after school tomorrow."

"I wanna play with daddy. Why doesn't he come home?"

I like to think Lex really cares about the children, but he gave up playing catch once he started working with Sally. He was afraid that catching a ball wrong would jam a knuckle. "Come on," I asked him, "Are you telling me that a six year old ballplayer is going to mess up your music?" He got all huffy and said he had to practice.

Lex probably wouldn't have called if Sally didn't tell him to. She wouldn't put up with him for a minute except for their duo. That day she told me she's appalled by how unaware he is of what goes on right in front of his nose, I asked her, "Is that what it takes to be a musician?"

"Probably."

Maybe it's a good thing that Lex never asks how I feel. That saves a lot of arguments, but one day I might tell him the truth. He would never understand that it gets so lonesome here that I decided to phone my boss. I didn't even know what I was going to talk about and I certainly wasn't planning to invite him over for dinner, but when he got on the phone it seemed to be the right thing to do.

It's the first time I ever asked a man out. After the call I stared out the window at the azalea bushes in the front yard, wondering whether it was sin that churned my stomach, or something deeper than that.

Dr. Cooper is a very charming man and a good boss, so I cooked a very special meal for him, tournedos Rossini. There was a special trip to the market for anchovies for a Caesar salad, and cinnamon and raisins for the apple pie. It took more courage than I usually have to get candles and light them for the table. How lucky I was that the children were invited to a classmate's birthday party overnight.

It was an absolutely delightful evening, which I would never tell Lex about, or anybody else for that matter. Among other revelations, I learned that Dr. Cooper's divorce became final a week before I started working; that he thinks I'm even more attractive than I am capable in his office…and that inhibitions need not necessarily last forever.

It would be a good thing if Lex didn't call again while this Alice is in Wonderland, and he won't be home for another two weeks.

33

Lex

Welcome Home Brunch

I had been back home less than two days and was suffering a case of acute jet lag when Vera roused me out of bed at 10:30 A.M. and asked why I wasn't up yet. "You've got to get moving. I told you Dr. Cooper would be coming for brunch today."

He was already sitting at the head of the table when I got downstairs. Vera and Sally sat on either side of him. Then came the kids. Vera had set me a place at the opposite end of the table. Was this her way to punish me for not wasting a fortune on overseas phone calls? "Maybe I should come up and join the party," I said.

"By all means," said Dr. Cooper. "I wouldn't want you to change anything on my account."

He already changed things. He's sitting in my place.

Vera went into the kitchen to put the finishing touches on her waffles, leaving Cooper and me to size each other up across the gap. The distance between us was like an empty football field. The five of them were the opposing team and they had sacked me in my own end zone.

I was a spectator as Dr. Cooper exchanged pleasantries with Sally. He looked her up and down as if preparing to do a physical. "I've heard much about you," he said. "Vera is a great admirer of yours."

"She's my Rock of Gibraltar. A true friend. How did you come to know her?"

"Vera's working for me part-time. She's the best office manager I ever had."

I injected myself into a conversation that was not intended for me. "I'd bet on that. What's the occasion today?"

Dr. Cooper and I glared at each other for a split second. Maybe he was as annoyed at my intrusion as I was with his.

"How did the concerts go?" Cooper asked.

I couldn't tell whether he was really interested or just breaking the silence. Sally answered for me. "Can you imagine playing in halls built for princes and being treated like royalty?"

Back from the kitchen, Vera joined the conversation. "You should play in the White House for the President." She turned to give me one of those taut little smiles that so often turn out to mean the opposite of what I think they convey.

"So you toured Europe for three weeks and everybody loved you," said Dr. Cooper. "Does that mean you never had a bad moment?"

Sally bailed me out again. "Not really. I goofed here and there, but Lex covered me. The audiences loved him more than me."

"What about you?" Dr. Cooper's eyes bored straight into mine. "Did you love the audiences too?"

"You can bet on that. I picked people in the second row to play for, and I could feel their reaction. There's nothing like a standing ovation to get love flowing both ways."

"It sounds like you were making love to the audience."

"It really was like that."

Dr. Cooper never took his eyes off me. "So you were making love to your audiences, and Sally too?"

Sally barely twitched, but I thought I heard a tiny gasp. "What the hell do you mean by that?" I asked, *sotto voce.*

"Please don't say bad words daddy." Jennifer interrupted. "Mommy doesn't like you to use bad words. She says it's not good for us to hear that."

"Shush up," said Aaron. "We're not allowed to interrupt when adults are talking, even if we want to ask what they're talking about."

"Aaron, Jennifer, you've both been very good. You can go play now." Vera stood up and hugged them as they made to rush off.

Dr. Cooper smiled at the kids and stole a glance at Sally, but did not linger long. He was bearing down on me. "What I mean is," he hesitated. "How could you be touring Europe with a beautiful woman, making music for adoring audiences and not be having an intimate relationship with her?"

"I'm married to the woman sitting next to you. What do you think I am?"

Vera looked back and forth at the two of us, jaw scrunched up, pleading without words. Cooper ignored her. "Didn't you say you shared a room with her to save money because the hotels were so expensive?"

"Yes I did say that. Maybe next time you'd like to sponsor the tour. Then we could each have our own room."

"You're telling me you were in the same bedroom every night and you didn't have any kind of relationship with her. Don't you feel anything, with all those rehearsals and concerts together?"

"That's right." I didn't want this, but this bastard never even gave me a chance to say hello. "See the woman sitting next to you? On your left. That's Vera. My wife. You think I'm going to ask you what you did with her while I was gone?"

Vera squirmed in her seat. Cooper wouldn't stop.

"How can anyone believe what you're telling me? Three weeks together in the same bedroom and you didn't even touch her. There must be ice in your veins."

I mumbled under my breath, "Must be, to put up with you in my house." I ought to kick him out, but then Vera would believe him for sure.

"What did you say?"

"Nothing you would understand. We have a musical relationship and that's what it has to be. I don't have any intention to make it any different."

"So you're still telling me that you concertized together and communicated in this very special language of music all that time, and you didn't touch her."

"You heard what I said."

Dr. Cooper turned toward Vera and Sally before looking at me. "You have the best defenses of anybody I have ever known."

As in the most upright of Puritan families, we finished our meal in silence.

34

Vera

Afterthought

I realized too late that it was not a good idea to have Dr. Cooper over to the house so soon after Lex got back, but he mentioned several times at work that he would love to meet Lex and Sally and hear about their concert tour. He told me he wanted to be a cellist, but his parents insisted that he go to medical school. When I asked, he said he still played, and he confessed to a tinge of jealousy that Lex could perform professionally while holding down a full-time job.

I had no idea that Dr. Cooper would be so blunt about his suspicions and I would rather not have heard them. It was uncharacteristically rude of him even if he turns out to be right some day. The good doctor should have known that some things are better left unsaid…and I am not at all sure whether he is correct about who has the best defenses in our family.

It's done now, although I regret that I didn't let Lex settle into our routine first before having Dr. Cooper over. Isn't it ironic that Sally and Lex will go on rehearsing in my home and that will be fine, but I'll have to make sure that my Lex and Dr. Cooper are never in the same place together again?

35

Lex

Interior Affairs

Outside my office in the Interior Department the gloom of an approaching storm smothers Washington. I ought to consider myself lucky that I'm senior enough to have an office with a window, but it comes with the brooding malaise of ten years working in a government department that doesn't get anything right. The budget for the National Park Service gets slashed with line item razor cuts that at first seem innocuous but eventually kill with the same certainty that a python squeezes its victims until they suffocate.

The Department consists primarily of drones in cubicles wallowing in a honeycomb of lost souls. In my section the only one who rises above all this is a boyish-looking Chinese named Roger Peng. He walks down the hall with a hint of a smile on his face and acknowledges everybody with a slight nod of his head and a soft spoken good morning. Other than that he says little, does more than is asked of him, and works harder than anybody. I'm one of the few people who greet him, but that's about as far as it goes. He has a slight accent, but he must have been educated here. Peng is an unsolved mystery. People seem to think he's from Pluto, and there is resentment that he has been promoted so fast.

I had cleared my desk and emptied my inbox before I left for Europe. I'll admit that was a little bit out of character, but I made sure to avoid giving anybody the impression my work wasn't completed. I also made arrangements for my job to be covered while I was gone.

Or so I thought. My desk looked like the front porch of a house whose occupants went away for the summer without canceling their newspaper subscription or telling the post office. Papers were piled so high I could hardly see over them when I sat down. I started leafing through this detritus and quickly discovered that nothing that should have been done got done. Every single item on which I had been listed for coordination or approval had gone no farther than my desk.

After about an hour wading through paper, my supervisor came into the office. Ray Klingaman is heavyset all around, with chunky flesh you might find on a teamster who worked the docks before the container era. He was a political appointee who found a patron somewhere and served him well. Bullying me and everybody else in the office was his reward. Jokers like him come in and start at levels higher than us career stiffs can ever hope to attain.

"Morning. Good to be back." I lied.

Klingaman frowned. "Not so good you were gone. You have a lot of catching up to do."

"It sure looks that way. What happened to Sam Ziegler? He was my backup."

"Out of commission for two weeks now. Heart attack. No telling when he'll be back, or whether he can come back at all. It's been pretty dicey."

"Weren't there any arrangements to move these items forward? It holds up the works for everybody."

"Heart attacks don't make arrangements."

"Oh." Much more could have been said, like how did he ever get to be in charge if he can't even arrange to get paper distributed so the work gets done? No doubt Klingaman would have said that's Kate Plunkett's job. She's the office secretary.

I asked, "What hospital is Sam in? I should go pay him a visit."

"Better stay here and get some work done. You've been gone almost a month and the first thing you want to do is take off again. You can visit Ziegler on your own time."

"I wasn't suggesting that …"

Klingaman stopped me in mid-sentence. "Why didn't you tell me you're back? Ever think we might have a few things to discuss?"

The door to my office slammed shut, a small act of kindness from a passerby who doesn't enjoy hearing Klingaman rant.

"Yes sir. I wanted to see what's going on first. It looks like a lot didn't get done while I was gone."

"You got that much right. Among other things your budget for an extension of the bicycle trail along the C & O Canal got knocked off again."

"What? That was highest priority. You told me it would be a slam dunk."

"It was, but you weren't here to defend it. It was slash and burn on the Hill and some stuff had to go. Sorry about that."

"Sorry? Doesn't the lowest priority stuff usually get cut first?"

Klingaman grinned. "You got it. That's usually the way it is. Amazing how priorities get shifted around when some people defend their budget proposals and others don't. I thought you learned that on the way up to your lofty position as my wandering concertmaster."

"It was almost two years since I took any leave. I would have lost it."

"Yeah, things go that way sometimes. Congress says make do with less. We might even have to cut positions in our department, and the Secretary doesn't look on bicycle trails as his highest priority. Drop by when you've gone through those papers." Klingaman slammed the door hard on the way out.

Weeks went by and we hadn't talked. Klingaman was always too busy blaming somebody else for his screw-ups.

I was goggle-eyed in the office, barely conscious, plowing through paperwork when the phone rang.

"Stan Goldman here. You up and running at this early hour? It's only 2:30."

That's Stan, short-term housemate, high flyer in the State Department, cynical, sometimes funny, and usually sarcastic. "Yeah. I'm here. What's going on?"

"Unlike you flunkies in the Civil Service, the Foreign Service owns me day and night and wakes me up in the wee hours to let me know it. Here I am a proven China-watcher and the wise men in personnel want me to take Mongolian training. I know the guy who sucked that lollipop fifteen years ago. He sweated six hours a day one on one with several teachers to learn the language, and we still don't recognize Mongolia. My reward for suggesting that's a waste is to get dumped in Venezuela."

"Congratulations."

"Bullshit. But get this. I'll be Embassy spokesman and Cultural Officer. Guess the personnel people found out about my eloquence and musical genius."

I wondered whether we should be throwing a goodbye party for Stan, but Vera cordially detests him. She won't do it.

"Get over here for lunch tomorrow and I'll give you more good news."

For no reason at all I told Stan I was tied up. "Can you give it to me over the phone?"

"Better in person, but if you insist. The culture vulture at the Venny Embassy here asked for help getting the word out that the National Symphony in Caracas is looking for a principal flutist. Big salary from oil money. Auditions in New York next month. It looks like a real good deal for a disgruntled government flutist."

Stan wouldn't know that when it comes to auditions, next month is like tomorrow. We spend years in conservatory preparing the difficult solos so we can try out for an orchestra job. I did all that, but it was more than ten years ago. Back then a bald assistant with a permafrost scowl on his face gave me the music and barked, "Start with Mendelssohn's "Midsummer Night's Dream." Would my low C# be heard? I practiced it for three years. There's no place to breathe. Where the hell can I breathe? Am I crazy to think I can relearn a whole list of the most difficult orchestral solos in a month and be able to sight-read others that won't be named in advance?

I want to make my life in music at least as much as I wanted to back when I was at Juilliard. The orchestra is the only way to play all the time and get paid for it, unless lightening strikes and you make it big as a soloist. So many times I've been told I'm good enough to do whatever I want on the flute, but can I be good enough again in a month, and lucky enough to win this blind audition that's like playing in a tomb?

We just bought the house two years ago when I got promoted. I have a steady job and a pension in twenty-one years. I have a duo that is getting concerts. So what am I doing busting my rear end to audition for a two year contract in Latin America in a job that promises to take years off my life?

36

Vera

Cozy and Not

Lex and I were relaxing on the living room sofa. He was sprawled spread-eagle on the cushions. I'm one to curl up and lean on the armrest. Together we must have looked like a pretzel, but this is not something we do as much as I would like.

A tape recording of one of Lex's European concerts had just arrived from Switzerland, along with a florid letter thanking him and Sally for a wonderful performance. He was so anxious to have me hear it that I saw images of a little boy who couldn't wait for the soda jerk at Bond's to prepare his first banana split with chocolate, vanilla and strawberry ice cream topped with marshmallow and fudge.

"Ready?" Lex jumped up and turned on the tape recorder, which he had prepared in advance. I wish it would have started with music instead of the welcoming applause, but this was his show. He came back and curled his arm around my waist. The clapping died down and Lex explained to the audience how he and Sally met. Then he introduced the *Entr'Acte* as the piece they played together at that fateful chamber music party.

I could feel Lex trembling with excitement in the replay. Right in the middle he got up and started conducting the music as if this was a live orchestra. It reminded me of that long ago December night when he sang and conducted Beethoven's "Ode to Joy" at Columbus Circle in New York.

"Incredible," he blurted, as he clapped along with the tape-recorded audience when they finished performing the *Carnival of Venice.*

"Shall we?" His eyes sparkled with excitement. "Make love?"

I got up to go to the bedroom. Lex reached for my arm and pulled me back down on the sofa. "I mean right here. We can even do it to music. I'll play the tape again."

The idea of making love accompanied by Lex's introductions to his concert brought me back to earth. I didn't want to share him with his audiences, even if it was only on a recording.

"OK" was all I could think of to say. I wanted him to introduce himself only to me, so I could get excited enough to please him. Instead of listening to introductions again, I went to get a beach towel.

The applause came on again over the speakers. "Here we go," said Lex.

Actually, it was quite good for love-making. He was so keyed up and considerate too. It was physically exciting to shut out the words on tape and see him so happy. I sprawled out on the towel contented, but crossed my legs tight as it flashed across my mind that Sally might have taught him something while they were on tour. She wouldn't do that…I don't think. Would she?

Of course the concert went on long after we were finished, but I was determined to enjoy holding his hand as the duo played on to ever lengthening applause. It made me want to play an instrument, but I've always known that would be a bad idea. I don't want to compete with him, either in rehearsal or for audience approval. Let Sally do that.

We didn't say anything, other than asking each other if we were OK when it was over. I could honestly say yes, happy for Lex. Pleasing a man is a worthwhile thing in itself, even though we women are used all the time.

We were still lolling on the towel when Lex propped himself up on an elbow and said, "I have a surprise for you. We're going to Venezuela."

"Venezuela? What do you mean by that?"

"Just what I said. We'll move to Caracas this summer. I'll be principal flutist in the Venezuelan National Symphony. Fantastic news!"

"What are you talking about? Why haven't you told me anything about this?"

Lex hemmed and hawed. "I didn't think I had an ice cube's chance in hell of getting the job, so I didn't see any point in discussing something that wasn't going to happen."

"So now it *has* happened. Did you ever think that the children and I might be part of this equation?"

"Of course you are. That's why I'm talking about it now."

"You hope to convince me with kisses to do things your way. Try telling me how all this came about."

"Remember that trip to New York I took two weeks ago?"

"New York? You said you were going to Albany for a conference with the state parks and recreation office. What does that have to do with this Venezuela business?"

"I guess…well…I better tell you. I didn't go to Albany. It wasn't for a consult on the state park system. I took the trip so I could audition for the symphony."

"Why do you always have to lie to me?" I wanted to choke the truth out of him.

"I don't know. Scared, I guess."

"Scared of what…that I would bite your head off?"

"I hope not. It's just that the uncertainty and all that…"

"Now it's coming together. Your flute wasn't on your desk and I discovered the music stand missing too. That seemed strange, but I assumed you took it with you to play in the hotel at night."

"I really dreaded having to tell you I was going to audition for this job and then fail to get it. I never dreamed they would choose me. I just wanted the experience."

"You were dreaming about getting the job all along, weren't you? The least you could have done was share that with me. Don't you realize this is what I'm here for? I'm your wife."

"I know. It's really stupid of me."

"Yes, you know all right. Now I see it. You were playing solos from the 'Leonora Overture' and 'Carnival of the Animals' over and over again, and that haunting melody in Shostakovich's Fifth Symphony. You're not in any orchestra and all of a sudden you're playing those famous flute parts. That's all you've been playing these days, isn't it?"

Lex looked down at the floor like he was about to crawl into our basement and hide.

"All that practicing for an audition you don't bother to tell me about. Now you deign to inform me that we're moving to Venezuela in a couple of months."

Lex was squirming, but it made no difference that he didn't know how to hide his discomfort. He didn't even realize that this is a very dumb move.

"I thought you might want to share some of the excitement of a new adventure," he said.

"Then why couldn't you see your way to telling me about it before now?"

"I said I'm sorry, but I couldn't bear to share another failure at what I really wanted to do ten years ago. What else can I say?"

"You are not a failure. You have wonderful children and a good job that provides us all with security. Your European tour was a smashing success. What more could you want?"

"I wish you were right, but I'm afraid things are not quite what you think."

"What do you mean by that? Can you just play it straight for once?"

I picked up my clothes and turned my back to him to get dressed. Maybe I ought to stalk out the door and not come back for a couple of days. I hear that is pretty effective medicine.

Lex reached out for my hand. I drew it away. "Okay, I'll tell you, but brace yourself. I'm being riffed. That's spelled RIF, and it means reduction in force. The reason I went to New York for that audition is big budget cuts at Interior. The powers that be decided my position is the one that has to go."

"They can't fire you just like that. I don't believe this."

"But they can cut my position, which is essentially the same thing. The boss said he fought tooth and nail for me, but I don't believe him any further than I can throw him."

"Do you think this is revenge for abandoning him for concerts?"

"You know I didn't abandon anybody. I earned that leave by slaving away for years. Those control freaks always said it was too busy. If it wasn't one idiotic crisis it was another. Finally I wouldn't give up the tour for that crap, if you'll forgive me for being crude about it."

"So you took the leave and they did you in. But you have your civil service grade. You can find a better job in the government and show them a thing or two."

"I'm not going to do that."

Lex left me standing there, trying to decide whether I should walk out while he headed upstairs, naked as the day he was born.

37

Sally

Me and Vera

When I asked Vera how she felt not playing an instrument, she said, "Jealous? Are you kidding? If I played we would just fight. You two play and Lex and I get along better."

It's almost like she was telling me I'm a partner in her marriage. Not a hugely comfortable role to play, but think of the alternatives. She could be accusing me of stealing her man. I don't want him, even though we make love from time to time. And don't think I'm going to steal him because of our music. We already have that and Vera supports it.

I can't really believe she doesn't suspect what's going on besides the music. Maybe she's just as good at pretending we're innocent as I am at playing chaste with her husband.

Vera tells me I make Lex happy. I tell her it's the music. "He wouldn't be any less happy if his guitarist was a monkey, so long as the monkey can play."

I was surprised when she invited me for lunch at The Guards down on 29th and M. We were friendly enough, but it was always rehearsals with Lex that brought us together.

Getting to Georgetown is a pain because the upper crust didn't want the hoi polloi loitering around their fancy digs, so they refused the city's offer to route the Metro through their turf. I walked over from the Foggy Bottom Metro stop and ran the gauntlet of drug addicts on the Pennsylvania Avenue Bridge over Rock Creek Park. Two panhandlers came up. I said, "I'm broke," and ran.

Vera was waiting for me, all dressed up in an office gray matching skirt and jacket that made my outfit look shabby. She greeted me with an enthusiastic hug. "It seems so right we should do something that's just for the two of us." We sat down. She straightened the lapels on her jacket. She looked a little nervous. So was I.

"How is it to be a super-mom and working too?" I asked.

"It is so good to get into the real world. I love children, but having nothing else addles the brain. My boss is really nice."

I wanted to know the real story about Dr. Cooper. He might just be a kind of insurance for me and Lex.

Just when the talk got interesting, the waiter butted in. Vera ordered a Jaeger Schnitzel. I hadn't finished looking over the menu and was pissed. The fancier the place, the more the waiters think they're the most important part of your intimate conversation. I didn't need this guy standing over us when I wanted to hear what's happening between Vera and her boss.

I went for the venison and asked Vera about her job.

"It's wonderful after so many years of diapers and baby talk. Dr. Cooper put me in charge of the office right away and the nurses are delighted to have me do all the paperwork. But you must have been even busier with all those concerts. Did you have to rehearse all the time between performances?"

"Pretty much that's the way it was." I wasn't going to tell her more, but I looked straight at Vera and knew I had to account for our time in Europe better than that.

"Our hosts were really nice about showing us around town. They made us into full-time tourists everywhere. Then in Munich there was an amateur string quartet made up of a priest, a lawyer, a druggist and a pastry chef. They had a Boccherini quintet for me and the Schubert quartet for both of us. Neither of us had played the Schubert before. It's got wonderful melodies, and those guys played as good as the pros."

"Lex has been punch drunk about the whole trip," said Vera. "Europe is all he talks about; how the audiences loved it and how the concert stage is all he ever wants to do. He says performing for an appreciative audience beats any high from marijuana or LSD, and going to the office day in and day out is death by a thousand cuts."

Of course I had heard all this from Lex. "He grouses about the office to me too, but I tell him to add up what we earned for the tour and think about the time and effort that went into it. Music wouldn't feed him even if he took every penny."

Vera shrugged her shoulders. "The money doesn't matter to him, even though he still complains there isn't enough when I want something. Does he really play that well?"

"He played beautifully, but that doesn't mean he can make a living at it. Lots of people play as well as the rich and famous, but the best they can do is teaching singing to brats in some junior high school."

Vera nodded. We ate a few bites before she said, "Try convincing Lex of that."

"I'll try. He's pretty stubborn, you know."

"That's no joke." Vera frowned. "He doesn't seem to have any idea of the sacrifices it takes to make a life in music. I can't help but wonder why you do it."

"Sometimes I wonder too, but it's the only thing I know how to do."

"You make me jealous. I wouldn't have the courage even if I had the talent."

"Courage? Sometimes I ask myself if I'm crazy, and other times I know it."

Vera looked around, as if to make sure nobody would hear us. "I was afraid you might say something like that. You have just confirmed that Lex is insane. He wants to quit his job. I asked whether he expects manna from heaven to pay the mortgage. Then he dropped a bombshell on me. I'll bet you know what it is."

"No, but if it's about relying on music for a decent living, he's nuts."

Vera took out a handkerchief and blew her nose. She didn't say anything for a while, and I was getting very uncomfortable praying that our silence wouldn't fester. Finally, I had to talk. "Do you mean that he asked if it's OK to do another European tour next year? We've already been invited back. I hope we can do it."

"No. That's not what I mean." Vera spoke very slowly. "I don't have any trouble at all with having one less boy to care for when you two take off for concerts. But Lex doesn't just want concerts in Europe. He told me he's quitting his job to become principal flutist in some new symphony in Caracas."

"Are you joking, or is he really a madman? Is it a steady job at least?"

"Lord only knows. I was too upset to ask, but he said the pay is good because the orchestra is subsidized by the Ministry of Culture."

"That would be a miracle if he could make a living doing what he loves." No sooner had the words come out of my mouth than I wanted to bite my tongue.

Vera stared right through me. "We bought a house here. Our life is here in Washington. We both have good jobs now. He even has his concert tours with you. Isn't that enough to satisfy him?"

Vera took out her handkerchief again. She sneezed, but I could tell she was covering up the tears. "I don't want to go."

I mumbled, "Hope I can help stop this nonsense."

"Tell him he's giving up everything for a ridiculous pipe dream. He can have it all here. I'm happy to see him play whenever he wants."

Vera wiped her eyes. "I know my husband. Who's to say he won't get as sick of playing in an orchestra as he is of the office?"

"What will you do if he insists on going?"

"I'm not going anywhere." Vera's voice was sharp-edged determination – something I had never heard from her before. "No!" She turned her head back and forth. I gazed at the burning log in the fireplace, now reduced to embers.

"What will you do if he runs off to South America?" She asked.

A trap I'm not going to fall into. "Guess I'll just have to find another flutist to do the tour next year. All I need is someone who will play for me rather than…"

Vera interrupted. "That's not what I mean. I want to know what you would do if you had a husband who pulled this on you."

"He's bananas…" and I think I know what she's getting at.

"I'm going to tell him he can't go."

"There's no harm in telling him what you feel."

"I can't believe he didn't tell you about this."

Vera was staring at me as if I might be the enemy. She doesn't make it easy to play innocent. "He doesn't tell me everything. Maybe he wanted to get your approval first. He did mention that Stan Goldman told him about the job, but I didn't know it had gone this far."

"Maybe I should tell him that if he goes to Venezuela I'll divorce him." Vera's eyes welled up as they bored into mine.

"But he can't be half as bad as my ex-husband." I couldn't think of anything else to say.

"You wouldn't know, I don't think," said Vera, never taking her eyes off me.

I tried to console her, but I did know, and Lex did tell me all about it before he told Vera. And I told him he had better be real careful about this.

38

Lex

Has It Really Come to This?

Vera and I were tight up against opposite ends of the sofa, trying to hold a civil conversation. "Why can't we just do a trial separation and you can come to Caracas later?"

"I don't see any point in delaying the inevitable."

"Must everything be inevitable for you? The only thing inevitable for me is death. Can't you think things over before making up your mind?"

Vera got a lawyer.

There wasn't any knock-down-drag-out fight. Vera was cold and straight to the point, like Miss Bubriski, the ninth grade English teacher who stared right through me as she detailed the "F" on the grammar exam, the automatic zeros for homework handed in late, the sloppy compositions – all the reasons she didn't give me the "B" I desperately wanted.

Vera never raised her voice during her steely cold recital of the facts. A sardonic tight-lipped smile crossed her face as she wrung my intestines out like a soaking wet washcloth. Finally she said, "Might you have wanted to ask me what I think about all this? After all, we're still married and that is supposed to be an equal partnership."

"Of course," and then I said something about me being the breadwinner and whither thou goest I shall go. Wasn't that somewhere in the marriage vows? At which point I think I made a mistake. Vera froze in time and place, not even a twitch from the big bang that did not happen until dark matter dominated our universe.

"Breadwinner. Such a nice sounding word," said Vera. "Might you recall that we were going to settle down and raise a family, so we picked a great school district and struggled to make the mortgage payments on a house we couldn't really afford? Finally we both have good jobs and some money left over every month to go out and enjoy ourselves and our children. Why are you running away from everything we strived for without even telling me about it?"

"I really wish we would have enjoyed ourselves like you say, but you never trusted anybody to babysit."

"How can you attack me like this? You still haven't begun to tell me why you want to ditch your family and life in a great city like we're dead fish to toss back into the Potomac."

"What makes you think Washington is a great city when everybody is defined by their rank in the government? Can you understand what it's like to go to a job I hate and get treated like dog turd every day?"

"You don't have to hate it."

"Want to know what it's really like? Try making daily payments to Scrooge McDuck to buy a coffin for the soul."

Vera smiled. "My dear Lex. I must say, you are a master of positive thinking."

Infuriating bitch. "Thank you so much for recognizing that, my dear. After years of slops at the government trough I'm finally thinking positive with this opportunity in Venezuela. You knew from the start I'm a musician. I didn't have the guts back then, but I do now."

Without any warning Vera burst into tears. Her sobbing wasn't loud at all, but she curled up in the fetal position. I reached out to comfort her, but she slapped my arm away.

39

Sally

Sisterly Sympathy

Vera is a homebody above all. How dull. She seemed willing enough to let Lex go off to Europe and do pretty much anything he wanted as long as she had her home and her marriage, if that's what you call it. Looks to me like it was an uncomfortable arrangement, the kind that goes on for years without anybody in it realizing how unhappy they really are.

Give the two of them credit for making a decent show of it. If you ask me, Vera had it easier than Lex because she was brought up not to expect much of a man, so she accepted that he was pretty much the standard. No gold or silver medal mate, but bronze enough to keep a roof over her head and buy second hand furniture.

Lex had almost learned to do his duty, until the Venezuelan symphony offer came along. He did a good job of pretending to be the faithful husband to an uptight woman. I'd like to think that Vera never figured out what was going on between Lex and me, but you know how women can hide it when they've been cheated on. Denial goes so deep that some people refuse to believe what happens right in front of their noses.

Music is so different from all the other reasons people screw around. You could say the duo excuses everything between us. It made our lives inevitable, and Vera is the kind who accepts what's foreordained. She's not curious about Lex and me. Thanks for that.

I can't help but wonder whether Vera might have known all along. Maybe it just wasn't very important to her, certainly not as important as her children and that roof over her head. Then there's Dr. Cooper, coming into their home and all but accusing Lex of perversion for not being my lover. Vera told me how much she enjoyed working for him but she never said a word about her feelings, which were pretty obvious at that horrific brunch where she seated the doctor at the head of the table and relegated Lex to the far end. Maybe she was thinking that symbolic insults are the best way to get Lex out of her life – let him bolt first.

Until recently I was really scared that Lex would blow our cover. Before Europe I trembled at the thought of what Vera might do if she thought we were playing around, but Lex was a pretty convincing actor. When we rehearsed he was nothing if not downright cold to me. Afterwards when we sat around the dining room table with Vera, he groused about what a hard taskmaster I was and accused me of telling him how to play every phrase.

"You could at least be nice," Vera would say. "She's just trying to help you." Or else it would be, "She's giving you the music you always wanted. There's a price to pay for everything. Thank her for it."

I've always been amazed at the way Vera handles herself. She doesn't know what passion is, but then she doesn't know despair either. Maybe she thinks life is an endless stream of disappointments and unfulfilled aspirations that you learn to accept.

Vera told me she never got any love from her mother, and her father didn't defend her from the maternal venom. When the neighborhood kids played doctor on her they explored her nude body and called her an incurable freak. An uncle and a cousin probed her intimate parts in ways those playmates never understood. She was never popular in school and wondered why, if her uncle and her cousin wanted her so badly, why didn't anybody else?

"Your eyes shimmer so, they're vibrant. Your face lights up. Why are you so alive?" She asked me.

"Maybe it's to hide the tears."

"Am I supposed to believe that?"

Vera doesn't have any idea about my loneliness. I can't tell her. She'd get suspicious about what I did with her husband. She hasn't asked either. I think she locks herself in a feeling-proof room that must be like a cabin class stateroom on the Titanic that's filling with water. But instead of drowning, Vera swims in a sea of coping and doing the right thing.

Me, I'm drowning most of the time, but whenever I get my head above water, it's pure exhilaration. Maybe that's what Vera sees in me. Music elates and performance is glorious, but somewhere deep down I'm terrified of it.

It's that fear that led me to ask Lex to come on the European tour. Going solo I would have missed notes and forgotten the music right in the middle. Maybe I would have been unable to go on. I don't understand this dread of playing for an audience. How come Lex the amateur performed like Paganini and seduced the audience?

Vera couldn't imagine Lex like that, and maybe that's why she couldn't see the electricity between us. She wanted a friend and let me be one even though I was making it with her husband. That's what husbands do. I had seen plenty of it. The difference between us was that she shut her eyes to it.

A couple of those husbands paid my rent for a while. When you're a musician and no money is coming in and people won't put a little money in a guitar case on a street corner, then temporary help from somebody else's husband who craves a sympathetic ear and some decent sex becomes OK. But if you think my vibrant eyes don't hide a vale of tears you are wrong.

Vera and I talked about that. Her curiosity must have built up for months before she asked me why I screwed around with a dozen men if it brought so much pain and so little reward. "Because all I ever wanted is to play the guitar and it doesn't feed me."

She looked at me with an expression of wonder. "What about marriage and children? Isn't that what we're supposed to do?"

I had to be careful what I said about that. I couldn't tell her she was shackled to her house and kids and a husband who was putting his passion into me every chance he got. "Children? I had to baby-sit brats as far back as I can remember. First my younger sisters. Then my father went bankrupt so I had to sit for anybody he could beg to take me on. I was miserable, hated it. Now I can't even take care of myself. How can I take care of kids?"

"But you're wonderful at it." Vera had that thoughtful look that revealed how little she knew. "Aaron and Jennifer are crazy about you. They keep asking when you will play with them."

We sat quietly for a while. Then Vera asked me, "Did you ever think about remarrying?"

"I already tried that holy matrimony stuff and it was a disaster, so why mess up my life again? Even with kids you're better off being unmarried and in charge. That tribe in the Chinese hinterland where the women pick the men to father their children and then kick them out has it right."

Vera turned and stared at me with an intensity that made me shudder. She put her arms around me and drew me to her until we came together. My cheek was against hers when she whispered in my ear, "I guess that's what I did with Lex, isn't it?"

40

Vera

For the Love of Music

Lex left our marriage just like a teenager who chucks his steady girlfriend when he hears the tenth grade beauty queen thinks he is oh so handsome. Music is some kind of satanic force within him that dictates everything he does, from jumping out of his seat when he's playing flute to skipping out of house and home. I wondered what I did wrong, where I could have saved this, but I don't think about that much any more. He's such a fool that my angst didn't last long. More than a week or two, certainly, though not so very much longer, and I really am OK now.

How could anybody blame me for this? I gave Lex everything he ever wanted, and even let him go on that European tour with a very attractive woman. At first I wondered what might happen between them on that trip, but she became a good friend and it was obvious Lex isn't her type. She only needed him for the music, and even if she did do what Dr. Cooper thinks they did, I could have faced that too. In truth there was no need to worry. Lex doesn't have much feeling at all, especially for women.

I admired his absorption in music, even though it stood in stark contrast to the lack of genuine warmth between us. He did get more adept and considerate, but it was a marriage that we were acting out rather than really believing in it.

I'm coming to know why someone might want to have an affair with somebody else. That doesn't mean I ever got used to Sally letting a dozen other men have her. Such wear and tear from men who don't care.

It was sad that Lex never knew what intimacy is. I really couldn't teach him. Looking back, I am a bit surprised that I stayed with him for so long. That must have been duty.

Sally has been so good through all of this. She seemed as shocked as I was to learn that Lex quit his job, or got fired, whatever the truth really is. I asked her to knock some sense into his head.

Sally cried when she told me, "I tried to get him to understand what it's really like being a musician. What it's like not to know how the bills are going to get paid. Like you never know where the next gig is going to come from. All Lex did was repeat over and over again that the symphony is a steady job with good pay."

"Didn't he say anything about me, or Aaron and Jennifer?"

Sally hesitated so long before answering that it was hard to know whether she was telling the truth or simply trying to make me feel good.

I slipped out of our hug. It had served its purpose and I had to let go of grief. "You don't think I was wrong to file for divorce, do you?"

"Do what's right for you," said Sally. "I told Lex he's mad. You know what he told me? If this is madness he wants nothing more than to be totally out of his mind."

I was starting to tear up and I didn't want to. "That's what I can't understand. I never once asked him to do anything when he was making love to that instrument of his. I did everything around the house. What more could he want?"

Sally put her arms around me, but I was limp. She must have sensed my discomfort because she let go and said, "He doesn't know what he wants. He just wants. He'll always want."

"Now he wants a trial separation. He thinks I miss him so much that I'll pack Aaron and Jennifer up and move down to Caracas to serve him again. I'm afraid I stopped missing him some time ago. He hasn't been here for a very a long time."

I looked around my living room and scanned the cardboard art on the walls, coming to the Degas poster that was Lex's favorite. The dancers would not have been impressed had they been able to see our ratty furniture. My living room is the same emptiness it has been since we moved in, a scene getting older but not growing at all. And my kitchen cabinets are in the same unreachable place they have always been.

Sally turned toward me, her gaze intense. "Do you think he really believes that you will just go to him?"

"That's what it feels like." I was embarrassed to tell Sally all this but, "The house was emptier when he was here than it is now. Even so, he's welcome if he comes back to reality."

"Do you think he will?"

"Probably not."

"Maybe divorce him sooner rather than later," said Sally. "No point letting this drag on."

I stared out the window at the oak tree in our front yard. Doubtless it had endured more than I could imagine. Like me, and I'm still standing too.

I wish I wasn't raised to believe that divorce is so absolutely wrong. My parents cordially hate each other, but they won't ever divorce, and here I am tormenting myself about doing what is right for me. I wallow in the stain on the record of my life, and see a decree as proof that something is wrong with me, even if none of it is my fault.

Sometimes I wonder if I have a good excuse. I can't claim cruelty or adultery, though he could if he knew what happened during his absence. I shouldn't feel guilty about that.

I hugged Sally. "Thanks. I needed you to tell me divorce is the right thing to do." I felt her tears mingle with mine on my cheek.

Not long afterwards Dr. Cooper invited me out to dinner at the Potomac House. Sally babysat. I told him about my decision.

"Good," he said, as the flickering candle danced light and shadow across the smile on his face.

41

Lex

Welcome to the *Sinfonia Nacional*

Could this ragtag man wearing only a T-shirt, shorts, and flip-flops really be the orchestra conductor who wrote that he personally would meet me at Maiquetia Airport? He looked more like the aggressive taxi drivers who tried to take my luggage as I struggled through the crowd until I saw the cardboard poster with my name on it moving slowly up and down as if on some kind of mechanical advertising device.

Luis Velasco held on to the poster instead of shaking my outstretched hand. He introduced himself as the emissary of the orchestra conductor, who was too busy to spend all day getting to and from the airport. Velasco was shorter and thinner than I, with coarse facial features and stubble on his chin.

He led me out to the airport parking lot through waves of equatorial heat and sticky asphalt pavement that tugged at the heels of my shoes. We got into a Chevy Nova that he must have bought for almost nothing. It wasn't because the car looked like a wreck, but because "*no va*" in Spanish means "doesn't go." Stan Goldman had told me about this exemplar of American business acumen in foreign markets.

For want of conversation, I asked Luis, "What instrument do you play?"

He looked at me as if I'm monumentally stupid. "I am your loyal second flutist. Our director insisted that all first chair players must meet the highest international standards, so you will have some foreign friends in the orchestra."

"We'll have to play some duets," I said, hoping to break the ice.

Luis didn't respond. We crawled through the coastal mountains towards Caracas in silence and growing discomfort. I wouldn't be too happy either if I was ordered to waste an afternoon in this traffic to pick up the man who relegated me to second flute.

"Is traffic often like this?"

"Usually worse."

Our conversation died there. I couldn't help but wonder why I was coming to Venezuela for this, but the orchestra was where the opportunity is, and I have a friend in Stan Goldman. In the U.S., my future in music could be interrupted by cops chasing me off street corners where I would be performing for coins tossed at my open flute case. When a famous violinist played at a metro stop near the nation's capitol to see what would happen, almost nobody stopped to listen.

The drive into Caracas took longer than the international flight from Miami. Eventually we arrived at the apartment that was provided as part of my contract. I invited Luis in, but he pleaded that his family was waiting for him to go to a party.

"The orchestra rehearses at 7:30 tomorrow and the conductor is expecting you." Luis left me and my overweight suitcases at the door.

Once inside, I went to call Stan Goldman at the Embassy, but there was no phone. I was greeted by minimal furniture and an envelope on top of a small table that would serve as my desk, breakfast nook and dining suite. The welcome packet had a map of the city and a number of typewritten sheets in Spanish. Although I was told that everything would be in English, the only thing I've seen in my native language so far is the "Tissue" label on a roll of toilet paper in the bathroom.

I had claimed my Spanish was good when I applied for this job because I took three years in high school and got Bs. If this was a test, I flunked. Wading through all this material with a pocket dictionary was not my idea of a welcome. Knowing the rehearsal time and place will be enough. The whole situation called for a nap.

The National Theater where the orchestra rehearses is just down the street. I entered the hall expecting the cacophony of instrumental solos that precedes every orchestra rehearsal I had ever been to, but this orchestra was playing the second movement of Mozart's symphony #40 in G minor. I stood in the back and watched some uncoordinated bowing from the strings. The conductor flailed away with sharp baton strokes.

Luis Velasco was sitting in the principal flutist's chair. He missed a cue and the orchestra played on until the conductor raised his hands in disgust and yelled, "Where is the flute? Where is the flutist?"

Musicians tittered at the tirade. The concertmaster pointed my way. The conductor whirled around and spotted me standing in the aisle, holding my instrument and waiting for a break so I could slither into the group. He shouted at the top of his voice, "Who do you think you are? We start our rehearsals at seven o'clock, not when you decide to walk in."

I stammered, "I thought rehearsal is at 7:30." Humiliation squelched thought.

"Seven o'clock," yelled the conductor. "Didn't you read the welcome kit?" His rant was in English, as if to confirm his disdain.

Velasco got up out of my principal flutist's chair and summoned me over with a bow and a sweeping wave of his hand. Laughter reverberated throughout the hall. Cymbals clapped as I worked my way through the maze of musicians. The conductor yelled again. "Stop. Luis will play first today. Gringo Flutist will listen from the last row in the auditorium."

I was so flummoxed by the conductor's outrage I hardly could tune in to my own memory, but now I was sure that Luis told me 7:30. I got to the last row and simmered as he played the Mozart and that great solo passage in the Leonora Overture. I felt the smirk on his face burn my cheeks.

When the rehearsal was over, I went up to the stage in hopes of apologizing to the conductor, but the concertmaster warned me against that. "Maybe in couple of weeks you can talk to him."

Luis came over and joined us. "Too bad you got mixed up. Come at 6:30 next time and I will introduce you to some of the players." He was all smiles.

I wanted to cram his fleshy flute lips into a shredder, but said nothing. Luis turned to me. "I'm president of the musicians' union. Mr. Principal Flutist, you are invited to join."

I asked about that, since it wasn't in my contract.

"We all belong to the union. It's the only way to protect the interests of the Venezuelans in this orchestra. The director is unfair. So is the manager. They yell at us like we're donkeys. You saw it tonight. They demand extra rehearsal time with no extra pay."

Luis was getting heated, but he still wouldn't look at me. "They never consult with our representatives about soloists. They take away our jobs and give them to foreigners."

I wanted to ask what would happen if I didn't join a union which seemed to be intent on forcing foreigners out of the orchestra. Luis must have anticipated this.

"All of your foreign colleagues have joined. They know the union is good for them too."

In the coming days I would learn more about the union from the principal horn player. Tony Ruiz grew up in Los Angeles speaking Spanish, and he was the first American to join the orchestra. "It's a shakedown pure and simple. If there ever was a union meeting, I wasn't invited, and I'm as Latino as any of these guys."

"I imagine we wouldn't be invited to a discussion about getting rid of the foreign invaders." I told Tony about the phony rehearsal time that Luis gave me. He wasn't surprised.

One of the promises made when I signed on with the orchestra was an appearance as soloist performing the Mozart D major concerto. I had wanted to do the concerto for flute and harp, but was told this wouldn't be possible. It turned out that the principal harpist is married to a tyrant who is so jealous that he tried to force her to quit the orchestra. There was no telling what he might do if she played with a man, even if it is only music. The management was not willing to see their harpist dead after the first rehearsal.

Months went by and nothing was said about performing a concerto as soloist. Very little has been said to me about anything. I was given a rehearsal schedule, that welcome packet in Spanish and keys to the apartment, and that's it.

Several other Americans were hired for the woodwind and brass sections, but all except Tony Ruiz were almost as new as I was. Steven Riddell, the principal bassoonist, said he was promised a concerto appearance too, but had heard nothing. Monroe Adcock, the oboist who sits next to me in the orchestra, didn't have a clue about his concerto either.

When I hadn't been paid after six weeks, I called up Stan Goldman at the Embassy and asked him how I should handle this.

"Not to worry," said Stan. "There's a lot of politics involved, but you'll eventually get paid. They just had an election here and the opposition won. The orchestra is a government entity, and that means everybody who ran it before has been kicked out."

Stan explained, "Even the elevator boys in government buildings are political appointees. When their *Accion Democratica* party lost the election they joined the army of the unemployed. That's for five years until the new bums in office get voted out and they have a job again. As for that concerto performance you're wondering about, chances are your new conductor doesn't have any idea what commitments the old one made."

42

Sally

Long Hot Summer

For years I had been working on the Pease Conservatory to make me their first official guitar instructor. Trevor Galena was a piano professor there and accompanist for my former husband. More important, he always liked me, and I took every opportunity to let him know of my interest. He was for the idea, but said there would be a lot of people to convince before it could ever happen.

I pretty much forgot about that until the night we were out together with friends and he told me I would be the new guitar department, complete with title. All I had to do is survive until school starts in the fall.

Vera is helping tide me over. She offered a room if things get really tough, and insists she can pay generously for my baby-sitting, thanks to Dr. Cooper. He pays her overtime to straighten out his office.

And his life, I'll bet. I remember his intense look at that brunch when he revealed that he was recently divorced after 35 years, and he sure was trying to skewer Lex into admitting enough adultery to make Vera want to have an affair. It all fits a man who made a mark in his field and has two adult children in therapy. If you think I don't have him figured out, Vera told me she's been seeing him socially.

She invited me over to celebrate my job offer. I brought Mischa Decker, a nice guy and good guitarist who got his real estate license and sells houses. He brought a bottle of champagne and we downed it in no time. Then Vera uncorked another bottle and we drank ourselves silly together. She laughed like a donkey. "I knew I wouldn't have to save you from the poorhouse. Good thing too, because I'm thinking of taking Dr. Cooper in from time to time to see how that might work out."

"Bet you were having a little fun while we were concertizing in Europe." I surprised myself saying that, but I was as drunk as my tongue was loose. Vera was totally sloshed, a lot farther gone than I.

"What would you expect? It amazes me that Lex could be so cold when you were together every day for almost a month. He's so full of shit."

"I told him I would cut his dork off if he made a pass at me. Remember when that lady downstate actually did it? Lex did."

"Don't worry. It's OK. You can have Lex and his dork too."

Mischa's jaw looked like it was hanging below his waist. We were giving him a real show, and Vera wouldn't stop. "Know what Lex was like? Fuck me when he wanted sex. Fuck intimacy, fuck everything all the rest of the time."

Enough, I wanted to say, but Vera was really in her cups. "You're not the kind who would blame me for having a little fun sometimes, would you? I'm sick and tired of holding off because the divorce isn't final yet. That fucking jerk walked out on everything he had."

I had never heard Vera use the F word before. "Have some more champagne," I said, hoping that would keep her busy.

"Sure. Celebrate that."

Then she passed out.

I wasn't about to visit Lex during the summer, even though he invited me. Vera is sleeping with Dr. Cooper, but why risk the friendship while epithets about Lex are spurting from Vera like blood from a severed artery.

I'll learn new solo repertoire and start at Pease fall semester. Then it's off to Venezuela to rehearse during winter break and tour the duo in Europe. International tours by faculty members make the reputation of the school. They can advertise that I perform worldwide. All I have to do is double up for a while on lessons to make up for the time away.

The plan was perfect, until I learned that I was being garroted with a guitar string. As Trevor put it when he called me in, "Our department budget just came back with major cuts. I'm afraid we're unable to fund your position right now, but I can give you students."

I choked so that I could hardly squeak. "How many?"

Trevor blinked, again and again. "I'm afraid we won't know until students register. We can't offer a guitar major until we try this out for a while and have a budget."

I gave him my best sardonic laugh. "How long should I wait for your budget when I won't earn enough to pay for gas?" Lucky my guitar was in its case. Otherwise I might have smashed the instrument over his head, just to see my world in smithereens.

Vera suggested that I call Stan Goldman in Caracas to see what employment prospects might be there. "He's such a jackass," I told her.

"Of course he is, but he's also the Cultural Attaché at the Embassy and he led Lex to the symphony. Lex even admitted that the pay is pretty good when we discussed a settlement."

Vera wants to connect me with Lex so she won't feel guilty about hooking up with Dr. Cooper. Maybe we're moving in tandem like the Bobbsey Twins.

Stan Goldman hardly even let me say hello. "Get on a plane and stay with us. There's more waiting for you down here than you can believe. Everybody loves guitar."

Stan used to strip me with his eyes and now he says stay with him when Lex is right there in Caracas. He won't let me put in a word edgewise.

"You'll be a huge hit. All I need to say is that you're a protégé of Segovia and the music world here will go nuts. This is the home of *El Sistema.* The government funds a huge foundation to turn slum kids into orchestra musicians, but you'll get to teach the *crème de la crème.* Take my word for it. You'll love it here."

After Pease and Trevor Galena, I wasn't about to take anybody's word about employment as a guitarist. "Can you check around and see what the real prospects are before I decide. I'll call back in a week or two."

"Don't waste your money. I'll call you. Official business. Get yourself a reservation. We'll surprise Lex."

I had hoped to catch up on the rent in a couple of weeks, but that was before Pease became an illusion. The eviction notice arrived in the mail yesterday and I don't want to move in with Vera. Stan's a boor, but Lex insists that his housemate of years ago is a loyal friend.

Good thing the telephone company waited until Stan called back before they cut my phone off. "Sally, just get on a plane. I've got a concert date for you next month at the Casa Bolivar. You must be there."

"What do you mean?"

"Just what I said. The date is booked. That's where you go to see the jewels and meet the money that will sponsor you. Send me the program. I'll pick you up when you get here."

I couldn't say anything because he wouldn't stop talking.

"Santiago da Silva wants you to teach his kids. He's like our Speaker of the House and his sons play classical guitar. Get it?"

"Send me a plane ticket." I wanted to take that back, but it already slipped out.

"We'll talk about that when you get here."

"I was joking. Forget it." It dawned on me too late that this would be a sure ticket to getting laid. Good thing I haven't maxed out my credit card.

Stan met me at the airport, loquacious as ever. "Don't even think you're imposing. We have houseguests all the time and a Colombian maid to take care of them. She's right out of 'One Hundred Years of Solitude.' Blames her sister for getting her pregnant, but we kept her on out of dumb sympathy. Who knows what we'll do when the baby comes?"

After an interminable crawl along the highway that runs like a spine through Caracas, we turned off on one of the ribs and drove up a hill into an area of homes boasting walls of glass supported by huge wooden beams. Stan's place featured a cavernous living room that dominates the house, topped by a cathedral ceiling. Stupendous acoustics and concerts for royalty popped into my head.

Stan must have seen me gape. "I have to do a lot of entertaining in my job. They call it representation. Naomi hates it."

"Nice digs for just the two of you."

"Three soon enough. We'll probably have to adopt the maid's baby. Otherwise she'll go screaming to the world that it's mine."

I heard my dead silence echo through the house.

"It all comes with the job," said Stan.

"What's that?"

"The house. The representation. The maid. In this country you either live in a mansion with servants or in a hovel with mudslides when it rains. If you can suck off the oil teat, you get the mansion. Otherwise curse the day you were born Venezuelan. Drink gasoline instead of eat cake. Gas is much cheaper than water, but one of these days this place will explode."

Late afternoon light gave the living room a golden glow. The maid shuffled in with her basketball belly and asked if we wanted anything to drink. Stan excused himself to make a phone call. The maid came back with orange juice and pointed to herself. "I have his baby."

"Where is the Senora?"

"Estados Unidos."

"When is she coming back?"

"Don't know. Master coming back. He doesn't like me to talk to guests."

Stan showed me a bedroom bigger than the master suites in the luxury homes where I babysat as a teenager. The dressing table looked like an office built for two, with a huge mirror. The sweet scent of luxury soap wafted out of the bathroom.

"Get rested. I'm having a party tomorrow night and you'll meet people who are really excited about having you perform. Lex will be surprised out of his wits to see you. Can't wait to see the look on his face."

I wondered whether springing this surprise at a big party is such a good idea.

"Prepare yourself for a shock about his living arrangements," said Stan, "but don't worry. You can stay here as long as you like. Uncle Sam pays the rent. It makes up for poverty in Washington."

Uncle Sam's tab or no, it's decent of him to invite me to stay. I wonder if the reason wealthy people take me in is because they hunger for art they cannot create. The patrons beg me to play for them so they can feel close to the making of miracles, they say. I guess all their money gives them only so much, and it is never enough.

Stan Goldman isn't like those people at all. He's a rooster trying to wake everybody with his cock-a-doodle-do, but he sure is playing the gracious host. Not sure whether he wants my body or I'm the trophy in his look-at-me success as the American Cultural Attaché. Maybe both.

I slept in the plushest of beds, and when I got up and made my way downstairs the maid came out and asked whether I wanted eggs or cereal. A note on the breakfast table read, "Wear a concert dress for the party tonight and plan to play for the guests. They'll insist on it." It was signed with a smiley face that looked pretty much like a heart with a broken arrow through it.

I practiced much of a day that was like most other days except for the maid service and plush surroundings. Stan Goldman's sofa is one of those big wraparound things shaped like an L with curlicues at the ends so a whole bunch of people sitting there face each other. It was too soft a seat for serious music, and the armchairs aren't good for my purposes either. There were several camphor chests against the wall that look like they came from China. I settled down with my guitar on one of those.

When Stan got home he tossed his suit jacket over the sofa and apologized profusely. "You're so good you don't need any notice to play. Every one of the guests tonight is in a position to arrange concerts for you. Start with the Minister of Culture. Then there's Cecilia Herrera who runs the series at the Casa Bolivar. The one I really want you to get to know is Santiago da Silva."

I was getting dizzy with the name dropping.

"He loves opera. There's more culture in him than any of them, even though he's Speaker of the *Leal Senado.* That's power in this country."

Every man I was introduced to at Stan's party sported a gold Rolex. They didn't seem ostentatious about it, but the shirtsleeves were shorter than I see back home. It's a good way to show off expensive watches, but Stan explained that it was more likely that their wives didn't really know what sleeve length to get when they went shopping in Miami and New York.

These women might not be good shirt shoppers, but they sure know what to get for themselves. Maybe all the diamonds, rubies and emeralds are meant to draw attention away from their creased faces caked with makeup. Most of them looked as if a pout were chiseled into their mouths, but they smiled and the wrinkles creased in a friendly sort of way.

I played in automatic. The women were intent on my hands, but the men couldn't get their eyes off my boobs. They are very hard to hide, so I just live with the stares and hope they enjoy the music too.

Everybody gushed and I should have blushed, but that's what we musicians live for. Ambassador Lucas came over and shook my hand so hard I thought he would break it off. He's the boss of our Embassy in Venezuela, a huge man who exudes confidence that I know who he is and am grateful for his presence. "Wonderful," he said. "We'll have to get you to play for my guests too." Just as quickly as he came over, he turned away and said a few words to others as he worked his way to the door and out of the party.

Santiago da Silva was surrounded by so many people that I lost hope of meeting him. A lady named Graciela whispered in my ear, "*Este hombre es el proximo presidente de Venezuela.*" No wonder he's mobbed. I'd like to meet the next President too.

After the compliments were over, I stood in the tumult of the party, trying to get my bearings while everybody was talking to somebody else. Santiago da Silva came over, his entourage in tow. "*Magnifico.* You must come out to the ranch. Tomorrow. My driver will pick you up." The hairs of his mustache danced as he spoke. "My three boys will study with you."

Stan whispered in my ear, "You're launched." But Lex was nowhere to be seen. His absence was a good thing, because I have a place to sleep that is as nice as I can imagine, and sleep is what I want to do.

I sank into the pillows of Stan Goldman's guest bedroom. As a child I used to hug the pillow, hoping it would provide safe haven from the gremlins and ghosts that populated my dreams and groped for my body. Now I had more pillows than I could get my arms around.

Hiding under the covers didn't always protect me from those dreams. Childhood fear returned sometime in the middle of the night. I felt crushed, I couldn't breathe. I reached out to fend off the nightmare. Something became entangled in my arm. A ghost of nightmares past whispered, "It's just me."

"Who are you? What are you doing?" I twisted and turned until I came face to face with the poltergeist next to me on top of the bedspread, hand clutching my wrist. Stan Goldman, stark naked.

"What the fuck are you doing in my bed?"

"Wha.. I must have been sleep-walking. No idea how I got here. Did I do anything wrong?" He sounded disoriented, but I couldn't tell.

"Bullshit. You're all bullshit." Faking or not, he wanted to make me in my sleep.

"No. Please. I really am a sleepwalker. It's so bad that when they discovered me halfway down the hall during Navy training they gave me a medical discharge. They said I would walk overboard at sea and that would be the end of me."

"Too bad they didn't put you on TV." I watched the show in fascination and disgust as Stan Goldman's generously endowed member wilted. He slinked out of the bedroom bent over just like it.

43

Lex

Surprises

"Where are my flute parts hiding?" I'm sure I didn't take the music home, but after I told Luis Velasco that I wasn't planning to join the union, the folder wasn't on my stand the next rehearsal. *"Stupido porco,"* screamed the conductor.

Luis whispered in my ear. "He said stupid pig. How could you forget the music?"

Had the librarian not noticed the folder on his desk while all this was going on, I would have been in deeper trouble than I already was. He understands English, so I went up to him after rehearsal and asked him if there was any way I might be provided with a phone and some decent furniture for my orchestra-issue apartment.

He offered to help in any way he could. Then he studiously avoided me for a week. "Very sorry, Señor, but the apartments provided for the foreign members are all standard. Anything else must be your responsibility."

Nobody at the telecom office spoke English, so I took a copy of every form they had and struggled mightily to understand them with a dictionary. Not knowing the language is like being deaf and dumb. Dependence like a baby on its mother's milk is not so kind to adults who need volunteers to navigate the basic necessities in a foreign country.

I took the forms to Tony Ruiz. "Whaddaya need a private phone for – not that you could get one before you retire. We all use the public phone and the desk will take messages for you."

Nobody told me this. When I went to check at the desk there was a message from Stan Goldman. "Save Saturday evening. Pick you up at 7:30."

That was last weekend. No point in asking the clerk why the message wasn't delivered. When I asked Tony about it he explained, "They hold messages for pickup, but delivering them isn't part of the job."

Stan blasted me when I finally reached him. "How come you didn't get your ass over to my party Saturday night? Everybody who's important to your future was here, and you blew it."

He echoed my "Oh shit."

"Good thing I didn't make a big deal out of your royal highness showing up. That would have made a fool out of me. Get over here tonight. I've got something for you."

He hung up. When the cabbie dropped me off in front of his mansion I wasn't anxious to face him.

"Hello Mr. flute player."

I tripped on the step and almost toppled over backwards.

"Remember your guitar partner?" Sally's smile was like we had just met. She was trembling. I touched her shoulders, hesitated, and finally lurched forward to kiss her on the lips. She turned at the last second and flabbergasted affection became an awkward kiss on the cheek.

"I thought you were going to Pease."

Sally looked down at my shoes. "It didn't work out."

Stan was standing behind her. He smiled momentarily, the curl of his lips a half smirk. "You want to take her home with you now, or should I keep her in my palace?"

I stared at him, speechless. Sally looked away.

"Come on in," he said. "You don't have to decide right away."

44

Sally

Body and Soul

It's cruel that music is all soul but depends entirely on a fickle body to produce it. Besides the eternal hours you have to practice to be any good, you won't believe how much time and effort I have to spend on my fingernails to produce just the right sound. A lot of guitarists use fake fingernails, but that's cheating. Their sound is tinny. To get a good sound you have to keep your fingernails in perfect shape. Not too long or they'll break. Too short and you won't be able to pluck any resonance. You have to have nails that are hard enough so they won't chip. That's part luck, part diet, part clear nail polish, but you don't want your nails to get brittle.

Break a nail and that's really bad news. You can't get decent tone quality if some of your nails are fakes. To keep them from breaking, you have to pluck the strings exactly right. Imagine how much fingernail care it takes to make the sound of fountains in "Recuerdos de la Alhambra."

Nail care is just the beginning. Fingernails are like the plectra that pluck the strings to make the harpsichord sound, but we don't have keys like a harpsichord. You have to shift your fingers all over the strings without making the awful scratchy noises you hear so often, even from big name guitarists. That's noise that spoils the music.

Don't ask how I do what others can't, but those fingerboard noises that other performers accept as inevitable drive me nuts, so I spend hours and hours practicing the hand and finger shifts until they're so quiet that even I can't hear them.

It's not just in the way the fingers move. If we're not like an atomic clock when we pluck the strings the music falls apart. Ever hear somebody play who didn't truly understand rhythm? It makes anybody who has listened to their heartbeat sick.

They say it takes ten thousand hours of practice to master a skill. Maybe that's why Mozart didn't compose any great music until he was sixteen. Imagine how many hours we spend tapping on a table in two with one hand and three with the other, just to get rhythm right. Try a passage that starts nicely with four sixteenth notes to a beat, then try to play seven, eleven, or thirteen of those sixteenths in the same beat and you'll see what I mean.

Then there's all the stuff it takes to convince an audience you really can perform. You have to come on stage with total confidence, sit just right, and project an aura of intense concentration as you prepare to play. Then make the audience believe in your complete mastery even if you blow a passage here and there like we all do. Don't forget to arrange the concert dress between your rear end and the chair so that it flows as gracefully as the music.

And if you think the rear end isn't a big part of the music world, you've got another think coming. For some women who get to perform it's the biggest part, pretty much like being a Hollywood starlet wannabe. Use it or defend it, because every male you meet in this business wants a piece of your ass, just like Stan. Always the same line. I can get you bookings, real concerts, big fees. Howzaboutit? You don't have any concerts now, but you gotta believe, and get fucked over good.

Or you can defend your precious rear end and close that career enhancer. Which usually means that you get out of music altogether and find a job that actually pays money. If you're faced with that grim prospect, it makes more sense to employ your sweet ass to support the music addiction. Beats selling it for drugs, though lots of musicians do that too.

Do you think I let those dozen guys make it with me because I loved them all or really wanted them to love me? Dream on. What I really needed was a place to sleep and food to eat and time to practice. Damned if I'll do that for Stan Goldman though. He's supposed to be Lex's friend, but I'm not fool enough to want his kind of friendship even though that means giving up his palace boudoir for a hovel. I moved in with Lex, for a while anyway.

That's not leading to a commitment, even though so many female musicians marry the first guy with money who will have them. Their fate is sorta like your aspiring starlet, except most musician hopefuls don't have Hollywood bodies like theirs to throw around from producer to producer. But don't think that decisions about how to use our sweet pussies aren't a big part of getting the chance to share what's in our hearts with strangers we hope will adore us.

I've learned to use my body for music pretty well, all the way from fingernails to toes. I say toes because Lex makes a ritual of rubbing them before we make love. That drives him wild with excitement. He says he really wants to nibble on my fingers, but the thought that he might hurt them scares him out of his mind.

Soul, music, body, sex, they're all connected. Sometimes quite nicely, but mostly it's a matter of survival. A lot of musicians died of consumption in the old days. Now more of them just go insane, unable to meet the demands of endless practice to make the soul connect successfully to the body and the body connect successfully to make the music. Some succeed, but fail the final test – the demand to make passionate love to people you detest, hoping that will bring the reward of opportunity.

Here I am in Venezuela with no money to speak of and scared silly that opportunity will disappear because I wouldn't let sleepwalking Stan desecrate my ass in more or less the same way I let it happen before. Was this out of loyalty to Lex? He might never have divorced Vera if I didn't show him how to engineer it so she did the divorcing. No knowing whether I really want him for myself or not.

After Goldman's palace Lex's place can only be described as a rat hole. His one bedroom apartment is squeezed into a maze of similar flats connected by a dingy hallway not quite dark enough to hide the evidence that nobody ever cleans them.

It's a good thing I'm in shape, because Lex's hospitality is a fourth floor walkup. The first thing I saw going into the kitchen was a placard over the sink warning about non-potable water. You can't drink from the tap here unless you have a particular taste for chronic diarrhea. That means hauling bottled water up four flights of stairs because the delivery people leave it in the lobby. The security guard explained that the union won't let workers take it up unless it's on an elevator that this building doesn't have.

The water comes in five gallon glass jugs that are a lot harder to hug than my guitar. Lex volunteered to haul these monsters but they usually arrive when he's out. The guard insists that if I don't come down and get them right away, somebody else will. So it was that I came to measure my strength and pride by the weight of those jugs. Five gallons amounts to forty pounds plus the weight of the glass, heavy even when I return the empties.

Everybody I meet here talks about *la lucha,* the struggle they face every day. Mine is getting upstairs with the jug and turning it over to fit in a cradle without dropping the whole thing on the kitchen floor and shattering it into a thousand pieces – to say nothing of flooding the place with those twenty quarts of supposedly pure water.

I've always been mesmerized by glass. There was a glass blower not far from home who let us kids watch while he dipped his big straw in a blob of molten stuff and blew it like we blew bubble gum. Then when I was eight my father took me to see a hypnotist who did whatever he did with a crystal ball and had me and other people behaving like monkeys. Dad told me afterwards that it was pretty lewd the way we were scratching ourselves like the animals in the zoo. I must have been in quite a trance because I didn't remember a thing. Not long after that he tried hypnosis on me and touched me in the wrong places.

When my mother caught him in the act she screamed at him like I never heard before. I was too young back then to really understand what the big deal was all about, but every time I saw crystal I had to stop and stare at it. Too bad I never could afford any.

Killing time in the airport on the way back from Europe, Lex wondered why I was so intent on the Svarovski pieces in the airport shop. When I told him I had always been captivated by glass he insisted on buying me a dazzling little cat with blue ears, even after I protested that it was far too expensive. It's a pin that I wear all the time. I turn it over and over when I put it on, following the shifting rays of light reflected in the crystal facets. Maybe it was the kitty on my breast that led me so quickly from disaster at Pease to Lex's ratty digs in Caracas.

As glasswork goes, the five gallon water bottle is hardly worth looking at, but its contents keep dysentery and other diseases in the Caracas water supply out of our apartment. You can't help but admire how this humongous bottle is molded into a tiny neck no more than a tenth the diameter of the cylinder itself.

Why they use glass bottles in Venezuela instead of plastic is a puzzle to me. Maybe to keep the glass blowing trades alive. Hard to believe that with so much oil they don't produce more plastic.

That's what went through my head as I tipped the bottle and manipulated to get it set in the cradle. Like always, I grasped the neck in my left hand to guide it into the wire frame – until I heard the tinkle of glass on the kitchen counter top and felt the jagged edge slice through the flesh of my middle fingers as water poured out of the bottle and turned red.

I recoiled as spurts of my blood bathed the tile floor crimson, but felt nothing at all until the bottle exploded by my feet. When I came out of my stupor, I screamed bloody murder.

45

Lex

Never Land

What in the devil is that blood-curdling scream? I scrambled out of my nap in the bedroom, ran through the living room into the kitchen, slipped and slammed into hard tile. Agony raged up and down my arm like I broke everything that once was my elbow.

Sally's hand was hanging limp, spurting crimson from her serrated fingers. Glass was everywhere, not just the countless shards that were slicing my hip. Blood swirling in circles by the floor drain seared an indelible image as I pushed myself up and took a sliver in the meat of my palm.

I never fainted in my life. When I was six the anesthesiologist told my parents he couldn't believe how much ether it took to knock me out for my emergency appendectomy. But when I looked up from that dive in my slimy kitchen and saw Sally staring blankly at her limp hand, my whole being dissolved in the pool of blood and water that was eddying down the drain.

"You all right?" Sally sounded like I was the one who was badly hurt.

"Maybe. Probably not."

"Then get off your butt and call the Embassy. Tell them to find the best doctor in town."

I couldn't take my eyes off the raw flesh hanging from Sally's fingers. Blood flowed thick in small spurts – cut meat like you see in the butcher stalls in the market, but a much larger life freshly slaughtered, bleeding to death in front of my eyes.

I know of this. A friend of mine in third grade had a grandfather who was a ritual slaughterer until a massive heart attack caught up with him while he was bleeding a sheep. Slice the carotid. Watch the animal sink to its knees. Slice the fingers. Watch a musician die.

"Stop staring. Call," Sally commanded. Both of us were numb in the face of a certain death, hypnotized by it. Maybe it is like this when airline passengers realize their plane is going down. We musicians are not trained to face it. Paralysis was more soothing than a hopeless wail, but a real leader takes over and barks orders. Brace. "Call an ambulance, idiot."

I grabbed a clean dish towel and helped Sally wrap it around her fingers to see if we could stem the bleeding. Then I ran downstairs to the phone and called the Embassy.

Stan Goldman was in his office, twiddling his thumbs and scratching himself, he told me later. "I'll get somebody who puts hands back together. Get your ass over to HOSPITAL MÉDICO-QUIRÚRGICO *de Emergencia* RICARDO BAQUERO GONZÁLEZ."

"What the hell is that?" I couldn't make out any of it.

"Why the fuck don't you learn some Spanish? Never mind, I'll send a car over. Be out there." Stan hung up.

Dr. Enrique Gandolfi looked like he should be on a Hollywood set instead of in a Venezuelan hospital. I cringed as he unwrapped the blood-soaked blue and white checkered dish towel from Sally's sliced fingers. He looked at me with deep sadness in his eyes. Then he turned away, and came face to face with Sally.

"You cut almost to the bone and severed the nerves," he said. "That's why you don't feel anything. I imagine you didn't feel much when it happened."

"Will I be able to play guitar again? I have to feel to play."

"If you're determined to play you will, but it will take months of hard work and there will be some pain. You are very lucky, because I just came back from training in new micro-stitching techniques in Philadelphia."

He studied both of us. I had trouble banishing the image of an Omar Sharif look-alike who isn't a real doctor at all.

"As far as I know I'm the only physician in Venezuela who can do this. I'll have to give you general anesthesia. This is very delicate work that has to be done under a microscope and the hand must be perfectly still."

"Anything. Whatever it takes." Sally and I spoke the same words, in unison.

In the weeks that followed we learned that Dr. Gandolfi wasn't telling us everything when he said that recovering any useful feeling would be a painful process. "It's like putting my fingers in an empty light bulb socket with the electricity on," Sally said. "Ever do that?"

At first Sally screamed when she put her micro-stitched fingers to the guitar strings. She couldn't continue. She must continue. She took to bathing her fingers in my mentholated shaving cream to ease the searing pain.

Sally cursed the world and her fingers. I couldn't help wondering if my name wasn't hiding somewhere in her ferocious vocal cords. She couldn't stand playing the instrument that is her life for more than a few excruciating minutes.

With time she screamed less. "It's not because the pain is any less, but I want to hear if this is sounding anything like music." She shared her fear that she would never be able to concertize again. Profanity graced our apartment for months, until she ended this concerto of grief with a towering chord, "Fuck it. I will perform again."

The electric shocks where the nerves were stitched did not go away. Dr. Gandolfi told her, "Your real choice is to get used to it. Those digits will get better with time."

I couldn't tell whether he was lying or not, but I could see the tears come whenever Sally put her fingers to strings and fingerboard. She would stop in the middle of a passage, cheeks streaked with drying salt, and chant, "Get used to it," over and over.

Sally refused to play with me, though I asked her to all the time. She insisted that I stay away when she practiced. "It hurts too much to face all I could do then and can't do now. Don't look at me like that. I must do this by myself."

Maybe it was arrogant to think that companionship would help. I slinked into corners and read "One Hundred Years of Solitude."

"Get out. Go get laid," Sally screeched. "Anything you want, but don't hang around here when I'm trying to force my fingers to work again."

The symphony wasn't a great source of pleasure during this time. The programming was OK, until Luis gave me a personal invitation and a front row ticket to the concerto he would perform and I wouldn't. The personnel director explained rather sheepishly that *El Presidente* had given the order that the orchestra was to feature native-born Venezuelan soloists. I should understand that it was not his fault that he couldn't keep promises made when I was offered the job. The government that made them was no longer in office.

Luis performed sloppily, but he still had plenty to say. "I hear that all the foreigners will be replaced as soon as their contracts are up. How long is your contract?" He knew full well that it's initially for two years, and his distressed sympathizer look couldn't have been phonier. "It's really too bad they enticed you foreigners here with such extravagant promises. How unfair to disrupt your career in the United States."

Under my breath I mouthed, "Snake."

Besides having to live with Velasco by my side in the orchestra, I worried that Sally would hate me so much for this accident it would be impossible to get along together. But neither of us had anyplace else to run to. Without this job, I couldn't pay the child support. With her injury, who knows what would happen to Sally?

The glue that held us together was becoming unstuck. "I can play as slow as you want while you retrain those precious fingers," I pleaded.

"Only I can do that. What if it were your fingers? How could you stand having me next to you playing so beautifully while you struggle with every note? All I feel is electric shock, whether I'm playing guitar or doing nothing at all."

I couldn't even get her out of the kitchen. "Please tell me I can help," but she insisted that was her place, except for doing the dishes. She wouldn't let me cook or prepare anything. I worried that if she didn't burn those fingers she would cut them off dicing potatoes.

Sally never blamed me for the accident, even though I told her in the beginning that hauling those water bottles was a man's work and I would pay the guard to do it. She didn't take kindly to that. "If you think I can't do a man's work, screw you," she said.

It's my fault that she can't play. What else does she know how to do? She wants to be loved, but I'm so guilty I can't get it up. I pawed at her like a puppy and offered to massage her back. That wasn't what she wanted. Eventually she took my hand.

After six months of this Sally finally allowed me to play with her for the few minutes it took to run through the "Entr'Acte" again. "It still hurts like hell," she said, "but playing is the only way I'll ever be able to play." A tear dribbled down her cheek.

Stan Goldman called from time to time to invite Sally to come back into the world of the living and perform at one of his diplomatic parties. She finally agreed, but only if I played with her. "Cover me, so people won't hear how bad it is."

"Better you return as a soloist. You're playing as beautifully as you always did."

"Just cut the crap and play with me."

"I mean it. Everybody's asking about you. You don't need me for this."

Sally clenched her jaws tight. "You're right. I don't."

Sally was rehabilitating herself on pieces she had played hundreds of times. It wasn't just the easy repertoire. She was addicted to Rodrigo's "Concierto de Aranjuez," and played the adagio over and over again. Maybe because it conveyed nostalgia and loss. Rodrigo's wife wrote that it was both an evocation of their happy honeymoon and lament at the devastating loss he felt when she miscarried her first pregnancy. I assumed Sally knew that, but neither of us ever said anything about it.

There is nothing I wanted more than for her not to need me this performance. Not after she spent all these months learning how to banish the horror of the accident and suppress the interminable pain of producing the sound she lives by.

Any honest musician will tell you that no concert is perfect. Sally's performance at Stan Goldman's party was no exception, but the sympathetic audience knew her story and heard what they wanted to hear. They applauded until she blushed crimson.

For once Sally didn't eat her heart out about the glitches. She actually smiled instead of wincing through it all. The sparkle in her eyes told me she was alive again.

Sally was surrounded by admirers when Dr. Gandolfi came over with two glasses of champagne and offered me one. We clinked a toast. I asked him if he was pleased with the fruit of his labors.

"I never could bring myself to tell you this." The doctor avoided my eyes, staring into the distance. "I just didn't have the heart, but you should know that everything in my medical experience led me to believe she would never be able to perform again."

46

Sally

Hot Pants

Anybody could have seen what I found hiding under a shirt in Lex's chaotic clothes closet. The black slacks were not men's trousers. I have a pair like that, but these weren't mine either. I gasped. I fingered them. I smelled them close up. A very faint odor of woman was still there.

I ought to leave him. I came here, took care of him, sliced my fingers, went through torture and was beginning to heal before I saw what was right there in front of my eyes all along. I tore the slacks off the hanger and laid them out on our bridge table cum dining set so Lex wouldn't miss this improvised bitch-in-heat tablecloth when he came home from rehearsal. Then I went to the bodega down the street and bought red candles. I dripped plenty of wax on the wench's pants and set the table so that Lex's dinner plate was right in that broad's crotch. Knife and fork sat perfectly on the inner thighs. Then I prepared the most beautiful salad I had ever created, along with mushroom soup and a perfectly cooked steak that would have made Ruth's Chris proud.

Lex didn't even notice at first. He gave me a perfunctory hug. I forced a smile and pointed at the table.

Lex turned very pale.

"How do you like our new tablecloth? Steak to celebrate it. For dessert I'm going to squeeze your nuts until you scream."

He turned away. "It's most unusual," he mumbled.

"Who are you fucking now? Look at me, damn you."

He covered his face with his hands. "I swear it was an accident."

I wanted to drag him through dog shit and shame him into getting down on his hands and knees to beg forgiveness. "Fuck you and fuck you again."

He reached out. I backed away. He pleaded, "It was…a spontaneous…I had no idea you would be coming here six months earlier than we planned. I'm not a monk."

"You're a prick, and too stupid to get rid of the evidence."

"I guess it's my turn to confess, like you confessed to screwing a dozen men on the first date. Can't we treat both as accidents?"

That was the last thing I expected him to say. Making it with those jerks was history, but trousers and underwear came into the present, folded on a couch, tossed on the floor, scattered all over the bedroom like leaves in the wind. Ripped off in haste. Trousers and underwear in so many incarnations burning in the crematorium of my past. "Fate forced that on me. You know that."

I went to get a scissors to cut up that pair of slacks. He followed me into the bedroom, then backed away quickly as I came out and pointed them straight at his crotch before putting them on the table.

"Did you ever think of having a little loyalty to your partner? I didn't come to Venezuela for this."

"Please listen," Lex pleaded. "The minute I learned you were here I called Graciela to tell her I couldn't continue. I was honest with her about you. That was before we ever said anything about living together."

"Thanks a bunch. What makes you think you have the right to get in some other woman's pants every time I'm gone for a couple of weeks? Don't do to me what you did to Vera, buster."

"A few weeks? You said you would be teaching at Pease and wouldn't get here for another six months. That's an impossibly long time for any man."

"You think you're Gary Hart and want to be President too, huh?"

"We seem to have the same urge."

If Lex thinks that's funny, it is not. I growled, but no words came. Lex interrupted.

"Can you be fair for a minute? I never asked you to stop anything for my sake. If pleasing me was why you stopped playing the field you never cared enough to tell me."

I could have spit. "We'll resolve this over dinner. No point in wasting good steak."

As soon as he sat down I yanked that pair of slacks cum tablecloth as hard as I could. Lex jerked backwards, but not fast enough to avoid the bowl of soup that flew toward his lap, spilling all over him like a flood of tears. For a moment, steak and salad filled the vast distance between us before splattering blue cheese dressing and mushroom sauce on his legs.

Lex tried to wipe himself off with paper napkins. "Enjoy your dinner, you bastard." I treated him to a torrent of "*cogno, corracho*," and every curse I learned studying guitar in Spain.

He got up from the table and grabbed me. At that moment, all we had to start over with was the kind of sex people have when they want revenge – a wrestling match right there on the living room floor.

Neither of us ever said we love each other, but our sex life at its best was celebration of a great concert. At other times it was respite from the grubby life I led between gigs. For Lex it was escape from his dreary cubicle by day and Vera's well-meaning prison cell at night.

You can choose whether it was love or hate this time. Animal is the correct answer.

I don't owe him anything and will not owe him anything. He owes me for his musical dreams realized. If the world gives me nothing more for my music than a bed that men want to crawl into while I'm in it, what the fuck am I supposed to do?

Lex will argue that it all comes down to his whore's pants versus the dozen men I was stupid enough to tell him about. If there's a God did he really intend for women to lose every important argument?

47

Lex

Affairs Sliced and Diced

Sally got up off the floor first. She screwed her eyes up tight and shouted in my face. "For you music is the love affair. If your guitarist was a robot you'd love the robot, for all you know about people. Did you ever think there is me behind the music? Me, a real me."

"I think about you all the time. Of course I want the music, but I want you too. And I want to know what you want."

Sally scowled and reached for the scissors she had pointed at me earlier. She jammed them far enough into my belly that I winced in pain. "If you really mean what you say, I want you to cut them up. Now."

"Cut what up?"

"That tablecloth. Idiot."

"Oh." I took the scissors and cut slowly and carefully through the crotch.

"More. Cut that woman's slacks into little pieces and throw them in the trash."

I cut up and down the legs and mumbled how sorry I was that all this happened.

"You better be sorry," and Sally burst out laughing. She took the pieces of cloth and scattered them all over the living room floor. "It's an emergency. I'll clean everything up later." She took my hand and led me to the bedroom, where we tasted the salt on each other's cheeks.

48

Sally

Revolution Anniversary

I listen while Lex makes no secret that orchestra life is becoming the winter of his discontent. He complains that the Venezuelans despise the Americans, but his real bitch is with his second flutist.

"That Velasco has a nasty habit of playing out of tune when we're supposed to be playing in unison. Sometimes he tosses in wrong notes and then he smiles when the conductor stops the orchestra and yells at me. It's always my fault when it's actually his, and I have no way to stop him."

"Isn't the conductor good enough to know he's the one who's messing up?"

"Maybe, but rumor has it they're cousins. Can you smell a conspiracy to get me fired?"

I wish I could do something to help him, but Lex isn't too pleased with me either. He keeps asking me to work up some new repertoire with him to put life back into the duo. I'm not ready for that yet. It was a monumental struggle just to get through the simple pieces I played for Goldman's party. My playing wouldn't fool anybody who knows guitar.

I'm not going to hold Lex back while I teach my half-dead half-electrocuted fingers to go to all the right places again. Dr. Gandolfi keeps telling me to teach myself to forget the pain and feel whatever else the fingers might feel. Self-hypnosis helps a little, but a tumbler full of wine before practicing is better, and two glasses helps even more. My playing sounds best late in the morning. Then I can sleep it off in the afternoon if I need to.

That means I'm back in reasonable shape by the time Lex gets home. He doesn't seem to notice, and I'm not about to tell him I'm sipping to deaden real agony.

When Lex makes beautiful sound he goes into a trance, but the spark in his playing is gone now. He's been in a funk, until he came home after lunch with Stan Goldman and strode across our living room with an air of confidence that I hadn't seen since before the accident. Without a word, he hugged me until I could hardly catch my breath. Then he took my stitched-up fingers to his mouth and ran his tongue over them.

"Beautiful scars all healed. I know because I was listening to you practicing from right outside the door before I barged in on you." Lex let go of my hand and started to unbutton my blouse.

"What's this all about?"

"Stan showed me a telegram that our Embassy in Suriname sent to every single Embassy from Mexico to Chile." Lex tugged at my jeans.

I grabbed them and held on. "Not until you tell me what this is about, flute-player."

"The anniversary of the Suriname revolution is next month. The Russians are sending a ballet troupe, the Chinese are sending gymnasts, and we're not sending anything. The USIA people in Washington say none of their rated artists is available. I guess they forgot about you."

I swallowed bile. "That Berberger bitch wouldn't give us a rating as a duo because you were a government flunky in Interior. She ought to croak."

"It's good news that she hasn't. She did you a favor."

"She hasn't done us any favors."

Lex tried to unfasten my bra but I brushed him away. "Talk to me."

"If the Berberger lady wasn't in charge of programs this never would have happened. The cable says Fidel Castro is sending his best troupe and Suriname will grant diplomatic recognition to Cuba if the U.S. doesn't send a show too. Washington won't be happy if Suriname becomes a Cuban satellite."

"What's that have to do with us?"

"Everything. Our Ambassador in Paramaribo is begging every Embassy to check around to see if they can find some kind of act to represent the U.S. at these celebrations."

"What idiots in Washington. They've got this huge bureaucracy for cultural exchange and they can't find anybody to play." I unhooked my bra to loosen up and vent my outrage. "Was Stan asking you to round up the Americans in the orchestra and put something together? Suriname's right next door, isn't it?"

"That's close enough for jazz, but Guyana is in between." Lex took off his shirt. "Are you ready to hear what Stan Goldman had in mind when he called me in?"

"Will it be worth the wait until you finish frothing political babble at the mouth?"

"I've been waiting too. Take off something else and I'll tell you."

"Don't touch me." I don't mean that.

"Here goes. Stan took the cable and went to Ambassador Lucas. He called the Ambassador in Paramaribo, Colin somebody or other. He was the Deputy here and heard us play shortly after you arrived. We're going to be the American celebration of the Suriname revolution. A week playing for the President and everybody else."

Lex went for my breasts, singing on the way, "Concerts in Suriname."

I didn't realize how much I missed that sort of thing.

49

Lex

Suriname

How much did I know about Suriname before the Embassy's Cultural Officer met me and Sally at the Paramaribo airport? Can I take the Fifth Amendment on that question?

Jeff Kincaid was easy to pick out in the crowd. He stood head and shoulders over everyone else at the cinderblock shed that served arrivals, departures, and people of all ages who came to gawk at the planes. He got us waved through customs and gave us a bit of background information on the way to the hotel.

"You'll be staying at the *Onafhankelijksplein.* Untie your tongue and that translates to Independence Square. Paramaribo was a thriving Dutch trading center until the nineteenth century but what you have left now is a polyglot mess dominated by an illiterate army. When the Dutch granted independence in 1975 a third of the population bailed out for Holland. "

President Henk Chin-A-Sen is of Chinese descent. Desi Bouterse, the Sergeant Major, coup leader and power behind the throne, has African ancestors. Then there are a handful of Dutch colonials who stayed, and the descendants of the Chinese, Indonesians and Hindustani Indians who were imported as contract labor when the slaves were freed."

"Stan Goldman told us the Dutch gave the English New York in exchange for Suriname," said Sally.

"That they did. Back in the 1660s New York was the pits, while Dutch and English planters in Suriname were making their fortune in peanuts. African slaves did the work, but many escaped to the bush and formed their own tribes. They're called Bosnegers or Maroons, and you'll be performing for them too."

After a boiled chicken lunch Jeff drove us to the site of our first performance. He said it was a big Tinker Toy structure buttressed with bamboo scaffolding. "A couple of weeks ago this was an open field. Now it's Bouterse's bleachers so a couple thousand people can celebrate the first anniversary of his coup. It's the biggest stadium in the country."

All kinds of people filed in, making their way up seven or eight rows of wood planks. If there were ushers, or any other signs of organization, I didn't see it. A dance troupe was warming up behind the performance platform.

"Where are we on the program?" Sally asked.

Jeff smiled. "What program? This is Suriname."

"How will we know when to play?"

"Let me go ask for a little notice so you can tune up, but don't worry about the program. All you have to do is create good will. The big questions are whether the development assistance we give them will be enough to fend off the Cubans, or is it all just a bribe that ends up in Swiss bank accounts?"

In the minutes before we went on, Sally told me to play the encores first. "Get the showpieces up front, and if there's a lot of applause repeat them. I'll tell you what to play and when we stop playing."

For the first minute or two the audience was listening as if they had been told to, but soon the chatter was louder than any noise we could produce, even with the brassy amps turned up full blast. We were right in the middle of a duo that Paganini composed for his lover when all hell broke loose.

"Don't stop," yelled Sally.

We played on as screams drowned us out. The flimsy scaffolding supporting a nearby section of stands gave way and the bleachers started to collapse. Native skirts flared and legs flailed as people tumbled all over each other in a scramble to get out. I gasped. We stopped.

Jeff Kincaid jumped out of his seat in the front row of VIP folding chairs and charged towards the stands. President Chin-A-Sen stood up and waved his hands wildly like some of the crazier conductors do, shouting at his security detail to go to the rescue.

The soldiers struggled mightily to prop up the scaffolding. The president pointed straight at us. "Play on." People got out of the collapsing section as soldiers buttressed the boards with their bodies. Everybody else clapped as if nothing had happened.

It was over before we finished "Carnival of Venice." The President came up and thanked us. Ambassador Colin Moodie told us nobody was seriously hurt. "They enjoyed your performance."

Chinese acrobats took the stage and checked their footing.

After the Chinese came the Russians. Then the Cuban troupe danced onto center stage; clarinet, sax, trumpet, guitar, keyboard and bass. They started out with African Flower and went on to showcase every Latin rhythm I had ever heard of.

The keyboard and bass players sang and hammed it up with the audience all the way. We flutists can't do any of that. We have to keep our lips to the pipe. There's something about the human voice that is more compelling than any other instrument. Advantage Cuba.

Next morning, Jeff Kincaid joined us for breakfast at the hotel. I asked if Suriname was trying to send some kind of diplomatic message by lodging us together with the Cubans.

"I doubt it," said Jeff. "International relations aren't a big part of their culture, not when the country is run by a ragtag army of gunmen who never learned how to read. Take a look at this anniversary souvenir and you'll see what I mean."

Jeff unrolled a poster featuring an upright M-16 with a rose sticking out of the barrel. "This is what you're celebrating as the representatives of the United States."

Sally turned to me. "Maybe we'd get more concerts if we had a poster with a rose sticking out of the end of your flute."

"I can get the Embassy photographer working on that." Jeff smiled. "Should I send a proposal back to the State Department and see if they approve it?"

There was a burst of laughter at the other end of the dining area. The Cuban troupe waved in unison, signaling us to come over and join them. "Can't do it," said Jeff. "There's been no contact allowed ever since the Bay of Pigs, but let's wave back."

One of the Cubans came over and introduced himself as Alvaro Gutierrez.

"Some other time. We have to leave for an appointment now," said Jeff. He stood up to go and we followed suit.

In the Embassy Jeff sat us down in a shabby office that didn't befit a diplomatic mission of the most powerful country on earth. "Now that you've had a taste of how things are done here…" The lights went out. "Sorry for the interruption. It happens all the time."

The generator started up and Jeff continued. "Back to our ever evolving program. The President is a lot more pro-American than the sergeant and his goons. He asked if you could play all around the country, which is why we invited you for a week. You'll be the true face of America. Most people outside Paramaribo haven't been anywhere near an American before."

Jeff looked worried. "It's best that I tell you now. There aren't any concert halls. There aren't even any towns of consequence. You'll be playing in the bush, out in the open."

"Can you find us some batteries?" Sally asked. "I'll need to turn my little amplifier up full blast so Lex can blow his head off."

"I hope you can be flexible. We have to keep the Cubans from getting a foothold here. That means playing for Bouterse's bush boys as well as the President at his white house."

Sally laughed. "Get that. We can put 'command performances for presidents and sergeants' on our promo materials."

"Just so you know, everybody in the whole country is invited to the President's garden party to celebrate. That's about 375,000 people, but this is a place where everybody knows who is welcome to come and who isn't. You make the cut if you own a pair of shoes, decent trousers and a shirt with all the buttons."

50

Sally

Maroons and Cubans

Jeff had briefed Lex and me on playing for the Maroons. "The Dutch call them Bosnegers. Like I mentioned, they're the descendants of slaves who escaped from the plantations and settled in the jungle. Their music comes from ancient African traditions."

My duty was to show them what a concert performance looks like. That means wear my purple taffeta dress. Lex said I was nuts. He had already put on slacks before I came out of the bathroom to announce my intentions. "If I can go formal you can too. Wear your tux."

"Are you serious? We're playing in the jungle for bush people. This isn't Europe."

"Do what you want, but I'm dressing for a concert."

Lex muttered something under his breath and took out his tux.

Jeff met us at the hotel and said I look gorgeous. He guided us to a jeep. "Sorry this is not a fancy limo, but we need four wheel drive to get to this village about halfway between Lelydorp and Brokopondo. One of our local employees went ahead to prepare the villagers for their first ever international concert. He'll translate for us."

I hugged my guitar tight all the way. I bet it wouldn't have survived if I let it ride the bumps.

The headman met us, wearing an ill-fitting suit that might have arrived in a CARE package. My stiff corseted concert dress didn't quite match his outfit, but I showed him respect.

He led us to a clearing in the jungle where the villagers were all a-titter as Lex and I arrived in our concert best. The women wore colorful bandannas and drab skirts while most of the men were in shorts and undershirts. A group of men wearing only loincloths beat unusual rhythms on African drums. "We want to give you a traditional welcome," said the headman.

Lex turned to me. "Do you think we might have overdressed for this performance?"

"Not on your life."

I had new batteries in my Pignose, but there was no telling how far the amplified sound carried in the soggy air. After the first piece the translator whispered in my ear and we stopped while the villagers chanted and danced for us. Then the whole village clapped and sang with our music and ogled my dress. The headman waved his arms and the drummers started playing along with us too. Lex transposed his parts up an octave in hopes of being heard.

After a program that got longer with every spontaneous dance and song, we thought our concert would be over. It wasn't. The translator explained that the celebration would go on into the evening. Jeff Kincaid egged us on. "This is very important. We can't just finish up and leave. Didn't I tell you the military strongman who runs the country comes from this village?"

"But we don't have any more music."

"All you have to do is make noise. Play the program again."

It didn't matter what we played. The villagers danced to it. As it got darker we just improvised. Smoke got in our eyes. We took turns with the drummers and the singers and the dancers – with everybody – making up stuff like drunks at a jam session until the headman announced the feast was ready. "Roast boar for our special guests."

I got scared about spilling boar juice all over the only concert dress I brought on the trip. Maybe the headman wasn't thinking about that, but as his cooks hoisted the boar into the air he presented me with a ceremonial skirt and took us back to his hut to change. The villagers roared approval when I came back out.

By the light of a huge fire we feasted with our fingers. Nobody cared what we played or how we played it. "So very important that you celebrate with the villagers," said the translator. "That is all that matters."

Next evening at dinner the Cubans were at a big table close to ours and you could see they were having a very good time. I overheard them complimenting the food before and after they ate it, though the meal was watery corn soup followed by dried-out chicken on rice drowned in gooey gravy that makes me think of dog food.

Alvaro Gutierrez came over to our table as coffee came out and told us he was a diplomat, not a musician. "I take Cuban cultural groups everywhere for goodwill exchanges. Everyone welcomes us except your U.S. government."

I was about to say that Uncle Sam is unfair to punish Cuban musicians that way, but Lex spoke first. "Might that be because you're an intelligence agent?"

Several of the Cubans guffawed. Sometimes I wish Lex would learn to shut up. Alvaro just smiled. "Of course. Isn't that what you do too?"

"Are you joking? I'm a flutist."

"That already makes you a better spy than most. It's good cover for all kinds of nefarious activities – like what your CIA tries to do to us."

It was four dinners of scorched chicken and rice before we accepted Alvaro's invitation to join his table, just to prove that we're friendly musicians and not spies. After introductions all around, Lex asked, "How can you stand the same dried out excuse for a meal night after night?"

All the laughter and smiles we had seen at the table dissolved into looks of bewilderment. I wondered whether Alvaro would come up with something funny to counter Lex's bitching. He had done most of the speaking, but his jaws were frozen tight.

Pablo the trumpeter broke into a huge grin. "Are you kidding? This is more meat than we get in months back home. It's special."

Alvaro's frown deepened. The table went silent, like a grand pause in concert. I looked to see if he was the conductor of this performance. A moment's hesitation, and the musicians went on without him. Heitor the bass player explained. "Everything is rationed so we all get enough to eat, but little meat."

The saxophone player, too thin for his clothes, spoke up. "It would be much better for you and us if you lifted the embargo. It's easy for us to be good friends."

"Yes. Being musicians really helps," said Lex.

Alvaro turned to Lex. "You are absolutely right, Mr. Flutist and secret agent."

"I assure you we are not secret agents. We don't have anything to do with the U.S. Government." Lex started to say more, but Alvaro spoke first.

"I thought you worked for the Department of the Interior. That's police and intelligence work, isn't it?"

Lex looked at me, then at Alvaro. "I never told you where I used to work." He picked up his knife and fork and dug into his chicken with grim determination. That must have convinced the Cubans he really is a spy.

51

Lex

For the President

President Chin-A-Sen sent word to come over for tea and music. Alvaro gave me and Sally the news at breakfast. "I told you I was a spy," he said, sopping up runny egg yolks with his toast. "You two are also pretty good at this game. Perhaps someday we'll know whose music he likes better."

Jeff was mighty upset when he learned that the Cubans knew about this before he did. "They're masters at the kind of influence game we're all here for. The Chinese to counter the Russians, us to stop the Cubans. You know they invaded Angola to install a Marxist-Leninist government there, don't you? Bouterse is in their pocket, and we've got to keep them out."

True to Jeff's prediction, the President greeted us at the door of the Executive Mansion, dressed casually in tan slacks and a short sleeve white shirt. He escorted us into a sitting room and settled us in wicker settees. Ambassador Moodie was already there.

The President anticipated our questions. "We're a very diverse country. My ancestors came over from China to work on the Panama Canal, went to Trinidad, and eventually ended up here. Why these revolutionaries who have the real power picked me to be President I'll never know. I'm just a doctor who wanted independence from the Dutch. Call me Henk, but Chin is my real name.

Ambassador Moodie leaned forward and broke in. "It has to be because the military who staged the coup want some legitimacy. You're the only one acceptable to all the factions. After all, you've cured everyone who's anyone of some tropical affliction or another."

"Odd, isn't it, because I never wanted to be either a doctor or a politician, but my father had my life planned out before I was three. I would rather have been a musician."

Sally smiled that seductive smile she puts on whenever she wants a new acquaintance to fall head over heels for her. "What instrument do you play?" Her eyes were glistening, just as they had been when she asked me that very same question.

"Chopsticks on the piano. A little of this and a little of that," said the President.

"He's far too modest," said the Ambassador. "President Chin is a terrific jazz pianist."

I saw a good-sized pile of music on the lid of the Steinway.

We played for the President for about twenty minutes, keeping it light: "Histoire du Tango," our arrangement of "Bachianas Brasileras #5," and the "Carnival of Venice."

I was about to take out the parts to the Paganini duo we had arranged, but Sally gave me that stiletto stare that said quit while we're ahead or I'll castrate you. I wasn't sure what to do next, so I asked, "Mr. President, we've played for you. Now would you play for us?"

Ambassador Moodie gave me a look like he was going to throw acid in my face.

"Maybe later," said the President. Do come and enjoy the reception tonight."

We arrived at a garden entrance for the Anniversary reception just as four swarthy guards were preventing three men in shorts and flip-flops from entering. One of them pointed to the main entrance and we were ushered right to the food tables, where deviled eggs, celery sticks, carrots, broccoli and dip were in abundant supply. Several Dutch cheeses were diced up and garnished with gherkins and toothpicks. We found sausage slices to accompany this and exchanged pleasantries with the Chinese Ambassador, who proposed that our countries should become very good friends. "We will be if you can overcome obstructionism and let our brothers on Taiwan return to embrace the motherland."

Sally turned to me. "I thought Taiwan is part of China."

"That's right. Your government recognizes that," said the Ambassador, "but you don't act as you promise."

"Can we let music overcome politics? I'll give you a cassette of our music." Sally fished in her bag for one of our tapes that she carries everywhere she goes.

"Your government should only be as gracious as you are. Let us drink to that."

Jeff was telling us it's time to leave when we spotted the Cubans with their instruments migrating toward the sitting room where we had performed in the afternoon. We followed, and found the President playing Duke Ellington on the piano.

"That's half his Cabinet looking on," said Jeff.

The Cubans slinked in one at a time and set up. The President played on. Two of the Cubans tapped lightly on their bongos, accompanying him. Alvaro signaled to his musicians to keep it soft. Then the bass player came in, and the sax. The improvising went on well past midnight. I wanted to join, but I didn't bring my flute.

Next morning, Alvaro asked at breakfast whether we enjoyed the music. I couldn't help but smile, even though both the company and the eggs were too runny for my taste.

"Super cool. I'll have to get an electric guitar to play with you guys," said Sally.

"Ah. Musician, spy, and femme fatale." Alvaro grinned. "We could use you."

"I'd love that, but I'm already being used by the United States. Can you guess which agency?"

Two weeks after our return to Caracas we were called into the Embassy. Ambassador Lucas personally read a cable from Ambassador Moodie, thanking us profusely for helping keep the Cubans out of Suriname. President Chin-A-Sen had convinced Bouterse and his thugs to stick with the United States and not allow them to establish an Embassy.

"Nice work you two. By the way, my guests also love music." Ambassador Lucas handed us an invitation to a party at his residence two weeks hence. It was perfectly clear we were expected to play for our dinner.

52

Sally

Miracle Man

I went to the hospital for a checkup to see how my serrated nerves are doing. Dr. Gandolfi always says the same thing, "You're healing beautifully." Then he gives me such a big smile you would think he's a dentist peddling orthodontics.

He could hardly contain his enthusiasm. "Your recovery is little short of a miracle. I've been asked to write about it for 'Annals of Neurosurgery.' The technique I use is quite new."

I winced at the thought that I have no right to have my fingers back. The heavens must have been aligned perfectly or those nerves wouldn't have been micro-stitched together. Dr. Gandolfi told me he came back from his specialized training only ten days before the accident. I was his first and most successful severed nerve patient.

"Your comments would be very helpful when I write about this. It would not have to be an office visit."

Dr. Gandolfi extended his hand and led me into his examining room. He took my forearm and turned it over so he could see the scars on my fingers. Then he kissed them.

I almost jumped.

"Precious hand," he said.

"Is that your idea of gallantry?"

"You're unbelievable."

"And you're pretty impulsive, aren't you doctor?" Images of Omar Sharif danced before my eyes. "Is this part of the cure?" I felt the warmth of Zhivago's breath, closer to my face than necessary to examine my hand. Gandolfi is the sexiest man alive.

"If it helps, of course." He looked at me as if I was the one misbehaving. "Don't you ever go to the movies? Well bred gentleman kiss the hand of royalty when given an audience."

"I'm not Marie Antoinette," the only royal name I could think of.

"And I'm certainly not your executioner."

"What are you then?"

Dr. Gandolfi turned away and looked out the window for such a long time that I really wanted to say something more. What would happen with Lex? Our only commitment is the music. I'm not about to say I do to domestic slavery.

Why not a spontaneous affair here and there? It teaches us how to make everyday life better. Wasn't that what Lex told me back in Washington?

"Who are you?" I whispered.

Dr. Gandolfi turned and faced me, his smile gone. "I am Enrique Diego de Gandolfi y Ruperez, born into a good family, trained in microsurgery, a physician who spent years perfecting the art of stitching together severed nerves like yours. I do not spend my life building a reputation to destroy it in moment."

I wanted to tell him I don't need any lectures about his genealogy and what he is building. We're consenting adults.

"Unfortunately you are in my office. This visit is strictly professional."

"Are you recording this for posterity or for protection?"

"Do I need to? Nobody would believe you."

"Why did you say I was unbelievable just now?"

"Don't be silly. It's your hand that's unbelievable…the way you can play after what happened to you."

"It's still waves of pain whenever I press the strings. I want to scream at those fingers." I turned away and spotted the picture on his desk; a stunningly beautiful woman with long jet black hair, a beguiling smile, two pretty young girls on her lap, and the doctor standing behind them.

"I could not believe how beautifully you played so soon after the operation."

"Flattery might get you somewhere, but you said this visit is strictly professional. When will the pain stop?"

"It's getting better, yes?"

"Your words are hypnotic, but the pain doesn't go away."

Dr. Gandolfi turned away and looked out the window again. He mumbled something, seemingly to himself, and then to me. "Maybe it is time I let you in on a secret. Nobody I talked to in the medical profession believed that you would ever be able to perform at a professional level again."

I slumped into his swivel chair, hating and loving him for not telling me this before now. "You bastard, playing games with me all along," and I was so glad he did that tears rolled down my cheeks.

Dr. Gandolfi sat down in the patient's chair. "All right. The pain might never go away. Some patients feel pain in a phantom limb long after it has been amputated. All I can say is suppress it, talk to it, curse it, and maybe it will go away."

"You think all my cursing makes it go away faster?"

"Perhaps. Do you feel much pain when you perform?"

I hadn't thought about that at all. "A good deal less."

"Mind over matter. That seems to be the key."

"So I should always perform."

"That would be very nice."

Such a smile had to be an invitation. I was tempted to take him up on it right then and there. Instead I said, "I'll be happy to help you with your article."

53

Sally

Ambassador Lucas' Party

Playing for our dinner can be a ticket to enter into the lives of the rich and famous. If you give a great performance or your name is Yo-yo Ma, the matrons fawn all over you. That's good news. Without the patronage of people with more money than they can ever spend, classical music would become a relic of museums.

Before Ambassador Lucas' secretary called to remind me about the party, Lex had suggested that maybe we shouldn't bring our instruments. "There's nothing about music on the invitation. He's a politician."

"You think you've been invited because you're a politician? How long would you like your career to last?" Sometimes I wonder if Lex packed his brains in his instrument case.

The Ambassador could help us, so I wanted to know everything about him. He was flamboyant, not the usual stodgy diplomat type. Embassy people had nicknamed him Wild Willy. The beautiful woman who accompanies him is a recent arrival, but she is not his wife. That's good for us.

I called Stan Goldman, even though I can barely stand him. "Tell me the Ambassador's tastes in music." If Stan could forget our little incident so could I.

"Keep it light. The boss man has been in a foul mood lately. First the President lied to him and he looked like a fool in Washington. Then a dozen bigwigs confirmed they would attend his last dinner party, but Wild Willy ended up eating alone with his deputy. Word leaked out that our fiery leader spent the evening reaming him out for inability to come up with an invitation list of people who would actually show up."

"Are you making this up?"

"Nope. These people have no concept of past or future, and that's what an invitation is. The only thing that counts is what struck them in the last few seconds."

I can't say I didn't feel a twinge of envy, to be able to live that way.

"Good manners in this country require you to say *'Si'* to everything," said Stan, "so the only way to live with that is to say yes and then do what you please."

From the gossip I heard, it's that "Yes" culture that is at the root of Ambassadorial apoplexy and all the cringing at the Embassy.

Ambassador Lucas greeted me at the door with a huge hug and kisses on both cheeks. He led us inside and introduced us to a gentleman standing alone. "Meet John Updike."

I had read about "Rabbit is Rich." Lex was stunned by his presence. The Ambassador scurried off to greet other guests. Mr. Updike seemed to have difficulty getting out a "pleased to meet you." Thank goodness the awkward silence that followed was broken by a waiter with drinks. He took orange juice and I went for the champagne.

At the height of the cocktail chatter Ambassador Lucas shouted for attention and called upon us to play. Thoughtful of him to set up folding chairs in a half-circle so the guests would sit and listen. I was delighted to see Santiago da Silva taking a seat in front. He blew a kiss.

I played solo first. Lex is good about that, giving me the stage before I have to accompany his fireworks. Mr. Updike listened with such rapt attention that it seemed as if he was wrapping his soul around my guitar strings. I must have been in a trance too. My solos are so much a part of me that my eyes were on him all the time.

Conversation at dinner turned to our adventures in Suriname. The way Ambassador Lucas gushes, you'd think we kept Cuba out all by ourselves. Lex said the real hero was me.

"Sally had the courage to wear the same concert dress in the bush that she has on now."

"You obviously understand what a good idea it is to look sexy for everyone," said Ambassador Lucas. "The critics don't say it, but it's an integral part of the performance."

His lady friend laughed and the guests followed her lead.

Ambassador or no, I let him have it. "It doesn't take a musician to understand that you dress properly for a concert whether you're performing in Carnegie hall or out in the jungle." More laughter.

John Updike was seated next to me, but he hadn't said a word. With everyone else laughing, he turned toward me and whispered, "I never know how to dress. Maybe it's because I cringe at the very thought of going out in public."

Santiago da Silva matched Ambassador Lucas' ability to stay at the center of attention. He announced, "You two make such a beautiful team. Why don't you get married?"

I blushed. Other guests went off on their own conversational way as I answered, "We've both been divorced, and that's not legal here, so we wouldn't be allowed to marry."

"I can take care of that."

I desperately wanted to change the subject. "Your sons are making tremendous progress. Pretty soon we can give concerts together like Pepe Romero and his brothers."

"*Estupendo.* We can do it at the ranch and plan a concert at the Casa Bolivar too." Santiago turned to talk politics with the other guests. I forgot the marriage talk as fast as I could.

As the Venezuelan guests left, Ambassador Lucas told us to stay on for a drink with Mr. Updike. He asked for orange juice again. The Ambassador and I had scotch on the rocks. His consort apologized for the joke about being sexy for performances, "But beautiful music is so much like love, isn't it?"

We chatted a bit about that, and Mr. Updike said he didn't quite know what to say in social situations. "I'm really quite a hermit. You lead a life. I just write about lives."

I stared in disbelief. He added, "Fame is such a distraction."

How I want that fame, but my reward has been more struggle to make music and worry before every concert. Lex believes he has fame already. That's the difference between us.

54

Vera

In the Mail

I received the strangest postcard the other day. The picture was labeled Maroon Village, but it was just two rickety shacks with corrugated tin roofs, clothes hanging on a line, a dirt clearing with a couple of log benches, and a lot of lush foliage that I couldn't identify.

The message on the back was all but indecipherable. I guessed that it came from Sally, even though she didn't sign her name. Finally I figured out her childish scrawl; "The latest design in concert stages. Played in the bush. Awesome. Your news?? Love."

I couldn't ascertain where the card came from. The postmark blended in with the most unusual stamp I ever saw, a rose sticking out of the barrel of a gun. It took a good deal of squinting and some research in the place names section of my dictionary before I figured out that the card was sent from Paramaribo instead of Paraguay. It wasn't until I read about Suriname's former colonial status that I located Dutch Guyana and Paramaribo in my outdated atlas.

Of course I knew that Sally had gone to Caracas. It was my idea that she get in touch with Stan Goldman to ask about opportunities there. She was pretty desperate after the teaching offer at the conservatory fell through. And I confess to feeling relief when she took my advice and went to South America. She's truly a dear friend who helped me get through the initial pain of the breakup, but I wanted my house and my children to myself – and I did not want a witness to my budding relationship with Dr. Cooper living in my home.

The divorce was reasonably smooth, if you can use those words to describe the end of a marriage. My lawyer talked Lex into deeding me the house in return for somewhat reduced child support payments. The day the judge approved the final decree I removed those nudes from the living room walls and called a contractor to redo my kitchen.

Dr. Cooper and I are becoming real partners in his practice and my home is becoming his respite from the one bedroom apartment he moved into after his own divorce. I'm so glad that Jennifer and Aaron like him. He dotes on them. Every time he visits he brings them a gift.

The postcard from Suriname was not the first I had received from Sally. There were several from Europe, and the Barcelona cathedral that looks like it could have been designed by Van Gogh after he was committed to an insane asylum is the one I particularly remember. I get upset with her cards, because there has never been more than a word or two about fantastic concerts and great reviews, and then she asks for my news.

I write letters, not postcards, and it strikes me as very unfair to provide so little information and expect a long letter in return. Besides, the only way I know to reach her is through Mr. Goldman at the Embassy, and the last thing I want is to give him the opportunity to open my mail.

But this card from Suriname sparked a curiosity that I could not put aside. I wrote back asking her what a Maroon Village is and why she was giving concerts there. Since she asked for my news, I also wrote that Dr. Cooper is no longer a mere casual acquaintance, though I am far more cautious about commitment than when I married Lex. I believe that's because Lex was once my knight on a shining white charger, but not long after we married acid began to corrode our relationship. I don't know exactly how and when that process began, but we almost certainly had expectations of each other that were not met and never discussed.

I wrote, "Sally, there was nothing you could have done to prevent Lex and me from divorcing. Believe me, you came into our lives and became my closest friend even as you were Lex's musical passion. Why that didn't translate into something more is something of a mystery, but thank you for being loyal."

I needed to be clearer than that, so I wrote more. "You didn't break up our marriage and we could say that Lex didn't either. It was the music that did it. He never seemed to realize that he could have a good job and everything for his family and the music too. Someday you might tell me if it was hard to put him off, or if you had a fling on that European tour. I still wonder how Lex was able to deny it so effectively, though Dr. Cooper didn't believe him for a moment."

When I think back, it didn't really matter very much to me that Dr. Cooper didn't believe Lex, so I wrote Sally about that too. "Anyway, I didn't need to know what passed between the two of you then and I don't need to know now. What I need you to know is that I don't resent you having such a profound effect on our lives. Once you brought music back into Lex's life your presence made me – and probably Lex too – realize that we were not good for each other. So follow the music wherever it leads with my blessings."

When I finished I wondered why it was that way and why I was writing Sally about all this. After spending almost half a day sharing more of my life with Sally than I had with anybody else, I read what I had written, folded up the letter, and put it in the wastebasket.

I wrote her a short note thanking her for bringing music into my life and helping me get Lex out of it.

55

Lex

Routine

Did life in Caracas become so routine because there were no more concerts in the bush, no Cuban spies, and no more jazz playing presidents?

After Sally and I got back from Suriname it was back to practicing the difficult orchestra parts in the bedroom while Sally did her scales and solos in the living room. She was reluctant to work on a new program, but we did try out a few easy pieces to see if her fingers would cooperate with unfamiliar music. I thought we sounded fine. She wasn't happy with the result.

I had Spanish lessons and orchestra rehearsals, while Sally had her students. Sometimes we partied with the American musicians, but most of the time life was practicing our art.

The Venezuelans didn't have a lot of patience with my halting Spanish, but Sally fit in stupendously well from the very beginning and often ended up interpreting for me whether she wanted to or not. She really mastered the language while studying with Segovia in Spain. I couldn't look up words in my pocket dictionary fast enough.

The orchestra life which seemed so glamorous that I gave up a wife and family for it…sucked. It wasn't that the local musicians were terrible. It was their resentment of the foreign players who occupied the principal chairs. False politeness didn't conceal the hostility.

Velasco told me the union was planning to petition the Ministry of Culture to recognize Venezuela's musical talent and make the National Symphony 100% Venezuelan. He took my hand and whispered his offer in my ear. "The best way for you to stay on is endorse me as co-principal now." He glanced away as I promised to look into that possibility and decided it would be best to do nothing. I don't need a co-principal, least of all Luis.

One lovely evening I discovered that all four tires of the old jalopy I bought had been slashed, right in the orchestra parking lot. The lot was supposed to be guarded. I wondered if this might have been the handiwork of Luis, and mentioned this possibility to Erik Becker, a clinical psychologist and supporter of the arts who we had met several times at Stan Goldman's. He was quite certain, "These people can't stand to see others happy. If you have more than they do, they will try to change that equation. That's why your tires were slashed in your protected parking lot, almost certainly by somebody who knows you."

The climate is wonderful in Caracas, sunny and rarely too hot, but other than that there is not too much to attract me and Sally. We don't have cathedrals and cafes like those in Europe, and there's not enough history to fill the kind of museums we like to visit. We didn't become eager tourists even though we had the car and gasoline was much cheaper than the bottled water which brought so much grief.

Sally's slashed fingers, my slashed tires, and weird who are we episodes dominated dreams that took me by surprise in the middle of the night, but I rarely remembered any of the details in the morning.

I must have been dreaming when Santiago da Silva called. It was a good dream, because we always enjoyed ourselves when he invited us over. He made us feel like close friends, real people for being us, not just entertainment for the evening. That was a shock at first, when one of the most powerful men in the country had us over for a barbecue and horse ride at his ranch. Instead of being lonely in a strange and powerful crowd, we discovered this was just us and him and his wife and the three boys. I never even imagined that happening in Washington.

Santiago spoke in a rush. "Everything is taken care of. You and Sally get to the *Palacio de Justicia* at 10 tomorrow. My driver will pick you up. Bring 300 Bolivars to take care of the clerk. Don't forget. That's necessary."

"Can you say that for me slowly please?"

Santiago switched to English. "Tomorrow my driver will take you to the Court and we will get you and Sally married."

I stammered, "Please hold a second."

I cupped my hand over the receiver and shouted at Sally in the kitchen. "Santiago wants to marry us tomorrow. What shall I tell him? It sounds like he won't take no for an answer."

"That's Santiago? I dunno. Do what he wants."

We didn't have time to think about it. Sally rushed off to the bank to get money. I had to work on Stravinsky's "Rites of Spring" and Saint-Saens "Carnival of the Animals." The third solo I went over all day might have been called, "I can't believe this is happening."

Sally was out so long that I took to thinking she had decided to disappear rather than go through with it. Santiago could be impetuous. He'd probably explode. I had to get to rehearsal and Sally hadn't returned. By the time I got back she was already asleep.

We didn't talk about it. Had we planned it that way? The day before we were to marry we passed each other like ships in the night. Sally's marriage taboo must have propelled what can only be called a silence between strangers.

56

Sally

Was It For Real?

As we were chauffeured to the Courthouse I pictured our wedding chamber. The judge would sit high behind a polished mahogany dais and peer out over the scales of justice. Flags would confirm his unassailable authority. Attendants with court papers would be waiting for a signal to approach. The sergeant-at-arms would stand jut-jawed at attention.

Not so the chambers of Maria Antonia Vasquez del Prado. Instead of wood-paneled walls there was bare plaster. The platform to insure that the judge sits above the court was concrete. The podium looked like it was patched together with plywood.

The clerk led us into the bare room to a leatherette sofa tilting unevenly forward from the rear wall. Its left front leg was bent inward. He motioned us to sit down and walked out without a word. I guess he was satisfied with the 300 Bolivars I gave him. As our weight came down on the sofa the damaged leg cracked and separated from the frame. I wondered if this would cost us more than the $70 that went to the clerk to make sure our wedding ceremony would go smoothly.

Santiago had assured us everything was arranged. I thought he'd come in person, but he left a florid note with the driver saying that *desgraciadamente* the *Leal Senado* was in special session and he had to conduct the proceedings. It must be that someone in such a high position can't appear before a local judge performing a prohibited marriage for foreign divorcees.

I smiled at Lex. Even though I promised I would never marry him, it seemed OK now that it was done for us. His hand was clamped over his mouth and he looked like a Greek philosopher in deep thought. He leaned over and whispered in my ear, "Look over there. This isn't going to be a private ceremony."

The couple standing in front of the dais was as rigid as mannequins in a department store. The bride to be was in a chic black pants suit, too shiny for my taste. The groom had on one of those elegant Latino embroidered shirt jackets that make a mockery of neckties and tuxedos.

"You'd think they would do these weddings one at a time," said Lex.

"Whisper. They don't need us to make them any more nervous than they already are."

"What's keeping the judge?"

"Don't know," I mumbled.

"Are you sure we should go through with this?" Lex asked.

"It's a little late for that now. I never gave it a thought when Santiago said he could get us married. Everybody knows *divorciados* can't marry in this holier than holy country."

"That's OK. We're not Catholic."

"Bad joke for atheists, lover. I wonder if Santiago paid off somebody a lot more than we got hit for by that clerk. Maybe he gifted a stud bull from his ranch."

"That would make it a pretty expensive ceremony."

"Shush up. Look." The sergeant at arms opened a side door and a woman about forty wearing a brilliant purple mini-skirt strutted in and settled in the high chair behind the dais. "Stand up. Quick"

The sergeant-at-arms ordered us to sit down.

I had to sneeze and turned away to cover up.

"Did you see that?" Lex put his lips to my ear. "That bald-headed guy in the pink shirt who just came in with the papers. I swear he bent over behind the judge and kissed her on the back of the neck."

"You've gotta be joking." But I sneezed just then and couldn't be sure.

A tall thin man in a pitch-black suit and tie came out and arranged himself in the far corner of the room. "Oyez, oyez. This court will come to order."

The couple standing before the judge trembled so that their clothing rippled. Lex leaned back. The sofa creaked.

I wanted to see what this ceremony was going to be like. What's happening?

"How dare you come into my court dressed like this," screamed the judge. "This is not a nightclub. Women do not wear pants in my courtroom. Who *are* you to think I would marry two people in pants?"

I tapped Lex on the shoulder and whispered, "Do you understand what she's saying?"

"It sounds like we're very lucky you put on a dress this morning."

The judge pointed a finger at the couple and shouted, "Get out, and don't come back to my courtroom until you are properly dressed to get married."

The bride-to-be sobbed out of control. The groom held her up as they slinked away and scuttled out the door. I felt very sorry for them. Was that fat balding clerk in the dirty pink shirt really kissing the judge-in-a-miniskirt on the back of the neck while I was sneezing?

Lex's breath was in my ear. "Do you think they might not have paid the necessary expenses in advance?"

The judge pointed a finger at us. "Come on up here." She scowled so hard I could see creases forming in her makeup.

"Good morning your honor," I stammered.

"Ev-i-dent-ly you want to get married. What about your silent partner with no manners?"

I jabbed Lex in the ribs.

"Good morning, your honor."

"What kind of gibberish is that?"

Lex said it in English. Maybe he wants us to get us kicked out of here too.

"What did he say?" The judge's voice was a gravelly growl.

"I'm sorry your honoress. I must be nervous."

"You sure speak lousy Spanish." The judge turned towards me. "Is he always rude?"

"Yes, your honor."

"Good morning, your honor. I apologize for not addressing you correctly, your honor."

"You better learn to address your future wife correctly or you'll wish you never came here." The judge smiled, lips curled up tight.

A tapping sound came from the corner of the room. The judge looked over at the stiff-necked man in the black suit and the tapping stopped. "Go on with the ceremony, before this man panics and runs," she said.

The man marched up to the dais and did a quarter turn to face us. He began reading in the properly pompous drone that you hear at dedications and funerals you didn't want to attend. Every other sentence – read in Spanish, of course – sounded like "*derechos de cogno.*"

Alfonso Oliviera, our photographer and witness, was turning red in the face, then deep purple. "*Derechos de cogno. Derechos de cogno.*" The judge was chuckling. Her sour sneer changed into a sarcastic smile.

Lex looked over at me in disbelief. The stiff-necked funeral director…I mean marriage man…kept reading in the same monotone about some other aspect of *derechos de cogno* that didn't quite make sense to me. Out of the corner of my eye I saw Oliviera clench his fist and grab it with his left hand. The judge laughed, bringing the ceremony to silence in her wake.

Derechos de cogno is not the same as *derechos de conjuge.* It just sounds that way. When spoken fast it's close enough to fool anybody whose Spanish isn't pretty good.

I started giggling. Couldn't help it. Lex covered his mouth. So, "rights of cunt" is what this is all about. It's supposed to be conjugal rights, but even Lex knew what was being given.

You can't miss the word in everyday conversation. The Venezuelans say "*cogno coracho* more often than we say damn or nuts, and that's literally cunt and balls in Spanish.

Everybody was smiling now except Oliviera. His face was so red he looked like he was about to catch fire. I was beginning to suspect that Santiago arranged for some stand-in to perform the ceremony because no law-abiding judge would do it.

"I now pronounce you wife with man. You can pick up your wedding certificate at the Clerk's office next Tuesday." She turned to face Lex, mock seriousness written in the lines on her face. "Now go out and enjoy those rights of *cogno.*"

The judge or whatever she was didn't convey any rights to me at all. Neither did the ceremony, if I heard it right. We left the cavernous Palace of Justice laughing. Outside in the bright sunlight, Lex kissed me. "You can have all the rights you want. Just start at either end and work towards the middle. Rights of *cogno* for me and you can have my *coracho* any time."

"Just remember I told you a long time ago that if we married, someday I'll leave you."

"You really mean that, don't you?" Lex half-smiled, half-frowned.

"Come on. Not today."

57

Lex

Married Life

Sally and I were loafing in bed the morning after the wedding. "Santiago really was giving us an order, wasn't he?" I asked.

"It doesn't matter now. Don't even dream of asking him who he got to marry us."

We joked about his phone call and my panicked proposal made with hand clapped over the receiver. There was no bended knee, no passionate kiss, and no engagement ring. We had never planned this. We didn't discuss our hopes and expectations of each other. Talk about children, raising a family, who did what in the house – I guess that just isn't us.

I had spent much more time thinking about Aaron and Jennifer, though I feel guilty about not writing them more often. When I wrote Vera asking if they could come in the summer, she wrote back asking how I propose to take care of the children. Now I have a wife to take care of, and I hadn't asked her about that either.

It struck me that Santiago da Silva's impetuous enthusiasm, his power, and his patronage were three pretty strange reasons for getting married. "What do you think it means?" I asked.

"What *it* are you talking about?"

"It marriage."

"Maybe everything, maybe nothing." Sally shrugged her shoulders.

I searched memory for something coherent, and found no story that would explain us. Our silence seemed to last at least as long as it would have taken to brew tea and search the leaves for answers. Without warning we broke into uproarious laughter.

"Can you believe we really got married?" We asked each other in unison.

"Only because you asked me," said Sally.

I doubled over again, unable to stop laughing. "Only because Santiago asked us."

"Thanks a bunch, Romeo. I should have said no way and fuck you too."

A little voice told me I'd better stop laughing.

Sally calmed down, but if she was trying to smile it was wan and tentative.

"Do you love me?" She asked.

"Sure. Why shouldn't I?"

"Plenty of reasons. Probably you love something I'm not. The kind of love you men throw out to snare us is the most screwed up emotion I know. So get it out of your mind that marriage means I'm going to be your baby breeder, cook, housekeeper, and sex slave."

"Hey. I haven't been thinking that way."

"Nothing is going to change. I'm me and you are you and we share a passion for music."

This was not the kind of passion I associated with music.

"How about a honeymoon?" I asked. "Isn't that what normal people do when they're in love and get married?"

"Who says we're normal?"

Stan Goldman shouted in the phone as I was trying to wake up. "Hey Paganini. Do you sleep all day?"

"I'm a flutist. It's Rampal."

"OK flute player. I have news for you, but you'll have to come to the Embassy to get it."

You might think Stan Goldman is like those people I had to deal with in the Department of the Interior, but that's not true. He doesn't call me into the Embassy to be highfalutin about his exalted position as a Foreign Service Officer. He does it because other people decide that everything must be classified so none of it can be discussed over the phone.

Stan prides himself on being the loosest goose in the Embassy, and it looks like the truth. His colleagues dress like old-style organization men. He wears a long sleeve shirt, but it's blue instead of white, and the sleeves are rolled up to his elbows. His tie is so loose that it looks like the knot is hanging halfway down to his belly. He must not be afraid to be seen that way, because somebody who was dressed like an advertisement for Brooks Brothers was coming out of his office as I walked in.

"Sit down and get this." Stan pointed at a leather chair with his suit jacket slopped over it. "The big secret is that every Embassy in Latin America wants to sponsor you for goodwill tours. They must have read Jeff Kincaid's reports about you playing in a loincloth."

"You're pulling my leg."

"I most definitely am not. Every one of us is starved for programs. You know what it feels like to be collecting a salary and getting *nada*, nothing to work with?"

"Are you talking about my old job at Interior, or yours?"

"Mine. Can you believe that most of these Embassies haven't been able to wring a single musical group out of the culture programmers for nearly two years? They send stuff to Mexico, Brazil and Argentina. Nothing for anybody else. Washington leaves us to twiddle our thumbs and wonder why we're here."

"It's that witch Berberger, isn't it? She still won't give us a rating as a duo, even though the excuse that I'm a government employee is dead and gone."

"She can rot," said Stan. "These Embassies want you. Some of them went to Washington with specific requests to fund you. They got shat on, which might explain why the messages are classified. Pretty much like every suggestion from the field gets a no these days."

"Sounds like some people here who get their jollies by shafting somebody else."

Stan interrupted. "Now you're beginning to understand why I'm going to be your very unofficial manager. We'll show Washington. The posts say they'll cooperate to put a tour together if you can be flexible on fees. They don't know how much money they can raise from local co-sponsors, but they can put both of you on travel orders with full per diem and make all the arrangements. What do you think?"

"Just don't tell any of your friends in South America that I really would play in a loincloth if that's what it takes to make it work."

58

Sally

Honeymoon Tour

We don't need a honeymoon or any other contrived charade that goes with marriage. If Lex wants our partnership to survive he better not treat me like he owns me. The only way we're gonna get along is behave like we're not married at all.

Lex offered to get me a wedding ring. I told him, "Hell no." He said he'd like to wear one. "That's stupid but do what you want, just so it doesn't throw your fingers off when you play."

Lex blinked. I looked him straight in the eye, "If you want a honeymoon, a concert tour around South America sounds as good as anything. We'll have music all around the continent."

"Now do you know why I like Stan Goldman?"

I couldn't hide my excitement. "Just think, we won't have to ask each other 'what am I supposed to do next?' like some people I know did on their honeymoon."

"We ought to call Stan and invite him to dinner," said Lex.

Stan insisted we get together in his palace. "No way," I said. "The Cultural Attaché from the Embassy needs to know how the other half lives." He relented.

I kissed him on both cheeks at the door, and sat him down to the best steak I could find in the bodega. "Stan, it's so nice to know that there are still a few brave souls who will tell the powers that be where to get off." I showered so much appreciation on him that I had to hope he wouldn't think I was offering myself up.

"Here's to the duo." Stan raised his tumbler of champagne to toast us. "I guess you figured out that everybody got sick of waiting for Bernice Berberger to throw them program crumbs with her so-called rated artists."

Stan relished telling the details of his coup as much as he enjoyed the steak. "That lady actually put out a cable saying that you had been rated 'excellent' as a soloist, Sally, but the duo had not been rated so there would be no funding for either of you."

"It looks like what we did in Suriname didn't matter a whit to her," said Lex.

"Or that everybody wanted to program you after what Jeff Kincaid wrote."

"Or that I'm rated and it's my duo." I whispered "fugging barbarian" under my breath.

"I heard that." Stan smiled. "Berberger is going to lose this battle. All the Embassies are willing to use their own funding. What they save by turning down the propaganda lectures that she wants them to pay for out of their budget will help pay for you. Don't tell anybody though. Innovative people in this outfit get skewered."

I filled our juice glasses with champagne again and we toasted some more. With Stan coordinating the schedule, we had six weeks of concerts. Bernice Berberger must be spitting venom.

59

Lex

Rock Stars

I wanted to ask what was in store for Sally and me after our concert at *Universidad Nacional de Paraguay*, but the Embassy Cultural Attaché who was supposed to have met us in the lobby of the Asuncion Esplendor was nowhere in sight.

Paul Aspinwall finally arrived twenty minutes late, looking almost too perplexed to speak. He apologized for the delay while still catching his breath. "Professor Strosser just called and said he couldn't arrange a rehearsal in the hall prior to the concert. I have an Embassy briefing for you instead and the Professor will meet us there afterwards to discuss the program."

"We sent the program weeks ago," said Sally. Didn't you get it?"

"We did, but the professor called just before I came for you and said he must talk to us. Something very important has come up."

Klaus Strosser arrived at the Embassy accompanied by two students who must have been brought along to help in case he stumbled. Bald and haggard-looking, he seemed far too old to still be teaching. I wondered if he was a Hitler Youth Corps graduate who got to Paraguay after the war, but his effusive welcome sounded too cultured to have come from somebody who committed war crimes, even though that combination of erudition and sadism was common enough in the Nazi era.

I put that out of mind as the professor apologized profusely for the inconvenience and described the hall. "It is Spanish colonial and seats 780, a very charming venue for recitals. But we have a difficulty. So many students want to attend your performance that the university issued additional tickets good for the second half only. These student representatives are here with me to ask a favor of you."

The intense young man on the Professor's left explained, "There will be a big change at intermission so both groups can hear you. Can you make each half longer so that all the ticket holders will get the full concert?"

Sally's lips moved ever so slightly, but enough to indicate that I should tell him we stick to the program.

Professor Strosser all but begged us, "We get so few concerts here. Back in Germany we had more musicians come to my small town in two weeks than we get in a year in Asuncion. The student union insisted on making tickets available."

Sally nodded halfway between yes and no. Professor Strosser was looking at me as if terrified that both pre and post intermission students would riot if they didn't get the whole concert – and he would hang for it.

From the briefing we got at the Embassy there was reason to worry. A junior political officer spoke of campus unrest and told us that students were openly challenging the dictatorship with demonstrations calling for free elections. The President's cabal had warned that the university would be shut down if students couldn't be made to toe the Colorado party line.

"Of course. We'll be happy to play the program twice." I would be nice to old enemies even though two uncles were killed in the war.

As our car approached the main entrance to the campus we were stopped at a checkpoint and ordered to turn back. The driver's explanation that we were the concert performers prompted a scowl. "So you're the cause of the trouble tonight. Go around back and maybe the guards will let you in there. I opened the window and craned my neck to see the main gate cordoned off by a phalanx of police, but there was no sign of trouble and no gathering of people.

"They're not taking any chances that the students will take advantage of the concert to march into town," said Paul Aspinwall. "Maybe the opportunity to assemble en masse explains why the student union made such a fuss about tickets."

The driver circled around and drove along a tree lined road to a gated access at the far end of the campus. We managed to get into the back entrance of the hall without being bothered by the people milling around toward the front waiting to be let in. In the dressing room, Sally asked me, "How are we going to go about this?"

"Just play the program, take a rest while they change audiences, and play it again. What else can we do?"

An hour into the concert, Professor Strosser rushed backstage as I took a break between numbers to get a sip of water. He was accompanied by a police officer. "The students outside are clamoring to get in. Please conclude."

Sally announced that we would end it with South America's most beloved composer. Villa Lobos' *Bachianas Brasileras #5* is sublime longing from beginning to end. We could feel the emotion as we performed. The foot stomping began while I was holding on to the final soaring A and Sally's chord was still reverberating in the hall.

"The professor said a thousand students are waiting outside," Sally whispered as we came back onstage to acknowledge the applause. "What shall we do to get these people to leave?"

"We can't let them go on like this without giving them an encore. They'll stampede."

We did, and another and another, and the audience wouldn't stop screaming for more.

"That ought to be enough," Sally said after three.

The truth was that I would play all night if people were willing to scream for it.

We played one more, and then did the entire concert again for the students who had waited outside. The police who came in to make sure the event didn't turn into a demonstration against the dictatorship stood by silently in the aisles by the exits.

When we finally crawled into bed Sally fell asleep before I could kiss her goodnight. But the excitement took command of my central nervous system and sleep was out of the question for me. I relived the entire evening. It must have been almost dawn before I finally dozed off. When Sally woke me up it was after nine.

We were lolling in bed, me still half asleep. "You really milked the audience," she said.

"But not the performer."

She turned and stuck her palm in my face. "Male chauvinist pig."

"But if farmers enjoy milking cows, why not…?

I didn't see it coming.

"Get some tissue and take care of your bloody nose." Sally smiled triumphant.

60

Sally

Encore

Lex lets applause go to his head. I can't believe he had the gall to play four encores when Professer Strosser begged us to finish up because of the mob outside waiting to get in. "You think you're a rock star," I told him.

"Why not?" Lex retorted. "A lot of rockers can hardly play their instruments and the audiences go wild over them. The way we played maybe we ought to be treated like rock stars."

"Get real."

Everybody but Lex knows you want to leave people wanting more rather than itching to go home. Two encores is the norm, but he drags me back onstage to play again. He can go out alone next time if he wants to conduct the audience in a Hallelujah chorus.

Paul Aspinwall told us that the Embassy had never programmed anything in Concepcion before, so he had no idea what to expect for our next concert. "It's a pretty sleepy town, but it was a crucial battleground in the 1947 civil war. Their version of a peace dividend is the embroidery industry."

We arrived to stifling heat and empty streets. Our concert was held in a hothouse of wilted people who must have been rounded up from old age homes to paper the hall. This wizened audience sat dead silent through the performance except for an occasional loud snore. At the end of an evening where nothing we could do generated a response, the applause was barely audible. What little there was came from the city government organizers who sat in the front row.

This should have been a good reality check for Lex, but he wanted to play an encore anyway, even though the feeble clapping had already stopped.

"Absolutely not." I saw people hobbling toward the exits.

"It doesn't cost us to be generous," pleaded Lex.

I grabbed his arm to keep him from going onstage again. "Are you nuts?"

"Somebody told them to be quiet during the concert and they didn't know what to do."

"Sure. Why don't you just come down to earth and stop behaving like hot shit."

After we got the cold shoulder in Concepcion, I wondered whether Lex would ever show a little humility. We flew over the Andes to Santiago.

In Chile the Embassy had us performing every day. Besides the concert in the just dedicated Claudio Arrau salon of the Teatro Municipal, there was a radio program to record and a performance at the Ambassador's residence for the Foreign Minister and other muckety-mucks. Then we were sent out to give concerts around the country.

With all the performances and master classes, Lex had another crazy idea. "Since we're playing so much why rehearse between gigs? Let's just go out and have a good time."

Lex is off his rocker, but counting each performance as the rehearsal for the next was a good idea. Sipping coffee in outdoor cafes in Santiago felt like Europe in summer. Strolling in Temuco was a feast of lush green. We won almost $200 at the casino in Vina del Mar and the beach was glorious. Strangers were friendly everywhere.

It looked like we would be forced to land on a rock pile dotted with date palms when we flew into the northern coastal city of Arica. Father Federico Fuentes, a handsome man who didn't look like a priest, welcomed us at the airport with assurances that we would never need umbrellas in this part of Chile. "It is always overcast, but it hasn't rained but three or four times in the last ten years."

As we drove inland, the last traces of cloud and greenery disappeared after a few minutes. Shimmering heat rippled across the sand of the Atacama Desert, creating a mirage of lakes in the distance. A thin line of green looked like a windbreak at the edge of a fallow field. Father Fuentes said, "That's lichen growing on the pipeline that brings water from the Andes. It lives off condensation, just like the palm trees live off coastal fog."

He said this is the driest of deserts. "Without the water from the mountains life would be impossible. There is never any rain between here and where you will play tonight. Calama's lifeblood is the river that flows from the foot of the Miño Volcano."

Father Fuentes took us to his mud brick church in the center of town. "I have a room to pray in and play the piano, a room for sleep, and this room for work." He motioned us to wicker chairs and plied us with oranges.

"I was sent here as a young man for a few years, but a replacement from the archdiocese never materialized. It was a form of excommunication, but what a blessed mission it is to live among these people and away from the church."

"That doesn't sound like a missionary at all," said Lex.

"I am, but I taught myself everything Bach composed for keyboard, so I have some idea of God's work and how many years you must have practiced before we were brought together in this place."

"Mastering Bach must be as lonely a pursuit as becoming a priest," I said.

"But his music brings us closer to God," said Father Fuentes. "I'm not lonely at all. Neither are the people in my parish, even though their understanding of our God and our Bach is only a thin veneer overlaying what they really believe."

He went to the corner of the rather large room, opened a simple wood chest, and brought back a burlap sack. "I'll show you one of the reasons these people are not lonely." He put the sack down on the table and lifted the covering to reveal a perfectly preserved mummy. The skin might have been tanned leather, but it was all there.

"Tonight you will play not only for the living. Your audience brings the souls of their ancestors with them and pays homage with music. This mummy is about 800 years old. His kin are found everywhere in this region, preserved bone dry like this specimen."

Mozart should have arranged to die here so we could know his whereabouts," said Lex. "Then we wouldn't be haunted by Emperor Joseph II's funeral rites decree that the sole purpose of burial is the rapid decomposition of the body."

"Won't the mummy decay out in the open like this?" I asked.

"No. There is zero humidity here. Take a look at your orange peels."

We just finished eating the oranges, and the peels had already dried out. I picked one up and it felt like a crisp soda cracker.

"That's why the mummies stay so well preserved. No moisture. That reminds me, what would you like to drink during the concert? You have to drink all the time if you don't want to end up as dried out as the mummy."

A case of mineral water and another of the local version of club soda sustained us. Lex went outside and belched up a storm during intermission. By the end of the concert we had polished off both cases. Afterwards we met some of the descendants of the mummy. They said their ancestors had magical powers in the afterlife. Something told me there were good reasons Father Fuentes didn't want to leave this place. I wasn't ready to leave either.

An Assistant Cultural Attaché met us at the airport when we got back to Santiago. Maria Palacios informed us that in less than 24 hours we would record concertos with the *Sinfonia de Vina del Mar* at *Television Nacional de Chile*. "The Minister of Culture called personally after he heard you play at the Ambassador's residence. Since you have a free day tomorrow…"

"That's wonderful." said Lex. "You're a miracle worker to arrange this."

I thought I would choke. He has no right to speak for me. I haven't worked on a concerto since the accident.

"Are you all right?" Maria asked.

No. I am not all right. I didn't need a mirror to tell that the blood had gone out of my face. I can *not* record a concerto on one day's notice.

I could barely whisper. "I think it's something I ate on the plane. Can I use the W.C.?"

How can Lex put me in a situation like this? Our programs and his milk the audience encores already were more than my miracle stitch fingers could handle.

Maria rushed after me to see if she could help. I all but slammed the bathroom door in her face. There was nothing wrong with what I ate, but I puked it up anyway. Lex knocked on the door. If I could have spit through it I would have. He was waiting for me when I came out. "Tell Maria that you are OK and will be delighted to play." His voice was a low growl.

I whispered, "Fuck you" under my breath. Lex can play two concertos if he wants to make a fool out of himself, but I won't.

Maria took us back to the hotel in an Embassy car. It's a good thing she kept me entertained explaining other events she had arranged for us. Otherwise Lex and I would have been snarling at each other like pit bulls.

When we got up to our room Lex motioned me to sit down. He looked like some godfather about to tell his capo that he was destined to be in a sack of cement dumped in the Hudson River. "How could you possibly be so stupid as to turn down TV performances?"

"You bastard," I shouted. "The real question is how you can be such a fool to play the Bach B Minor Suite on national TV when I've never heard you practice it."

"And how many years have you been practicing the *Concierto de Aranjuez*? Tell me. Ten? Twenty? Probably more but why give away your age?"

I was about to tell him he can make an ass of himself before the whole world if he wants to. I don't play concertos on one day's notice no matter how well I know them. But Lex ranted on before I could get it out. "By the way, what do you practice for, the pure joy of it?"

"Not for the pain, damn you."

Lex's face twisted into knots of anger. "Didn't you tell me you always dreamed about soloing with orchestras?"

Sure. I practiced a lifetime because I want to play, but I worry about screwing up. Lex doesn't worry. Mr. Cockiness plays Paganini and knows his showmanship will wow audiences. All I want is to recover what I had.

Lex was yelling, "Answer my question. You know that concerto by heart. What for if you won't play it when you finally get the opportunity?"

He didn't wait for an answer. "Tomorrow night you will be ready."

I was still foaming at the mouth when Maria Palacios knocked on the door and delivered the solo parts. When she left I cried and cursed until I was spent, but once the orchestra started playing with me as soloist I felt nothing but joy in my fingers for the first time since the accident.

61

Lex

Discovery

Coming into Cuenca, Ecuador, I wondered if this trip was to be my shortcut to the afterlife. How could a 727 dive out of the sky from 25,000 feet and land on a runway that looked hardly long enough for a Piper Cub? As mountain peaks rushed by almost close enough to touch, I asked myself what Aaron and Jennifer and the rest of the world would remember me for.

Afterwards, the pilot told us he was the only one who could land on a Sucre coin and slow the plane enough to turn off on the taxiway. "Every so often someone goes over the cliff at the end of this runway. It's so short that none of the IATA carriers will fly in here."

We had more adventure as we wended our way through concert halls and gracious hosts in Ecuador, Bolivia, and Colombia. I'm not sure how many wind players make a life for themselves at 14,000 feet, but we were grateful to our Bolivian sponsors for giving us a day and a half to contemplate that possibility.

Sally and I both adjusted to the altitude well, though she will tell you that focusing on anything for any length of time was a struggle. I spent much of that respite looking for new places in the music to breathe, because I had to take breaths twice as often to play it. We were told that President Zuazo would be watching our program, and that the TV studio was in El Alto, a thousand feet closer to heaven than La Paz. We gulped thin air on both counts.

In Medellin, I got desperately ill after lunch, just hours before the concert that evening. I was exploding from both ends and who knows what the fever was in the middle. Soledad Casablanca called a doctor who met us at the hall, where I was writhing in agony when I should have been rehearsing. I have no idea what was in that syringe, but in the struggle for life I knew nothing like that elixir. Barely in time. Ten minutes before we were supposed to go on stage, I was still in the bathroom, muttering hope that it would be the last time.

The urge to music is no less than the urge to live. Probably it was a narcotic that stopped the vomiting and paralyzed the peristalsis. I can't tell you whether it was the doctor's adrenalin or my own that propelled me through that concert, but it began and ended in some kind of out of the body experience and felt like it was the best I ever played.

And then the lights went out. The concert was over. We made our way in the dark, and learned later that the rebels had cut the electricity to half the city. It seemed considerate of them to wait until we finished playing.

Our Barranquilla concert was cancelled. M-19 guerillas were creating havoc there on a regular basis. Since one of their complaints was government subservience to the CIA, the Consulate said it was best not risk going ahead with an American-sponsored event.

Our hosts took us to the airport at five in the morning and told us to watch for nails and spikes on the road. Gleason Stone, the Vice Consul who accompanied us, offered cold comfort on that hairy ride. "That's how the M-19 disables cars, robs and kills the passengers, or kidnaps them for ransom. It depends on their mood that day, but don't worry, they're not usually out this early in the morning."

I tried to convince myself they don't harbor any grudges against musicians.

The flight was delayed an hour while the army swept the runway for bombs. We tried to hide our apprehension behind jokes about concluding our grand tour of South America with a spectacular display of fireworks. Thoughts of bombs and splattered flesh intruded. Although flutists develop much larger than average lung capacity, I couldn't hold my breath all the way back to Venezuela.

The day after we returned to Caracas I went to the Embassy to tell Stan Goldman about our trip. The Marine Guard kept me waiting until Patsy Baras, the office secretary, came down to tell me, "Mr. Goldman left at the beginning of the week."

"That's strange. He didn't say anything about taking a trip."

"It was very sudden. They desperately needed a Public Affairs Officer in Taiwan. The job is a plum and he said he got it because he was the only Chinese speaker they could pull out and send on a moment's notice."

"Do they really do that to people?"

"It goes to show how important we are, doesn't it? I'm sure he had no idea this was coming. We certainly didn't, and I'm the one who sorts all the cable traffic for the section. He left you a note."

I read it aloud: "Went to a dinner party at the ersatz Ambassador's in Taipei. Trust you know where that is and won't try to swim out. P.S. You also need to know that you don't call the head of the American Institute in Taiwan 'Ambassador.' That title is only for our man in Beijing."

Stan Goldman was in touch a few weeks later. With his usual acid humor he wondered how long it would be before I got kicked out of the orchestra.

He didn't have to wait very long. Luis Velasco was right all along. José Maria Buenadia called me in after rehearsal to confirm Luis' prediction that my contract would not be renewed after this season. "*Desgraciadamente* we have been commanded to make the National Symphony truly Venezuelan."

We have a few friends here, nearly thirty students between us, and some concerts scheduled around the country, but without the orchestra job our money will run out soon enough.

In many ways the life of a musician is like a broken record. Both are scratchy, running around the turntable over and over. We tour here, we tour there, and we do it again. We practice the same concertos for a lifetime, but few musicians ever get to play them with an orchestra. After we reach an exalted level of proficiency many of us spend more time looking for jobs than we did to learn the art we want to share. I might be out of this orchestra pretty soon, but any musician – even my Juilliard classmates – would count me as being among the lucky ones.

62

Sally

Different Kind of Miracles

I've come to like it in Venezuela. Lex too, when we get concerts, but in between he agonizes about what we will do when the orchestra stops paying and kicks us out of the rent free apartment. Wandering the streets of Caracas looking for work and shelter doesn't appeal to either of us.

We pondered the merits of going home to mooch off Lex's parents while we look for work. They barely know who I am, since we never got booked for a concert in the New York area and they didn't come to Washington to hear us perform. I remember Lex telling me about a huge scene when his parents came home early from a weekend trip and found him playing house with a half-naked French woman, but even if he was persona non grata then, this would hardly be the same thing. I'm his wife.

Which reminds me. It would be a very good idea for Lex to get in touch with his parents and tell them we're married – and better if he doesn't reveal how many months it took him to get around to it. The least he could do is write a letter. So far he hasn't, and his parents reciprocate the courtesy, meaning that we don't know if they're dead or alive.

It's not that much better between Lex and his children. Vera writes occasionally to report how well Hank and Jennifer are doing at school, but she was ticked off after she made arrangements for them to come down and visit and he wrote that he couldn't take them because of our tour. Lex writes them, but tells me he doesn't know what to say. I don't hear from her even though I send her postcards from everywhere we play.

In the midst of big time confusion about our future, Patsy Baras called from the Embassy to say that a letter from Stan Goldman arrived in the diplomatic pouch. Lex went in to get it and showed me the capital letters written all over the first page. "LEX AND SALLY, GET YOUR ASSES OUT HERE." Just like Stan, foul-mouthed, sex starved, crude and hungry, but he helps us time and again. Putting on programs must help his career, since he also wrote that he got promoted on the way out of Caracas.

The letter explained how the Taiwan government had built concert halls and culture centers all over the island. Lex read a word at a time, "The Chairman of the Council for Culture is a Cabinet Minister with a huge budget. He asked for help getting American performers to Taiwan. Do you understand? That sounds like a gold mine."

You never know whether to believe Stan Goldman – not after all that bullshit about sleep-walking when he was really after my body.

Lex told me to believe; "He can set up a tour for us. He says the government's new 'Experimental Orchestra' needs international principals for the woodwinds and brass."

I still wasn't ready to tell Lex that Stan tried to rape me in Caracas. "I bet he does this so he can put his name on it. The American Embassy presents. The United States Information Service presents. It makes him look good. He's got programs and we promote his career just like he promotes ours."

"He told me that himself," said Lex. "You might not like him, but he does what he says he'll do. We're going there, so be nice."

The Pan Am captain announced that we would be the last plane to land at Taiwan's Chiang Kai-shek airport before the approaching typhoon struck full force. "For the information of passengers, the forecast is that this will bring up to twenty inches of rain to Taipei. That's rather more than we get in hurricanes back home in the U.S."

Planes were already being diverted to Hong Kong and Okinawa. We fluttered like a wounded butterfly going in and skipped like a frog on touchdown. By the time we got into the terminal raindrops the size of golf balls were splashing against the windows.

Stan was there to meet us. "You brought good weather."

"It's the way we make our presence known," I said. "You could have told us it was coming."

While we were waiting for our suitcases Stan opened a cardboard tube and pulled out a poster. It was all in Chinese except for the numbers, but the picture was of us. "This is for your debut concert tour here. Caracas sent me the photo. You're beautiful. Hope you don't mind."

Lex gushed, "Mind? It's like manna from heaven."

"Glad you like it. Eat, drink and be merry, because you start tomorrow."

I was going to puke. How could he do that to us? Twelve hours time difference and more than twice that to get here.

Stan put an arm around my waist to hold me up. "You've got almost a month to get over jet lag before you have to play. For now it's get to Taipei before it's under water."

63

Lex

Taipei Routine

How did it happen that Chinese musicians in a developing country get to practice western music in an opulent palace? The Experimental Orchestra rehearses and performs in the National Concert Hall, which looks like a structure transplanted column by column and tile by tile from the Forbidden City of the Emperors in Beijing. The National Theater is a twin, facing across a plaza that somebody like me would mistake for Tiananmen Square, though I know this is smaller. Overlooking both, as if surveying the whole empire, is the Chiang Kai-shek Memorial, erected by the President to honor his father, the President.

Whatever they say about the dictator, his son knew how to honor the arts. Go to a concert of the Experimental Orchestra and it looks like an ensemble of teenagers with a few foreign teachers playing the first chair woodwind and brass parts. What really blows the mind are the audiences for Western classical music. It's mostly teenagers and younger kids who come to concerts, and I can't help but wonder how many Americans would take to traditional Chinese music like these people take to ours.

My second flutist, Renee Chang, told me, "The goal of the experiment is build a world class orchestra quicker than anybody. We want to become a developed country even faster than Japan did."

We foreigners call ourselves the international section. Bob Clark sits next to me as the principal oboist. Andy Thornton and Jack Hoffman are just behind on clarinet and bassoon. We're all assigned eager students who take lessons with us as part of our contract.

Our purpose is as much to train home grown talent to take our places as it is to fill gaps in the orchestra. Andy said he has already been thanked for his services, since a young returnee from Vienna will replace him next season. Unlike the Venezuelans, the Chinese are upfront about their intent, and gracious about replacing the foreigners with locals. Andy was offered a professorship at the National Academy of Music.

Kao Shih-wen, the personnel director, told me about that during our first meeting at his backstage office at the National Concert Hall. "We are so grateful for your contribution to our musical development. Our best students will come from all over Taiwan to learn from you."

It wasn't just polite talk, even though I thought I was being introduced to contestants in a beauty pageant when I met my first students from the National Academy of Music; Rebecca Chou, Sandra Lin, Annie Wang, and A-lien Chang. Besides the demure beauty which led to a dream about Miss China finalists, my nymphet flutists share another common trait. They focus their complete attention on how I play the magic instrument and on everything I say about it. Jack Hoffman told me what to expect. "These kids practice eight hours a day. It won't be long before some of them have better chops than you do."

The girls are quite shy, but they are willing to let me take their fingers and adjust their hand positions on the flute for a more fluid technique. I have taken to doing that whether the adjustment is necessary or not. Then they come so close to see how my embouchure adjusts for two octave jumps that I only need to sway a bit and we would be kissing mouth to mouth.

These students come in with their parts memorized. They practice twice as much as I ever did and play with grace and femininity that sends shivers up my spine. Their lithe bodies sway in perfect rhythm with the music, like the flow of silk streamers that other beautiful women swirl so gracefully in traditional Chinese dance performances.

I also dance when I play, not with anything approaching the beauty of my students, but in a way that conveys my passion. Lately I find myself weaving in synch with these girls as we play duets. We brush arms when they turn the pages. My elbow grazes their shoulders. Our hips touch and I feel the electricity all the way up to the nape of my neck. What would happen if my students came to know what goes on in their teacher's head and loins?

Stan Goldman laughed at that. "Teachers here are revered. They can do whatever they want with their students."

"My girls seem to be willing to let anything happen, or is this how they behave when all they really want is flute lessons?"

"It might be a little risky for a foreign flute player to try to find out, but then there's the consul who gave hard-to-get U.S. visitor visas to good looking women in exchange for sex. The women didn't complain, but his staff was so disgusted they blew the whistle on him. It still took a whole year to get him transferred to the Philippines where he could play the same game."

"What does that tell me?" I asked.

"Nothing in particular, but watch out. There are just a few more temptations in this oh so traditional society than your typical American liberated woman will stand for."

64

Sally

In the Vanguard

Here in Taipei Lex is lucky he plays the flute and not the guitar. He's got plenty of students. There's no tradition of classical guitar here, and that means I have just four curious beginners. This leaves me with six empty days in my week, and I'm left alone a lot. Lex is busy with the orchestra, but you won't find guitars there.

Being alone so much means musicians don't make friends like other people. By the time I got to junior high it was already obvious I was a lot different, not a little. Other kids played sports or hung around with their friends after school. They goofed off until dinner and watched TV unless their parents butted in and told them to do homework. I didn't do any of this. Once school was out I went home and practiced guitar.

My record collection was so different you can hardly imagine. Everybody else went wild over Elvis and I didn't even know who he was. OK, I knew he was the guy who swiveled his hips like he was screwing on stage and shouting asinine songs I wouldn't call music. Elvis the pelvis and Enos the you know what. I was worshipping Segovia and listening to Dietrich Fisher Dieskau singing Schubert Lieder.

I barely survived ninth grade, but in Spain with Segovia we students were all together in the music. For the first time I discovered like-minded people my own age. Our own gang falling in and out of love with each other. We had been alone with our instruments for so long that we shared our lovers when we finally found a group we could belong to.

For a while I had hopes this body and soul life would last forever, but soon enough we were pitted against each other for recognition and a future in music. Win a big international competition and you get a major tour. Second place is easily forgotten, and nobody even asks who all the other contestants were. Julian Bream and John Williams made it big time. I came in second, but I'm not finished yet.

Imagine you're a musician and you have a lover and one of you survives all this and makes it into an orchestra and the other teaches Suzuki to four year olds. If you're the one who succeeds, it's like my friend Ginny in the Baltimore Symphony. She's so busy making a living there isn't much time for anything else. And that says nothing about the insanely jealous husband she has to go home to after rehearsals and performances.

I might have suffered from my ex-husband even more than Ginny, because there's no bigger putdown than being told you are playing an illegitimate instrument. That's Michel Sevigny for you, even though he had no reason to be jealous and his idol composed duets for the guitarist he loved.

Like Ginny and I discovered with our exes, chamber music forces intimacy on the players like nothing else – and the music world is littered with relationships that disintegrated. Our own friendship survived all the tension that lies just below the surface of music's thin skin because we didn't have to play together, so we didn't lose respect for each other's musicianship.

Ginny shared my elation with the success of that first European tour with Lex, but she also confided how jealous she was of us performing as soloists in those glorious halls while she slogged away on second violin parts in the symphony. When I told her about going to Venezuela to prepare for another tour, she wondered aloud whether it made sense for me to tie myself to Lex when I was becoming known in the U.S. "Surely something good will happen here," and then she hit me with what she really had in mind. "Why not take me to Europe next year instead of Lex? The tour dates coincide with a break in the orchestra season."

I didn't know what to say. Ginny was my closest friend, but she's an orchestra player and that is not the same as chamber music. It would be starting all over, and what if I didn't like her playing? That would destroy us.

If it wasn't for Ginny dragging me along to that party at Katya Tenbroek's, I never would have met Lex. The only way I was able to handle her request to tour Europe with me was to share these thoughts with her and hope she would understand. Lex and I needed each other as a duo, and it was for more than just music.

Ginny had the last word. "When you get famous you can perform with anybody you want."

I could barely hold back the tears as we hugged.

After I went to Venezuela we exchanged letters almost every month. Ginny shared the trials and tribulations of raising a rebellious daughter who refused to be musical. I wrote about concerts we had, and made up stories about others because I couldn't reveal to anybody back home what happened to my hand. That would have ended any prospects of performing in the U.S. Nobody would chance it, so I never told her about it.

I did tell Ginny all about Santiago da Silva and the craziness of our ten second decision to be united in a wedlock that was all about rights of cunt. Good thing our rights are turning out to be reciprocal and I'm OK this time around.

I also sent Ginny a couple of tapes we had recorded for Radio Caracas. Then I didn't hear from her. I thought the tapes had revived the jealousy she revealed to me just before I left for South America.

I never dreamed Ginny would go to New York just to deliver our tapes to a friend whose sister worked at Vanguard Records. "I had a hunch," she wrote, "and some weeks later my friend passed the message that Vanguard would be willing to produce and market a record of you two if you reimburse the costs of production. It would be the first recording of an American flute and guitar duo on a major label."

I couldn't believe what I was reading. Vanguard, the company with people like Menuhin and Rostropovich on their list, would record us as "Romanzas." I could hardly wait to tell Lex and I've got to write Gene Dinkel, our all but useless manager back in the States. It's about time he did some serious work for us instead of the handful of U.S. concerts he lined up for next year.

The filet mignon I bought was my lucky charm to get a concert in Alice Tully Hall. Then I spent more money than I had on a bottle of Moet & Chandon bubbly. The shop owner said I could pay her later. I didn't find tapered candles for our candlelight supper. The monk in the Taoist temple on the way home gave me votive candles free when I emptied my purse and came up with nothing. These people are like all the strangers who took me where I needed to go when I used to get lost in the maze of Taipei's lanes and could hardly speak a word of Chinese.

Lex hugged me when he came in. "Smells wonderful. What's the occasion?"

"Just us." I held back the big news. Instead I told Lex how happy I was to be invited to get together with a famous pipa performer. "Finally getting to play with people is worth celebrating."

That was enough to fool Lex. We celebrated each slice of medium rare while I gabbed about the beauty of Chinese traditional instruments. Then I brought out the champagne. "Open it. This is for us." I smiled as innocently as I could.

"Good Lord. You're pregnant."

"Come on. I'm a musician, not a mother. It's much better than that."

"The Culture Council asked you to give a solo recital at the National Concert Hall." Lex's face was a question mark.

"Still better. Guess again."

"That Dinkel guy you have managing us in the States got us some concerts."

"That too, but it's even more than that. We're being offered a recording contract." I got Ginny's letter out and read it to him.

"Great," but then Lex looked at me puzzled. I was sure he knew about Vanguard Records. Nobody has the sound quality they do.

His smile seemed to be twisting in the wind, turning into a frown. He squinted, his expression darkened. "What's this about us having to pay all the expenses?"

"It doesn't matter when we're on the same label as Menuhin and Rostropovich."

"They get paid. Why not us?"

"What do you care if they get paid? Everybody I know would give an arm and a leg to be in that kind of company."

"I know, but look at it this way. Vanguard has our radio tapes. They want us. They should pay us like they pay everybody else. Dinkel's a professional manager. He ought to be able to negotiate that."

Lex frowned. I wanted to cry.

"Can't you figure out what this would do for our career? You're not Rampal and I'm not Segovia. If we ask for money Vanguard will tell us to go fly a kite." I swallowed the thought on my tongue: *You are so stupid, Lex Kennan. I didn't get champagne for this.*

"It's a matter of principle."

The bubbly was coming up. I swallowed hard to keep it down. "Just because Gene Dinkel got us booked at the World's Fair and a couple of concert series doesn't mean that anybody else knows who we are. Vanguard is doing us a huge favor, even if we do pay for it."

Lex stood up from the table. "Ever hear the Chinese talk about face? If we're good enough for Vanguard, then we're good enough to get paid like everybody else. At the very least we don't pay them for making money off us selling the record."

I swallowed bile and clenched my fists. Lex stared me down. I grabbed the half-full bottle of champagne and shook it as hard as I could and squirted the bubbly in his face. "Celebrate! I don't want to be crude, Mr. Hot Shit Flutist, but you are fucking insane."

65

Lex

Waves of Affection

"Why didn't I just say I couldn't accept it?"

Maybe because I had to get out of the house, but Adolf Hsu's invitation to dinner with his family made me really uncomfortable. I couldn't help associating him with Hitler. He insisted, "It's five thousand years of Chinese tradition to give a special welcome to guests from afar."

His daughter Penny is a sweetheart, but she's a long way from being my best flute student. Adolf comes to get her after lessons. He asks me how she's doing in English as fluent as mine. That makes all the difference in a world where my Chinese is laughable and my wife is sour. I couldn't refuse the invite.

It took some courage for me to ask him how he got the German name. He explained while I chewed nervously on minced pigeon wrapped in lettuce.

"My father was an Army Colonel sent to Berlin in the thirties. German advisors had been training our officers for years, and Generalissimo Chiang was a great admirer of the Nazi regime. By the time I was born, Hitler was revered for reasons you certainly can understand. Officers named their sons after him."

I did not swallow the pigeon easily.

Adolf continued, "Some say it pleased the Gimo and meant faster promotions, but that's not me. I've wanted to change my name for years, but I can't do it while my father is still alive."

"How did you learn to speak English like an American?"

"My father sent me to live with an uncle in Washington as the Communists were closing in on us at the end of the Civil War. That made me one of those 'little overseas students' whose parents sacrifice everything so their children can learn how to get rich like the Americans. I got my engineering degree at the University of Michigan and came back to make Ambassador golf clubs for Wilson."

It was easy to see how well Adolf Hsu met his parents' expectations. He invited me to go golfing on Sunday at the fanciest club in Taiwan and picked me up in a Porsche. I couldn't really play the game, but Adolf took a coach out with us and said he enjoyed being with his American friend. For me, it was a real respite from sullen Sally and I think the rhythm went right from my flute to my golf swing.

Adolf said I was a quick study and we played often. He rewarded my first birdie with an introduction to his friend Eileen. She was trim and quite cute in a mini-skirt and pony tail hairdo, though the crow's feet by her eyes suggested that she might be approaching forty.

Once Adolf was provided with a masseuse, Eileen led me past several men on recliners getting their toenails manicured, into a cubicle barely large enough for a massage table. As soon as the door was shut she said she never expected to be working in a massage parlor. "Waves of Affection not right name for this place."

When I asked her Chinese name, she turned away from my gaze. "Must give you best massage, but not my name. I am number fifty-one. People ask for my number."

"Why won't you tell me your name?"

"I tell already. Eileen. Please get undressed and lie on table. I massage your back now."

I did as I was told and wrapped the large towel she gave me around my waist.

She dug her knuckles into my neck and pressed hard. Then she worked her way from the top of my skull down my spine, lingering at length on all kinds of sore muscles along the way. We said nothing until she blew softly in my ear and whispered, "You want another session? Very special."

"Only if you tell me your real Chinese name," I was confident that this was the way to pry it out of her.

She frowned. "Sorry. If you want me next time ask for number fifty-one. That is my name here."

"How many names do you have, anyway?"

"Many names. Hope you understand. In massage parlor we don't tell anybody our real name, not even boss at desk. That might lead to trouble."

After more weekend golf with Adolf, Eileen gave me her Chinese name on the third visit to Waves of Affection. I have no way of knowing whether Lotus Blossom is her real name, but she made me promise not to reveal it to anybody. I tried to pronounce it and the tones came out all wrong. It was the first time I saw her smile.

"How did you get the name Eileen? It doesn't sound anything like Chinese at all."

"You wrong." She elbowed me hard in the buttocks. "So I tell you. Teacher gives us names, but I no like Annie, so when I leave school I pick my own. Eileen sounds like Chinese words for love and soul. I dream about that but it never happen. Men think they in love with us but we just masseuse do our job."

She pressed hard against the muscle leading to my calf, just below the back of my knee. I clenched my teeth to suppress a scream. "You call this a massage? How does so much pain help anybody?"

"Pain when I do that, feel so good when I stop. Very good for sore muscle."

I grabbed the back of my knee and dug at it with my fingers.

"You say stiff neck from playing flute all a time. I work on that."

I must have loosened up because I was drifting off to sleep. Next I knew I was spread-eagle on the massage table and she was stroking my buttocks lightly and running her fingernails up and down my legs. Every so often she swept her hand in between.

I was hard, surprised, and embarrassed. The tingle sent shivers up to my neck and scalp. I reached for the towel she had slid up to my waist and covered myself as I turned over, but there was no hiding my arousal.

Lotus Blossom paid no attention to it. She came up on the massage table on her knees and dug her fingers into my muscles just below the collar bone. Then she squatted over me and ran her fingers through my chest hair, circling my nipples and down my belly. There was no way I could hide my reaction. I reached down and tried to cover up. She took my hand and squeezed hard between my thumb and forefinger, then swirled her fingertips ever so gently back and forth from my brow to my sex until I was throbbing.

Nimble as a dancer, Lotus Blossom stood up on the massage table and dropped her halter top and mini-skirt. Perhaps I was too intoxicated from the pleasures of being stroked, but there was Venus de Milo with arms, positioning herself on top of me, guiding me into her body, allowing herself to settle on mine, a feather from heaven.

I couldn't move. She leaned back. Such perfect curvature of belly and breast. I closed my eyes to stop the whirling cameras of my mind to record the still image in permanent memory. She reached for my thighs and stroked, then in between them. She stopped, maybe sensing that I couldn't bear to end it all here.

It was her turn now. A slow dance on my stage. She gyrated from the waist, pony tail swirling around her head. Tilting back, then forward, flying freely from side to side. Then a small sound, suppressed as if she wanted to make sure it wasn't heard in the next room.

What seemed to be pain on her face loosened into a smile that radiated pure joy to my lips and loins, though she had not kissed me there or anywhere else. "Thank you," she whispered. "I have need too. You a kind person."

Lotus Blossom helped me get dressed without saying a word. I pulled a bill out of my pocket to tip her, but she frowned and refused to take it. "You not understand," she said. "If you pleased with me, remember number fifty-one. Fifty-one is my real name."

Adolf dropped me off in front of our apartment building, but I couldn't face the possibility that Sally might smell some trace of where I had been and what happened there. I took off as soon as he gunned his Porsche around the corner and walked around the city until I was drenched in sweat.

66

Sally

And Yet…

Lex is principal flutist with an orchestra that draws wildly enthusiastic audiences and plays encores every concert. We perform as a duo and as soloists in new cultural centers all over Taiwan, and autograph a lot of programs afterwards. Our students are a pleasure to teach. Some of them travel hours on the train just to study with us.

We're treated as VIPs at the National Academy of the Arts. The pay is good, and the people are as friendly as you can find anywhere. The Taiwanese are really grateful to Americans for their newfound prosperity and for not selling them out to the Communists. It's an ideal situation. But don't ask me to describe how often stony silence reigns in our household.

Lex is so different now. I'm not particularly surprised that his success as a performer has gone to his head. The problem is much bigger than that, and it's bigger even than his pompous rejection of Vanguard's recording offer. Now he hardly ever looks at me, but he can't take his eyes off the Chinese women. We walk down the street and he gawks at any decent looking skirt until she disappears from sight. It's not because they wiggle their hips like you see in the movies. They don't.

There is a hunger in him so strong he doesn't even know it when I tell him he makes people uncomfortable. He insists, "I'm just taking in the scene."

"Can't you see how women bow their heads and look straight down at the sidewalk when you stare?" Lex ignores my plea.

It's not fair these Chinese women arouse him so by just going about their business. I give him everything he wants. I'm a really good cook. He tells me I'm a great lover. He doesn't have to ask, I'm willing. All I expect is that he take care of me too, but I have to beg him.

What kind of a jerk sees his wife lying naked on top of the bed and doesn't take it as an invitation? No wonder Vera told me he doesn't know what he is doing.

That's not the only thing. I've met some of the top performers on traditional Chinese instruments and have fun playing with pipa, arhu and bamboo flute. When I told Lex I'll be doing an East-West concert with a pipa player he asked why I would waste time on that stuff. I told him to buzz off. He can't get beyond Western music, and doesn't even realize that it's the traditional Chinese instrumentalists who are making the innovative music over here.

It's almost fun to see how pissed off he gets when I'm playing Chinese music instead of practicing duos with him. He can't get over the fact that I have my own music to play and he doesn't own me. We've got plenty of time to rehearse, but if he thinks I'm going to sit around and play his stuff all day, he's crazy.

There's no reason we can't have Chinese music and traditional Chinese instruments too, but Lex won't have any of it. I bought him a bamboo flute and he never touched it. When I take out a pipa and experiment with it he takes off in a huff. He could be playing along with me and improvising too, but that has never happened.

Lex can be so stupid. He's been touting an offer from *Chang Yang Records*, the local company that pirates every American and European record they can get their hands on. That just hardened him against Vanguard. It's getting like he would ruin our career if he only knew how.

67

Lex

Misunderstanding

I don't understand why Sally is half sloshed when I come home. It doesn't matter whether it's after an evening concert, in mid-afternoon, or when I take a walk in the morning and come back with the croissants they do pretty well here even if we are a long way from France.

She still asks me how everything went, cooks a good meal when she cooks, and tells me she can't practice our duos, she's played out. That's when she's in a good mood. When she's in a bad mood I get home to find her in the corner of our living room, staring at a blank wall. Her lame greeting sounds like some whispered echo of a past that never existed. She says she's meditating.

One morning in May she complained about the heat, stripped off her clothes in the living room, and went into the bedroom without a word. I went out for breakfast and a walk and came back an hour later to find she was still sprawled out on the bed naked, just as she was when I left. I kissed her on the cheek and said, "Maybe you shouldn't drink so much. Best get some sleep."

Next morning I slept in late after a performance of Beethoven's Ninth and found her sitting on the living room floor cross legged by the phone, cheeks stained with tears. The Chianti bottle by her side was empty. I reached for her hand. She looked up at me, glassy-eyed, and whispered, "You'd fuck anything in a skirt." She dropped her gaze and turned away.

"You're smashed out of your mind, aren't you?" I went out for a long walk by the river.

The apartment was empty when I came back.

I went to bed quite early that night. It didn't faze me that she hadn't come home yet. Sally had been spending a lot of time recently with pipa-playing friends who drink *hsiao hsing* wine and gab until the wee hours. Then she sleeps until who knows when.

I turned over in the morning and discovered the other side of the bed was empty. It was still empty when I returned from a full day of lessons and another all-Beethoven program in the evening. This must have been the weekend of her East-West concert in Taitung, six hours by train down island on the east coast. She could at least have left a note before she took off. A Sunday concert means she won't be back until mid-afternoon Monday at the earliest.

She wasn't. Not Monday night either. After our Tuesday orchestra rehearsal I asked the French Horn player Sally befriended if she had seen her. Wendy Silverman shouted at me. "Are you telling me that she's been missing for four days and you haven't done anything about it? Do I have to report it for you?"

I shrunk. The embarrassment was so great I couldn't talk to anybody. At home all I could do was get drunk on Sally's wine and try to go to sleep.

I tried to ignore the knock on the door but couldn't. The man facing me stood stiff in an officer's uniform, with gold braid on his cap. "Foreign Affairs Police. We have a report that your wife has not been home in several days."

Damn Wendy Silverman. "I was about to report it myself. No, I have no idea where Sally Pendergast might have gone, except she was supposed to have a concert in Taitung sometime around now."

The police officer's frown suggested that I was a fool not to know the whereabouts of my wife. Then I remembered the name of the pipa player, "Chang Su-mei."

"She is a very well known performer. You will have to come in and file a missing persons report. Right now."

When we got to the police station Officer Wang led me back to a small cubicle and called in two of his colleagues. "Do you drink alcohol? Did you have a fight? Was your wife angry that you frequent the Waves of Affection Massage Parlor? Is she a jealous person?" They grilled me about everything but the size of my desire.

None of the policemen told me outright that I was suspected of foul play, but their hints that I would be watched were not subtle.

Three days later the knock on my door was louder than ever. This time officer Wang was accompanied by a baby faced kid in uniform who must be a rookie in training. "The Bureau of Exit and Entry informs us that a Miss Sally Pendergast departed Taiwan on a flight to Tokyo with onward reservations to New York. You should have told us right away that your wife might have left you."

68

Sally

Your Baggage, Miss

When we were having a passionate affair right under his wife's nose, I promised Lex that if we ever got married I would leave him someday. I should have given that more thought when Santiago da Silva told us to get to the Palace of Justice.

We didn't marry by choice so much as by chance. Ten seconds to decide when one of the most powerful men in Venezuela is on the other end of the phone telling us what to do and when to do it is not quite choice.

Why do we bow to power and let other people commandeer the most intimate parts of our being? Don't ask why I let so many men into my body without knowing what I really wanted. I have enough trouble taking responsibility for myself, and I wasn't born to coddle infantile men or raise children.

Somehow I must have known all along that to become a human being I have to be independent. For a while, that imperative receded deep into my unconscious, suppressed like Freud might say. Maybe I completely forgot about it. Lex and I had tremendous excitement in our life together. We lived our dreams of a performing career on stages all over the world. We were new, fresh, exciting, masters of our niche bringing back a lost art. Flute and Guitar had been all but forgotten for more than a century, like Bach was forgotten until Mendelssohn revived him from the dead.

We also brought the dead back to life – musicians whose names I love, like Ferdinando Maria Meinrado Francesco Pascale Rosario Carulli and Mauro Giuseppe Sergio Pantaleo Giuliani. Best of all, living composers were writing great music for us. We offered so much variety that even the strangest new works got a fair hearing. Don't get me wrong. We only performed real music, not the awful noise that some people wanted to pass off as their genius.

I wanted to kill the curse of that promise to leave him. Ever since our first concert I was determined to banish my flight not fight responses to the pain of living a life. We were so alive that I actually thought I had succeeded. Until Lex left me naked and betrayed.

You understand why I left. Lex fired us up to do things we never dreamed of. He led us to those fifteen minutes of fame that people talk about. But in the end I discovered in Lex's dizzy rush to perform for the many that his passion was all for the music and none for me.

Sure there was the intense affair in the beginning when he was married and I was lost. Excitement drove us. He wallowed in ecstasy on stage, falling in love with his playing and his audiences. I fell in love too, but didn't realize he was forgetting that I was there with him.

That's not all. Ego is one deceit, but betrayal is something else entirely. I'm not talking about his dalliance with that Venezuelan woman. We had no commitment then and I couldn't ditch him for one affair when I had many more.

What was fair then is outrageous now. I offered Lex more intimacy, love, and partnership than he'll ever get from any woman anywhere. I also offered him plenty to look at if he wanted to stare at a real female body instead of cardboard hanging on his walls or Chinese women walking down the street. I stood naked before him with doors open to body and soul, and he turned away. I called him at the studio that time he said he had students, but he didn't show up at all. It's bad enough he was screwing around, but when he rejects my all, that's it.

I took the guitar and packed a suitcase. I'm terrified, but something new will happen before my credit cards melt. Better to carry good memories than to live bad dreams.

In the end it was lonelier with Lex by my side than it is waiting at the airport on standby. The counter agent calls out Sally Pendergast as I'm discovering who I really am. The only sane choice is get on a plane. Don't let anybody carry your baggage.

69

Vera

I Didn't Need to Go Anywhere

I hadn't heard from Sally in a dog's age when another of her picture postcards arrived. She was in the middle of the picture with her guitar, surrounded by mariachi performers in elegant silver studded charro outfits and wide-brimmed sombreros. Her hair was tied back in a bun with a purple ribbon, the same color as the bowties the men wore.

The postmark was Mexico City, and the message was cryptic. It read, "You were right to dump Lex. I never should have married him."

Sally had never mentioned Lex in her postcards. Lex never mentioned her either, but that wasn't a surprise.

I sat down at the dining table to give a quick response and get this out of the way so I can get on with my life. I wrote, "Dear Sally. Marriage isn't such a terrible state of affairs, even my ten years with Lex. Unfortunately we had such different needs and ambitions that we were unable to bring them together in the same place, even though you were right here in Washington to fulfill his music dreams.

"To this day I do not know what he was running from, just as I have no idea why you are fleeing now. Once you went to Venezuela, I couldn't imagine that music would not have kept you together, regardless of your cynical view that marriage is slavery.

"To bring you up to date, I owe you much for guiding me to independence. I shall maintain it, though it is best expressed in true partnership. I discovered that Dr. Cooper was so considerate of my real needs that I could not keep him out of my life. He is wonderful with Jennifer and Aaron, and they are closer to him than they ever were to their father. Dr. Cooper bought a catcher's glove so he could make a pitcher out of Aaron, and he goes shopping with Jennifer. He gave them both music lessons right away, and they give us music. Jennifer plays piano while Aaron is making great progress on the cello. Lex would be proud of their talent, and I will invite him to hear them when I locate him.

"I was as wary of entanglement as you must have been with Lex, but Dr. Cooper melted my defenses with kindness. We married last year. Now there is new life in our family, a baby boy born on March 21st. We have watched in awe as Sherrod has almost doubled his birth weight."

I signed the letter "With Love," and sealed it in an envelope. Only then did it register that there was no address on Sally's postcard.

70

Lex

Trockne Blumen

Will Sally come back? Weeks went by and there was no news of her, but that was no surprise. We're not letter writers and she won't call. If Sally decides to return, she will pop in on a day of her own choosing, like she did in Venezuela. She'll smile as if nothing happened and signal with her index finger that it's time to jump into bed.

We didn't plan to marry and I don't have the courage or humility it takes to chase down and capture the heart of a deserter. I can imagine how a visit to a massage parlor can be magnified in the gossip mill of hurt, but it's not the same as humping any skirt. I leave it to you and the moral philosophers to judge whether a massage, even of the kind given at the Waves of Affection, constitutes infidelity or relief from pain. I don't understand why Sally abandoned the lessons of her dozen men and me to become a moralist so righteous as to leave without a clue about her intentions.

When I was seven my parents bought me a kaleidoscope. I turned the cylinder very slowly for hours on end, searching for a galaxy distant beyond my imagination. Time passed slowly in an inner space that was as empty then as it is now. I lost the kaleidoscope along the way, but the patterns of my life still moved glacially when I graduated from college, auditioned in vain, went into the government, married Vera and had children.

Of all the places to be hypnotized again by shards of glass in a tube, the souvenir shop in the Chiang Kai-shek Memorial was as unlikely as any. The salesgirl handed me the toy and I felt the tremor in my hands as images flashed by with such speed – glistening eyes, glorious sex, abutment, encounter with death, Sally's miraculous recovery, fame making love onstage in twenty countries – I got dizzy. In our music, flashes of lightning revealed the heavens but I didn't see the storm brewing in Sally's ominous silences. Nor could I understand such profound change with each turn of the toy of my life.

I don't live alone very well. Whatever I'm doing, practicing, reading, watching TV, I want to be making music with people. I think constantly about the girls in my puppy-love years. Those early loves were explosive fortissimos, as driven as Stravinsky's "Rites of Spring." Lydia came first, an elusive lullaby as pubescent boys bayed below her window. Then Carol-in-the-bushes and Peg O' My Heart and Evie Sevarin. I was passionately in love with one teen musician after another until the flames were extinguished because I wanted them too much.

Then practical Vera won my mother's heart and became my wife. Those raw urges to make a life in music faded into a distant background rumble – until Sally Pendergast asked, "What do you play?"

Why did Sally think I wanted her too little? With her gone – another rejection, more emptiness – I was tempted to make a play for Rebecca Chou. Before I could act on my fantasies, the student who had come to dominate my daydreams was the successful candidate in auditions to replace me in the orchestra. She broke the news with a hug so tight I could scarcely breathe. She planted a kiss full on my lips. I gasped. She wagged her tongue in my open mouth like a puppy dog. Might that have been more than a momentary burst of passion realized? But as Rebecca Chou metamorphosed from my student into my replacement, I couldn't grasp it.

After the concert season was over I went back to the States and soon learned that our duo couldn't possibly break up when what we had going for us was the envy of everybody. Gene Dinkel insisted that our reputation as a duo doesn't mean a thing when it comes to making a go of it as a soloist. "This is a business. Count the number of solo flutists and guitarists getting bookings. I can sell 'Romanzas,' but go it alone and you'll go begging. It's suicide."

The premier string quartet of the era performed for adoring audiences for years after they stopped talking to each other and wouldn't even rehearse. Ralph Greenberg said the players in Ars Nova detest each other. Some people can make music without love, but I cannot, and yet I still couldn't bring myself to chase after my disappeared partner.

While our duo lasted, passion burned more brightly than ever, fueled by performances for presidents and peasants, on the world stage and in the bush. Though Sally was gone, that ember was still glowing, so I signed up to audition for second flute in the National Symphony. As a newly unemployed musician it mattered little that I wondered whether counting far more measures of rest than I would get to play would wear me down.

So many of my friends who once basked in their talent had already given up on music as a career. A Times article on my Juilliard class reported that several classmates even sold their instruments, one committed suicide, and another was selling jewelry. I wasn't contacted for that story, but I would have told the reporter that my passion made it to the stage and strutted in front of adoring audiences, but all I ever really want to do is make music with like-minded people. Would non-musicians understand the depth of that desire and the enormous gulf distancing talent from the business of music? Is it true that the most successful flutist of the day became famous only when he recorded "Annie's Song," the John Denver ditty that I could teach a ten-year-old beginner to play in a matter of weeks?

I was mulling all this while strolling aimlessly in the National Mall. As I stared at the Washington Monument an Asian man whose face was familiar walked up and planted his feet right in front of me. "Don't you remember? I'm Roger Peng from the Interior Department"

The name without the face would not have rung a bell. He was a brilliant Chinaman whose parents immigrated when he was a kid. I had no idea whether he came from China or Taiwan, or maybe Hong Kong. He was all work and never said much, but he got promoted really fast and there were snide remarks about diversity programs in the government.

Roger smiled and asked how I was doing.

I wanted to change the subject. "Have you made the Department work?"

"Still trying, but you know as well as I do it's tough to find decent help in Interior. Present company excepted, of course."

I choked up. Now I'm unemployed, with a one in four hundred chance of getting a second flute position that I'm way overqualified for. That kind of security isn't easy to get excited about. I should have stayed in Taiwan.

"You'll never guess why I stopped you like that."

"I have no idea." We used to greet each other, but we weren't at all close in Interior.

"You won't figure this mystery out, so I'll tell. It's to thank you. My niece, Rebecca Chou, wrote about her American flute teacher. I recognized your name immediately, even though I had no idea that you are a great flutist and teacher. She wrote that she owes you a profound debt of gratitude for helping her make it into the orchestra."

"I'll be…" stunned, I didn't know what else to say.

"By the way, there's a GS-15 slot coming open in my division. Schlotzky's retiring after 42 years. We'll advertise it of course, but the position reports to me and you have the qualifications, so the outcome is predictable. Perhaps you learned in Taiwan that relationships are everything in our society."

Before I left Taipei, Friends in the Experimental Orchestra tried to convince me to stay on. They argued relationships. They said my students loved me, that teaching is my destiny, and that enlightenment can come only by subsuming self into the entire universe. "But what I've experienced on the concert stage seems like enlightenment too," I said, "though it's subsumption of the universe into self."

Randy Chen, a double bass player who would rather be carrying around my instrument than his, corrected me. "Any Zen master will tell you that your version of enlightenment is a totally self-centered move in the opposite direction."

"Where will that lead?" I asked.

"To reincarnation over and over again, living the same torments, making the same errors. You'll be trapped in endless lives."

Would accepting Roger Peng's offer be the beginning of another cycle of surrender and disillusionment? Ten years in the government was enough to know its disadvantages and bitch about them. Could I believe Roger's promise that I will make a real difference, that thousands of people will be grateful for the network of bicycle trails that I'll establish.

And where does second flute fit in the search for enlightenment? I started out that way in the student orchestra and could hardly wait until rehearsals were over so I could get out of there. While I didn't precisely calculate how rarely I had a real part to play, counting the measures in between them was endless purgatory. Maybe that explains why the second flutist in a renowned orchestra for forty years never picked up his instrument again after he retired.

I played principal flute and had a solo career. Music is a business, but I always played it as an act of larger love. Now I realize it is second flute that would be my reincarnation trap. Sally and Vera might say that my fatal flaw was not giving any thought to relationships being everything. But if learning that now means starting over working with Roger and pursuing my passions in free time, then reality is worth the compromises it requires. Looking back, Vera was right in that respect. Give her credit for raising the children well, and turn the kaleidoscope.

I went to Roger Peng's office with him and forgot all about the audition that afternoon.

Not long afterward I located Ralph Greenberg, who told me he was still the best amateur cellist in the world and he would be happy to round up string players for quartets and old time's sake. "And Katya Tenbroek is still giving parties for musicians. You're invited this weekend."

Katya's wallpaper had not changed. The entrance hallway was still populated by naked nymphs, along with a flaming redhead whose eyes sparkled in the dim light. She introduced herself as Rosanne. "I majored in accompanying," she said.

"That's rare among pianists, isn't it?"

"That's what I like to do more than anything. Do you have the Prokofiev or Poulenc Sonata with you? Maybe Trockne Blumen?"

"You mean the Schubert variations on that poem by Wilhelm Müller?" I asked. "About those flowers of lost love we carry to the grave."

"Yes," said Rosanne, "but when he composed this masterpiece he must have been thinking of my favorite stanza. 'And spring will come. And winter will go. And flowers will grow in the grass again.'"

To think I played this music so many years before I ever read the poem.

Acknowledgments

Two Musicians and the Wife Who Isn't owes an enormous debt of gratitude to Judy Angsten. She went through the manuscript word by word, making perspicacious suggestions that I could not have imagined. She challenged me to dig deeper into the characters of my women protagonists and to make every sentence count. If I did not fully succeed in this essay into passions and souls, the shortcomings are mine alone, not hers.

Rosanne Cerello's detailed comments added insight, as did those of Dan Bloom, Genevieve Cimaz, Helen Cochrane, Georgia Court, Gerald Fox, Dr. Norman Katz, Susan Knopf, Aviva Layton, Alice O'Grady, Ken Sherman, and Linda Stenseth. I appreciate the contributions they made to my understanding of the story and the process of getting it written. David Bell offered a precise historical timeline of important events mentioned in the book.

Erin Tyler designed a cover which truly captures what I want to say.

Profound thanks also to Chang Hsiu-chen, the wife who really IS, my dream partner who took over my chores and gave me the time and space to write this book.

About the Author

Syd Goldsmith's first novel, JADE PHOENIX, was a finalist in two major international competitions. His second explores the hearts and souls of three passionate people in TWO MUSICIANS AND THE WIFE WHO ISN'T.

Syd's op-eds on the U.S.-China-Taiwan relationship have appeared in the Christian Science Monitor, the Los Angeles Times and the Asian Wall Street Journal. Some forty commentaries on the 2008 Presidential election and the American scene during the early months of the Obama administration appeared in the opinion pages of the China Post.

He has enjoyed multiple careers as a diplomat, musician and entrepreneur on both sides of the Pacific. As a leadership and strategy consultant to American and Chinese companies in China, Taiwan, and Hong Kong, Syd served a stint as temporary CEO of a Taiwanese multinational manufacturer with 8000 employees in Taiwan, China and Thailand.

Syd was trained in New York as a concert flutist and has performed in twenty countries. His lifelong passion for music led deep into the desires of his characters in Two Musicians and The Wife Who Isn't

Syd and his wife Hsiu-chen Chang live in Taipei with their two teenagers. They can be found in upstate New York in summertime, cavorting with writers and other fascinating people at the Chautauqua Institution.

www.ingramcontent.com/pod-product-compliance
Lightning Source LLC
Chambersburg PA
CBHW050032180626
46810CB00002B/684